Transparent
Web of Dreams

Transparent Web of Dreams

Toni Armstrong Sample

TATE PUBLISHING
AND ENTERPRISES, LLC

Transparent Web of Dreams
Copyright © 2014 by Toni Armstrong Sample. All rights reserved.

No part of this publication may be reproduced, stored in a retrieval system or transmitted in any way by any means, electronic, mechanical, photocopy, recording or otherwise without the prior permission of the author except as provided by USA copyright law.

This novel is a work of fiction. Names, descriptions, entities, and incidents included in the story are products of the author's imagination. Any resemblance to actual persons, events, and entities is entirely coincidental.

The opinions expressed by the author are not necessarily those of Tate Publishing, LLC.

Published by Tate Publishing & Enterprises, LLC
127 E. Trade Center Terrace | Mustang, Oklahoma 73064 USA
1.888.361.9473 | www.tatepublishing.com

Tate Publishing is committed to excellence in the publishing industry. The company reflects the philosophy established by the founders, based on Psalm 68:11,
"The Lord gave the word and great was the company of those who published it."

Book design copyright © 2014 by Tate Publishing, LLC. All rights reserved.
Cover design by Harold Jason Branzuela
Interior design by Jake Muelle

Published in the United States of America

ISBN: 978-1-63268-196-6
Fiction / General
14.06.17

To God and to my friends—old and
new—you know who you are,
I dedicate this book to you.

Without your love over the years, your encouragement,
your help, and your time, I would
never have had the
desire or motivation to write
about women who have gone through
struggles and come out the other side.

Some struggles remain our secret.
Other troubled times we have shared
and have moved through together.

Some of you continue to be my closest of friends, and
along the way some of us have been
separated from each other.
That too is part of life.

This book is for all women, who with God's help,
have come to realize
their value in this world
and their purpose.

Whether you are actively in my life today or not,
your very existence is my inspiration.

Special Mention:
It is a pleasure to express my gratitude to
Tate Publishing and to copy editor Yvonne Menchavez
for applying her amazing skills
to make this book all that it could be for you, the reader.

Transparent. When light encounters a transparent material that appears clear, it can interact with it in several different ways.

Web. Loose, irregular, tangled obstacle courses that may have a disorienting effect making one more vulnerable.

Dreams. Dreams are successions of images, ideas, emotions, sensations, and events generally outside the control of the dreamer. Dreams can be a source of inspiration.

Vision reaches beyond the thing that is,
into the conception of what can be.
Imagination gives you the *picture*. Vision gives
you the impulse to make the picture your own.

—Robert Collier

Contents

Accidentally	11
Attempting Forgiveness	26
Exactly Like a Date	34
The Thrill of Looking Back	56
Oh, Baby!	72
Taking It with You	81
Plan B	91
Grey Streak	109
The Follow Up to Plan B	123
Before the Special Day	133
A Change in Plans	146
Plans Continue	153
From the Roadside	170
Fatherhood	187
A New Routine	197
Melding and Dividing	211
What About Mel?	225
Reader's Aid and Book Club Synopsis	239
Characters	241
Book Club Discussion Items	243

Accidentally

> A little neglect may breed mischief…for want of a nail, the shoe was lost; for want of a shoe, the horse was lost; and for want of a horse, the rider was lost.
>
> —Benjamin Franklin

Hank stands before me in the middle of the room. His muscular legs are spread slightly as his hands are grasped together behind his back.

I have never in all the years we have been together doubted that Hank loves me. He just said those words to me again, "Helena, I love you."

His next words stopped me cold. "I will always love you, Helena, but I'm leaving you."

I heard what he said, and then my mind stopped on those last three words, "I'm leaving you." It's like when a doctor gives you bad news. You stop listening. I know Hank was still talking because in the background I could faintly hear mumblings, but my mind refused to put form to those sounds. I didn't want to hear any more words. I was stuck on the fact that Hank had said he was leaving? Why? What could possibly have happened that he would do this to me?

Although Hank spoke quietly, and with obvious remorse, I felt like I had been hit by a physical punch. I look up at him through the tears that are streaming down my face, and I look into those glorious green eyes that have always been filled with love. Now those eyes reflect pain and pity. He stands there motionless knowing full well that the words he has just spoken will end our life together. He has admitted his infidelity, and now he waits for, what? Does he expect absolution? Is he looking for my blessing?

I sit, frozen in place, on the side of our bed, fully dressed in the blue jeans and plaid shirt I had put on that morning. This is the bed Hank and I have shared for thirty-two years. This is the bed we made love in and conceived our children in.

Why did he have to choose our room, our oasis to tell me?

I look around the room I have just finished redecorating. I think about how long I searched to find just the right shade of pale yellow for the walls and the navy blue patterned curtains and spread for our king-size sleigh bed. The plush white carpeting was laid yesterday. It's easier for me to concentrate, if only for a moment, on the atmosphere I created for this room than what is happening in it.

Shaking my head slightly, I think about last night. When I went to bed, I believed that my life was perfect; and now as it turns out, it was actually the last night Hank and I would ever sleep together in this room. Last night, we made sweet, sweet love. Hank knew it would be our last time. I didn't.

Why is Hank doing this to me?

I look straight ahead at Hank who is standing in a pool of morning sun as it streams through the floor-to-ceiling windows that fill the entire end wall in our bedroom. If I were to get up and walk to the windows, I would see the beautiful rows of live oaks that run down both sides of our front drive.

Hank's next words fall on me like pelting shards of glass. His voice is filled with deeply sorrowful emotion as he says, "I didn't mean to fall in love with her, Helena." He stops and looks at me with such sadness as his voice trails off. "It just happened."

He paused, and when he continued, he was pleading for me to understand. "If I could turn back the clock to the time before I met her, I would. I can't do that, Helena, because I've already gone over the edge. I'm so sorry, Helena."

Things like falling in love, going over the edge, they don't just happen. You make them happen or allow them to happen, but they don't just happen. And he has a choice. If he does love both of us and has to leave one of us, why is it me he is leaving?

Why is he standing here telling me he loves someone else if he still loves me? Why does he think I'd want to hear that he loves someone else? I don't want to hear it.

If he had an affair with someone, he could have just ended it with her, whoever she is, and I'd never even needed to know. I wouldn't have wanted to know.

He took marriage vows with me. He hasn't taken any vows with her. I'm the one he's supposed to stay with. He said the words to me, "till death do us part." I'm not dead. I want to be right now, but I'm not.

This pain I'm feeling in the place that I call my heart is agonizing. I can't stop the tears that are falling freely down my cheeks. I know I'm only hearing part of Hank's words. I can see the emotional pain he is experiencing; it's plainly evident on his face. If he is hurting so much because he is leaving me, then why is he leaving me? I'm not married to a stupid man, so why is he acting reckless and irresponsible? Beyond being my husband, he is also the father of our children and a grandfather. He told God he would never leave me. He can't do this.

Why would anyone throw away a wonderful life and hurt themselves and so many people they love for someone they didn't mean to fall in love with?

I look up at him through eye lashes that are so soaked with tears that he appears blurry, and streaks of sunlight flash off my vision and make Hank look like he is a shining star.

My voice has a little quiver as I ask, "You are going to throw away everything we have had all these years? You are going to hurt me beyond reason and our children for someone you didn't mean to…"

I couldn't go on. I couldn't say those words. My heart would not allow me to say that he loves someone else. I have heard Hank tell me he loves me for so many years; I just can't believe that his love for me is now taking second place to the love he has for someone else. I can't believe that he would hurt me like this.

I am still sitting on the side of the bed. The realization of what Hank has told me causes me to recoil with the strong emotion that is sweeping over me. I want to rise and go to him and smash him with my fists and beat him and hurt him the way I am hurting. I want to hurt him physically like he is hurting me emotionally.

Understanding rapidly surfaces of how someone can seriously hurt another person in the heat of "passion," in a moment of "insanity." This thought is more frightening than Hank leaving me. I take in a deep breath to calm myself. My own previous thoughts are more frightening at the moment than Hank's deserting me.

I don't want to hurt Hank. I just want to never have heard the words he has spoken. I want this to have been a bad dream, a nightmare, and soon I'll wake up to the beautiful sunshine, and Hank will be kissing me like he did last night. The memories of last night wash over me. What at the time I believed was an act of love now I see very differently as an act of dishonesty. I gave him my body as my assurance of faithful exclusivity. Hank made love to me knowing he was in a relationship with another woman, and that he was leaving me today. I feel defiled.

I don't feel like I can even stand up. I sit there and think about how quickly it took my love for Hank to be covered over by pain, which in not much more than an instant had now turned to anger.

Hank comes over and kneels on the floor in front of me. This is what he did when he proposed marriage to me. How ironic that both the beginning and the end, thirty-two years apart, I would find him on his knees.

For some reason, God seems to think it's time for him to intercede. I know this because my thoughts, although not charitable, turn to wondering why Hank hadn't spent a little more time on his knees during our marriage, and in particular, recently. Perhaps if he had spent more time with God, he would have been more content with our marriage and, with God's help, would have placed more value on the vows we said. Maybe he wouldn't have "accidentally" fallen in—I hate to say the words—in love with another woman.

Accidentally my foot. What is it that attracted him to her that ceases to attract him to me?

I begin searching inward. What is wrong with me? What have I done wrong to cause him to want someone else? My inside voice joins the argument. *Quit that, Helena. There is nothing wrong with you.*

I always want to take the blame for everything. I rush in and say "I'm sorry" even when I know I've done nothing to be sorry about. I've taken the blame for things all my life, but this time, I have to understand that it isn't about me. I am fine. It's Hank and this other woman who are at fault here.

I'm the same person I've always been. It's Hank who has changed. I may have put on a few pounds over the years, but I had two children. What woman doesn't change a little from her early 20s to her mid 50s? That's part of life. Our bodies change. I wonder how old this new woman is and how thin she is.

I had to interrupt my thoughts when I realized that Hank was saying something. "What did you say?" I ask.

Hank took my hands in his and repeated his last words. "Helena, I've changed."

I have no pity or compassion for Hank at this moment, and I shoot back, "So what kind of excuse is that? Bully for you, Hank, you've changed." I know my voice along with my words reflected my disgust. Here I was accepting responsibility for Hank leaving because I had changed, and now he's telling me it's because *what?* Because I haven't changed.

I continued, "Hank, are you telling me that you're leaving because you've changed and I haven't? Is that the problem?" I paused looking at him with the loathing that filled me at the moment. "Is there something wrong and unfavorable with being consistent? Suddenly all the things we once valued, like being dependable and stable, are bad things? Are you telling me that I haven't kept up with you?" I was feeling the dizzying effects of not breathing, and as I gulped air and hiccupped, I continued, "Do you mean I haven't grown, and so you had to find someone else to 'accidentally' fall in love with? Well, isn't that just great for you? 'You've changed.' Well, Hank, I haven't. I'm still the same woman who you said vows to. Remember? Vows to love, honor, and cherish till death do us part?"

I knew my words were hitting hard and slashing into his gut as his words had torn into mine. I wanted them to. I was mad. I was livid, and I wanted Hank to understand just how furious I was. But I couldn't leave those last stinging words be the last words I spoke just then. With the heat of anger cooling, replaced by my desperate need to try and save our marriage, I ended, "Hank, I still love you, and I don't want you to leave me."

Although I didn't say it I didn't want to hear this conversation, and I didn't want to face that Hank was leaving me. I did not want to become another American statistic as a divorced middle-aged woman. I had just read an article that most single women over forty never marry again. From fifty-five until God took me home to him could be a lot of lonely years. I didn't want to face those years alone.

I also didn't want to think that Hank might be going through something significant, and I hadn't picked up on the signals. Maybe it was my fault that he had wandered off to find someone else, whether he had meant to or not. Had I failed to make Hank feel important, desirable or attractive, and that life wasn't sliding down the far side of the mountain? Well, it was sliding down that mountain for both of us. I know that at fifty-five, most people don't want to admit that they are middle-age, but unless we live to be a hundred and ten, most of us hit the middle of our life somewhere in our forties.

We are at a vulnerable stage in our married lives. I'm not stupid. I know that. Our children are grown-ups, and we've been experiencing what Dr. Phil, Dr. Oz, and Oprah call empty-nest syndrome. I'm sure those three gurus of daytime talk shows would be quick to tell us that Hank is experiencing male menopause, and his hormones are making him do crazy things. Well, I'm going through menopause too.

The difference is, I'm not anxious to become a cougar, one of those women who search out younger men to satisfy their needs to feel young again. I didn't run out and "accidentally" fall in love with some guy twenty years younger than me.

I wonder again how old this new love of Hank's is. Please, God, let her be younger because if she's my age, then what am I going to come up with as a reason why he would choose her and not me? Then I am really going to have to do some finite self-examination.

Women hate when their husbands end up with younger women, but it's a lot easier to say that "he left me for a younger woman" than "he left me because I wasn't meeting his needs as a wife."

Hank is a good man. He's a churchgoing man. He's a good father. He's been a good provider. That's what is making this so much harder to believe and understand and accept. If he had run around on me during our marriage, which I know he didn't, maybe I'd be prepared that this day could eventually come.

How could I have been so self-absorbed that I didn't see this coming? And yet, haven't I known for quite some time that something was amiss? It was right after Hank's fifty-third birthday, when we went on the cruise, that I began to have an inkling that Hank was going through some life-altering changes. That was three years ago, and I had to admit that for those past three years, there seemed to be growing some distance between us that hadn't been there before.

Haven't I wondered why he frequently seems to be coming home from work later? It has been an unspoken question in my mind why his tennis matches take all afternoon on Saturday when they only used to take a couple hours? It's given me pause to wonder when he's called to tell me he has another late meeting at work. Haven't all these things niggled at the back of my mind?

The final question may have been the real tip off if I had cared. Why he doesn't seem interested in making love to me as often as he used to. That one has not been a concern to me. I've actually enjoyed that Hank hasn't wanted his usual sexual favors because my libido has been far from hot lately. I just chalked that up on my part to what must happen when a woman begins menopause. I didn't think about his part. Why had I pushed all of those clues as far back in my mind as I could and ignored them? Was I that confident in our marriage, or did I just not want to acknowledge that this day could come?

Today, right now for the first time, I realize I shouldn't have ignored the signs.

I do remember five years ago when Hank turned fifty that my mother, God bless her soul, decided it was time to give me the "mid-life crisis" talk. It was kind of like the sex talk she gave me when I turned thirteen. I didn't pay much attention to her either time. I should have, both times.

We had gone out to lunch, just Mom and me, right after Hank's birthday; and while we sat there sipping our iced tea, she said, "Helena, men get to a certain age where they start to feel old. I think Hank might be there. They don't like that feeling."

"Oh, Momma," I said, "Hank doesn't feel old. He isn't old."

"Never the less," Momma continued, "some men begin to look around, not that I think Hank would. "

"No, Momma," I interjected almost offended, "Hank has no reason to look around."

She smiled, that all knowing I'm your Momma smile, and then these words came,

"Hank is a good-looking man, and it would not be unusual for some young thing that thinks he's attractive to begin a pursuit. Being pursued is very flattering and hard to resist. When that happens, it awakens a man's teenage hormones. It feels good to a man to feel like a stud again. It's not a feeling that most red-blooded men are about to oppose."

"Oh, Momma, stop it. Hank is not going to cheat on me. He's not going to be pursued by some hot bodied young thing that will turn his head. Hank loves me. And, Momma, I can't believe you just used the word stud. Are you for real?" I sat back looking at Momma, feeling very assured with my marriage and acting like I was shocked by her choice of words.

Momma was not about to leave it at that, however. "Helena, I'm not a dinosaur. Even if you think I am. We both know men, and we both know the word stud. You're a horse woman, so that word cannot possibly shock you even if I did use it in the context of your husband."

Mom smiled, rolled her eyes, and continued. "Please don't be the kind of wife who acts like an ostrich and buries her head in the sand. Too many women are divorced today because they didn't pay enough attention to their husband's needs. You have to realize that what I just said could very well happen. When Hank's head is turned by a younger ankle, you need to be aware enough of what is going on to take decisive and appropriate action. It takes a sharp wife to keep her husband from straying."

I remember nodding my head and smiling and thinking that mom didn't need to worry about Hank and me. Looking back at that now and recalling it so clearly, I should have listened more closely to Mom.

I think Mom must have had firsthand experience to have been able to describe it so aptly. But she and Daddy stayed married more than fifty years. No one would have ever guessed that either of them even remotely understood what is happening to me right now. But somehow I'm quite convinced now that she did know. Had Dad strayed? Had she noticed the signs that I tried so hard to ignore, and did she take action before it got to this stage. Somehow I think she did.

Poor Mom, I wish she would have shared more about that with me, but how very difficult it would be to admit that the man you love wants someone else. And how could a woman ever tell her daughter that she hadn't paid enough attention to her father, and that she almost lost him because of her inattention? That time was coming for me only it wouldn't be *almost*.

I wondered, would my children blame me for their father leaving? Would they think that I hadn't been a good enough wife to him?

I wish Mom were still here. I wish Dad were still here. It's so lonely without them. It was so very difficult when Mom died three years ago of cancer. That was about the same time I noticed the subtle changes in Hank. Dad followed Mom to heaven within the year. He had a massive heart attack in his sleep. I really think he died of a broken heart.

Those last three years have been recovery years for me, and I know I haven't been the person that Hank was accustomed to. I have been melancholy and removed and depressed. This introspection was difficult as I realized that recently I have been very different from the woman Hank married and loved.

I didn't realize how difficult it would be to lose my parents. I have really just recovered from both of their losses, and I still miss them so much. I would give anything right this minute to run to them and have them hold me and tell me everything would be all right. Dad would tell me that "This too will pass," and I would believe him and be comforted. I didn't have those arms, or Mom's, to run to anymore.

All the layers above me are gone now, and I'll be the next to go. That's probably how Hank feels. There is something awful about losing your parents. Hanks parents died several years before mine. Since I still had mine, I wonder if I provided for Hank the solace that he needed at the time. I loved my in-laws, but it wasn't until my own parent's death that I truly understood what Hank must have gone through. Losing your parents isn't just tragic because you love them and miss them, but you realize that there is no longer a layer of protection between you and the great beyond. They were always that layer, and now you are that layer between death on this earth and your children. My thoughts moved to the children.

How will we tell the kids? I don't want to tell them. They'll look at me, and I will have to tell them that I failed. I don't want them to see me as a failure. There I go again. Taking the blame for what their Dad is doing. It's not my fault. I'm not a failure. Listen to the voice, Helena. *You are not at fault. You did nothing wrong.* But did I do anything right? I wonder what it would have been like if Mom had failed with Dad. What would I have felt if she had told me that Dad was leaving her for another woman? I know I would have been madder than a hornet with Dad, but how would I have felt about Mom? Would I have thought she had failed? I honestly didn't know the answer, but that thought that kept popping into my head would not be pushed down. Would the children think I had failed their father?

I prayed that our children would realize that it didn't have to do with any failure on their part. It was something strictly between their dad and me, and we both still loved them dearly.

I look up. Hank has quit talking and is just looking down at me. He's no longer on his knees. He's looking at me very strangely. I know that my thoughts had taken me away for what must have been a considerable number of minutes. I shake my head as Hank asks, "Are you all right, sugar?"

I can't believe he just called me sugar. Using that word, now, in the middle of what he is doing is the final straw.

"Sugar, you just called me sugar. Hank, don't you ever call me sugar again. You have no right to call me sugar." Sugar meant I was his sweetness. I am not any longer his sweetness.

Using that term incensed me, and I spit out more angry words that landed on him with the vengeance I was feeling. "You want someone else, Hank, well you go right ahead and go to her. You call her your sugar if you want, and while you're doing it, I hope you choke on those words. I hope every time you call her some special term of endearment that you used on me that it makes you think of me and how much you have hurt me."

Hank steps back like I have just sucker punched him. I have never in the thirty-two years we've been married ever spoken back to him, raised my voice to him, or admonished him. Well what does he expect? He just stuck a knife into my heart and twisted it. Does he have any idea what he's done to me?

He can go. Right now, the way I feel, I don't want him anymore. Amazing. In just a few short minutes, I went from loving this man to not caring what he does. I think if I say it enough times, I'll believe it. I don't want him anymore. What I really want to do right now is to hurt him as much as he's hurt me.

It's time for me to throw some grease on the fire and I do, knowing that as it lands, it's going to burn. "How do you plan that we'll tell our children that you have left their Momma for another woman that you didn't *mean* to fall in love with?" The words are hurled out of my mouth and landed right where I intended them to land. I see the words penetrating, and I see him as he appears to crumble and grow smaller in front of me.

"I don't know, Helena. I hadn't thought that out yet. I was more concerned about telling you and hurting you, which I never wanted to do; but I knew that I would, and I know that I am." Then almost instantly, he seemed to gain confidence, and I could tell he was ready to end this and move on.

Hank sucked in his stomach, and his shoulders straightened, and he said, "I think the best thing for all of us—you, me, and the kids—is to meet with them together after the two of us have accepted what's happening."

I looked at him with incredibility. "Well I don't intend to ever accept this."

Hank continued. "I know, Helena, that this is so unfair to you what I am doing. I am truly sorry, but I am doing this, very selfishly, I'll admit. I'm doing it for me."

He paused and then began again, "You know, Helena, our children are both adults with spouses and homes and children of their own. Gabe and Gilliam aren't children anymore. You keep calling them children like they are still little kids. They aren't. We both love them and will till the day we die, but they have lives of their own now. How often do we even see them? Not that often. It's not like we sit down together every night with them for dinner. When they left for college, their new lives began and our old lives changed forever. It has been years since they've lived under our roof. I think they will understand. I'm sure they won't like it, but I think they will understand enough to forgive me for leaving their Momma. Maybe they won't forgive me right away but eventually. I'm hoping that eventually, you'll be able to forgive me. And, yes, Helena, I do think we need to tell them together."

I looked at him as though he had grown horns and gone crazy. "I still don't understand why you think I would want to help you tell our children that you are leaving me and them, no matter how old they are or under what roof they lay their heads at night. Even if we don't see them often, we still spend special times together, holidays, birthdays, and vacations. You won't be a part of that anymore. All those special times that parents and children and grandchildren spend together, you won't be a part of. Have you thought of that?"

My tears stopped. I'm not going to be this crumbling little bit of nothing in front of Hank. I am going to show him that I am a strong woman, and he is not going to break me. I want him to know that he is not just leaving me, he's also putting at risk his future with our children and grandchildren. I'm using them against their father. I know it when the words spew out of my mouth. I'm being vengeful and nasty, and I know that I shouldn't. I can't seem to help myself. I'll use whatever weapon I can to fight this, and right now, the weapon I have at hand is our children. I pray that they will forgive me.

I stand up, and I look at Hank with absolute contempt. "Get out of here, Hank. You are not the man…" But my words trail off. I don't want to say them. I don't want to say he's not the man I've loved all these years because he is, and for me to say them would be to say a lie.

Hank looks at me, totally defeated. "Honestly, honey, I am so sorry. I never wanted to hurt you."

I look him straight in the eyes, "Then why are you hurting me?"

He looks at me, shaking his head from side to side with his lips tightly pursed together. I watch him as he studies my eyes. I know he sees all the emotions that I am feeling. I know he sees the pain, the confusion, the reaction to his unfaithfulness, and mixed with the anger he probably also sees the love that has to still be lurking somewhere behind all those other feelings. With his usually pulled back shoulders again somewhat slumped in a posture of defeat and rejection, he turns and leaves the room.

Well what was he expecting? Did he want my blessing on this new venture in his life? This wasn't a new job. This was a new woman, a woman who was taking my place. Well she wasn't getting my family too.

I hear him go down the hall, past the family room, and I hear the front door close quietly.

I sit back down on the edge of the bed, looking out those beautiful windows, and I see his blue pick-up truck as it moves slowly down the driveway and out through the gates. I gaze as it continues down the dirt road, kicking up a little dust as it continues its progress. I stare until there is nothing left to watch. He is gone.

Attempting Forgiveness

> Sometimes you have to stand alone
> to prove that you can still stand.
> —Anonymous

Hank walked out that door and drove down that driveway eighteen months ago, and as today begins, I am a divorced woman. I received the phone call yesterday that it was done. Hank filed, and I didn't contest anything. We both had attorneys, and we both did everything we could to make this ending as pleasant as an ending can be. It was amicable with neither one of us wanting to rip the other apart physically, emotionally, or through the assets we had spent so many years building together.

After the initial shock of that horrible day in our bedroom wore off, I grew to be less resentful and less hateful; and with God's help, I learned to forgive. Moving on is more difficult.

I remember the words from the movie *Sleepless in Seattle* when the radio interviewer asked the character played by Tom Hanks how he was getting on after his wife's death. He said something like, "I get up every day, put one foot in front of the other, breath in and out…" So that's what I did.

Hank and I had worked together to build what we had, and so a fifty-fifty split, or something close to that, seemed appropriate. Hank insisted that I keep the house and most of our investments, and he took his half mostly in the business that he had spent his life building. It was fair. We had worked our entire lives together. I had spent most of my time in our marriage, making a home, and Hank had spent most of his time operating his business. We worked together raising our children. Hank had been a good provider, a good husband, and a good father. I could not fault him in those roles. Neither Hank nor I was greedy, and there were enough accumulated assets for both of us to move on with some sense of security at our age.

My share of our divided life would allow me to continue living, without worry, in the style I was accustomed to living. It wasn't in the style of the super rich, but it afforded luxuries, like my horses, and it was very comfortable. I didn't long for furs, or diamonds, or even a super chic New York City wardrobe. I loved my hair pulled back, my blue jeans, and my riding boots. I got everything I needed to continue my life, except Hank.

Within a month after Hank told me that he was leaving, we met with the kids and broke the news to them together. As it turned out, it was the best choice. Once the disbelief and distress of what was happening between Hank and me passed and I had a chance to realize that the circumstances weren't going to change, I was forced to accept the inevitability of the situation. I wasn't happy with Hank leaving me, but my anger subsided. You can only live so many days hanging on to emotional agony; it is not a lifeline. Hank's leaving me for someone else bruised my ego considerably. I have always been comfortable in my skin, but now I no longer seemed to feel an appropriate level of self-worth. I felt old and used and useless.

To say that the children were angry with their dad would not be accurate. They were furious and resentful, but mostly, they were as sad and as hurt as I was. I have been as generous toward Hank, with the children, as my spirit will allow. I have encouraged the kids to forgive their dad and even made excuses for him. I explained that although for years they have looked on him as being their super dad, he is, after all only a human. Humans are susceptible to temptation, and not giving in to temptation was never one of Hanks strong suits to begin with.

Gabe and Gilliam didn't understand what I was trying to say. They looked at their father, up until that time, as one who could do no wrong and had no faults.

Ah, the innocence of youth. What a blessing it is to have your offspring think you are perfect. Yet that is a tall pedestal to stay on top of, and most of us will eventually tumble.

I told the kids a story about their father, not for any malicious reasons, but as a way to help them understand a little more of the true essence of the man. About the time that Gabe was starting to walk, when he was about eleven months old, Hank was going through the classified section of the newspaper on a Sunday morning, and he saw a Corvette for sale. Hank was just beginning to make a profit from his business, and we, like most young families, were struggling to afford the combination of the house and the pick-up truck payments each month. A Corvette was definitely out of the question.

Hank was salivating as he begged me to agree that we could just call the man and take the car for a test spin. It was very difficult for me to say no to this man I adored, but I knew there was no way we could swing another payment. I wouldn't give in. I think it was our first significant disagreement since we had gotten married. He left the house angry that Sunday afternoon, and that night, he came home the owner of the Corvette. He sold it three months later. We really could not afford it. The only thing was, for even just a short time, he owned a Corvette and drove it around town like he was the king, a very guilty feeling king, but nevertheless, a king.

As much as I have forced myself to do this little dog and pony show for the kids as a way to show them we are all fragile and they should forgive their dad, I know that I have not yet reached that point of generosity of spirit. I have encouraged Gabe and Gilliam to understand that what happened to their dad could also happen to them if they are not careful in how they nurture their love for their spouses. I have also encouraged them to understand that their father still loves them. I have even shared with our children that I am very confident that Hank also still loves me. That is the really stupid part. He loves me but he wants a different life than the one we lived together.

I will never truly understand what happened. I'm sure it has a lot to do with reaching fifty-five and the fear of being turned out to pasture like they do with used up old horses. I believe in my heart that Hank is scared. He is looking at his vulnerability and eventual demise, and he's not liking that it's inevitable and moving closer and closer to actually occurring.

Whatever the situation or the reason, the one thing I am very sure of is that my life did not stop when Hank left. I'm sure of that fact by the pain I can still feel in the place I call my broken heart.

I have friends who think I am grieving too long over this lost relationship. They say things like, "If the man is too stupid to know what he had, Helena, then let him go and good riddance." I wish I could feel that way, but I haven't stopped missing him. How do you rid yourself of the comfortableness of a relationship you spent your entire life in? With Hank, I didn't have to be anything except what I was, and I cannot imagine going through the process of breaking-in a new relationship. Like breaking in new shoes, there will be blisters and some achy little pains, and maybe you'll have to turn them in for another new pair. Ugh. Just the thought of going through that, not just once but possibly more than once, was totally unappealing.

I have seen Hank out and about several times when I've been in town, and it is very evident that he is thinner. It's kind of the Jack Sprat fairytale story. Jack could eat no fat, and his wife could eat no lean, which, of course, means that while Hank is thinner, I am a little plumper.

The last eighteen months, the upheaval, and the divorce have taken their toll on us, and we both look older. What I resent most about looking older is that Hank can wear it better than I can. I'm thinking face lift. I say that as a joke, and yet maybe a face lift would pull me up out of the malaise I'm feeling and help me to move on. Perhaps it would have been better if Hank had had a face lift then he wouldn't have needed a younger person to help him recapture his youth.

Last week when I was in town, I saw Hank for the first time with his new woman. It hurt. It was like a knife being thrust into my heart. To know about her was one thing, but to see them walking down the street with their arms around each other in our town was excruciating. Maybe I'm not as far along in the recovery process as I believed myself to be.

She is younger. She is much younger and very thin. She looks to me like she's a vegetarian. Well that would serve Hank right since he has always been a meat and potatoes guy. As charitable as one tries to be it is still rather self-satisfying to know or imagine that maybe this perfect person you were left for isn't meeting all your old mates' requirements as well as you did. It's rather like grasping at straws, but oh how satisfying those straws can be to one's psyche.

We live in the same small area, but when you live on an island, the whole area is small; so running into Hank or her, now that I know what she looks like, is going to happen. Being a person who grew up in the church where I learned about God's gifts of faith, hope, and love, I should love that Hank looks so happy. Honestly, when I see him looking happy without me, I would be lying if I said I loved that he was happy. In my heart, where I still have not reached the absolute point of forgiveness, I want him to be lonely and confused like I am. In my very critical and selfish heart, I would like Hank to experience having no one to come home to or share a meal with or snuggle next to. This is what he has left for me, and I would like him to understand my situation; so he will acknowledge it, if only to himself. What he did to me was so unfair. I want to forgive him. I pray that I can forgive him, but that time has obviously not yet come.

I have noticed that when I see them together that Hank looks like the peacock he used to look like in the early days of our relationship. Maybe it's real, and maybe it's an act. I know that many of his friends have been unhappy with him for leaving me.

The women especially have not been kind to Hank, and I'm sure their husbands don't want Hank's fallout reigning down on them, so they too have been cool to Hank. Sometimes Hank will see me at the same time that I see him, and his puffed out happy look turns instantly deflated and sad.

I know that Hank must be filled with self-loathing that he hurt me. I am almost certain that what he really wanted was to have both of us and to keep her and me happy. I imagine she gave him an ultimatum, me or the highway, and so I'm the one who got dumped. Of course, if I had known about her like she knew about me, maybe I could have been the one to put forth the challenge, and maybe the situation would have turned out differently. Perhaps that's what mom was trying to tell me five years ago when she had her talk with me.

I hadn't thought about that talk Mom and I had for a long time. "Mom," I think now, "did Dad have an affair and almost leave you?" I'm sure that he did and Mom did not want me to suffer the pain, anger, anxiety, guilt, and self-questioning that she had. I understand those emotional twists and turns now, but I didn't have the foggiest idea then what she was getting at.

Dad didn't leave Mom, for that I am very grateful, but I think it must have been a really close call. Mom did everything she could to warn me while still being faithful and protective of the man she loved. I, like Gabe and Gilliam, would have been so angry with my dad. Mom would never have wanted me to feel that way, and so she did what she could to advise me without allowing me to feel less than the full admiration I had always felt for my father.

Relationships can be so complicated. Some people truly treasure what they have and wouldn't do anything to jeopardize it. Others stay with what they have but never learn to treasure the person or the relationship. Couples stay together many times for the children, or to spare themselves the criticism of their friends and family, or because they don't want to change their lifestyle. Both women and men like Hank may at times long for something more, and in some cases, they may "accidentally" get it. Life is certainly not easy and notably so when the choices we make evoke so many personal changes and affect so many lives.

    I sit looking out my window in the same bedroom where eighteen months ago, Hank told me he was leaving. I see all the beautiful live oak trees and the splendid driveway. My eyes take in the stunning gardens filled with spring blooms of purple Iris's, bright yellow Daffodils, the stark Paper Whites, red Tulips, and more yellow repeated in the Forsythia. This time of year, the flowers are not as soft in color as those found in a Monet garden, but each flower and each vibrant color is every bit as heavenly. The vividness of the colors wake our drowsing spirits and jolt us into realizing that a new season is about to begin.

    As I gaze out upon this beautiful landscape, I pause to thank God for his faithfulness in walking beside me through one more difficult occurrence in this life. In all probability, this won't be the last time I call on God's strength and peace to get me through a tough time. I just pray the next one won't come too soon.

    I am grateful that I can still look out this window and see the beauty that surrounds me. I am indebted that my sight is not clouded by bitterness. Amidst the disillusionment and the lingering pain and loneliness, I do seek to understand and forgive Hank.

    I'm even trying to forgive Autumn. Yes, Autumn. It's actually rather ironic since I have never liked the fall of the year. When September and October roll around each year, heralding that summer is over and winter is approaching, I take it as a strong indicator that things are either hibernating or dying in preparation for the long spell of cold about to arrive. Ruminating upon it in that manner, it becomes so clear that Hank's Autumn is no different than any other autumn in my life. Autumn the person or autumn the season heralds that new things are looming. Autumn is the perfect name for Hank's new love.

Exactly Like a Date

A friendship that makes the least noise is very often
the most useful; for which reason I should prefer
a prudent friend to a zealous one.

—Addison

This afternoon I'm going riding. For many years now, I've had my Blue Blue and Grey Streak housed at Victoria's Riding Stables, which isn't far from our home. I really don't like mucking stables or doing the other routine chores required to maintain a horse.

Hank had offered to build a stable for me on our rather extensive piece of property, but I declined his generous offer. What I love to do is ride, and I'd rather spend my free hours on the back of my horses rather than putting down clean straw, filling water troughs, and taking care of tack. It's important to know your likes—and your dislikes.

I love the wind in my hair and feeling the horse beneath me. I am always stimulated by the sounds of ventilation expelling from the nostrils of my mammoth beasts. In the winter, I don't just get to hear the sounds, but I get to see the great puffs of air heated from their masterful lungs as it is ejected forming a foggy mist. My girls are many times larger than me giving me a sense that I am both powerful and powerless all at the same time. Riding is almost like a drug. I feel quieted and more peaceful and yet invigorated and alive as I walk one of my babies back to her stable after I have curried her at the completion of our time together.

I plan my schedule so that I get out to fully exercise each of them several times a week. Blue and Grey are big, strong, and gentle. At one time, I used to look at my horses and think of Hank. Hank always towered over me. He is broad shouldered and narrow at the waist. He would pick me up, hold me several feet off the ground, and swing me around in a wonderful moment of laughter, happiness, and celebration. Now I only have my girls, Blue and Grey, to give me that feeling of being overwhelmed and awed by a robust brawny body.

It is so amusing to watch my girls when they are feeling playful or are anxious to get going. They will usually butt me gently on my shoulder or back followed by a short snort; and if all else fails, they will begin to paw at the ground, flicking their heads upward, letting me know that they are ready to run, and that they don't like being held back. When the girls reach that stage of impatience with me, I put my left foot in the stirrup; and swinging my right leg up and over the rump of either Blue or Grey, I settle myself in the saddle. With reigns in hand, I will give them the appropriate signal for the direction I wish them to take, and I am off riding with my good friend.

I live on Jekyll Island not far from Brunswick, Georgia, about half way between Savannah and Jacksonville, Florida. Hank and I moved here shortly after we were married. We are both Georgia natives, but neither of us had even visited the island before moving here. After living on Jekyll for more than half my life, I cannot imagine spending the remainder of my life anywhere else.

Shortly after we moved to Jekyll, I discovered that I was pregnant with Gabe, our son. It was a difficult time for me, and I was so depressed, I was fearful that my moodiness would harm my unborn child.

My doctor suggested I take an antidepressant or at the very least a tranquilizer on really bad days. I refused. I remember the scare back in the sixties when mothers took the tranquilizer Thalidomide. Although the manufacturer, the doctors, and the mothers were not aware that there would be complications, many babies were born with significant birth defects. Like all mothers, then and now, I wanted my children to be born whole and well. Years ago, mothers smoked and drank during pregnancy because they didn't know not to. Now doctors are very aware of fetal alcoholism, and that many seemingly disconnected behaviors of the mother before and during those nine months of gestation can be harmful to the fetus.

Hank was a saint back then. He was patient and kind and would sit for hours in the evening with his arm around my shoulders and my head leaning peacefully on his. He'd talk about how his business was coming along and how excited he was about the baby coming. He reassured me constantly that everything would be all right.

He talked with some of the guys at work and had their wives give me a call and invite me to lunch. Hank wanted me to be happy and to make friends and to feel good about our move here. I tried.

I think much of what I went through then was hormonal. Pregnancies can do that sometimes. I was never sick like some women are, but I just felt sad all the time. I was pitiful, and I am amazed that Hank stayed with me until the baby was born.

Hank was more than aware that coming to Jekyll was all about him. He was busy at work from seven in the morning until seven every night, twelve plus hours a day. He did understand that I was a newly married pregnant woman who had been thrown into an environment where I knew no one. Life was far from easy for either one of us.

Once I got our house settled, a small little cottage that Hank thought would make a great starter home for us, I was left with nothing to do but think about how lonely I was. I wondered why I thought getting married was such a great idea. Here I was pregnant. I only saw my husband in the evenings, which made for very long days. My family was too far away to just stop over and hang out with.

That was the stimulant for Hank buying me my first horse. Hank really did care about me, and when Beauty and I met for the first time, it was instant love. I had never ridden before, but I couldn't wait to get started, and Dr. Harris, my OB/GYN doctor, gave me permission to ride from my fourth until my seventh month. Since I was three months pregnant when Hank bought the horse, I only had to wait thirty days until I was given the okay to ride.

Hank had arranged for me to board Beauty at Victoria's. Hank named her. He said he named her after me. I met Victoria, Celeste, Old Bill, and other people at the stables, and I began to feel like life here on the island would be okay. It turned out to be a lot better than that.

Gabe's birth was so much more than I ever could have anticipated. I became the Martha Stewart of motherhood. I wanted to do everything right and do it all myself. It's a good thing that Hank's job was requiring a lot of overtime and travel when Gabe was born because if he had been present, he would have been totally ignored. I was completely enamored with my baby boy. The tables turned, and my days were filled. I loved it.

That overwhelming adoration I had for Gabe, which my new friends laughingly equated to obsessive compulsive disorder, dissipated when I gave birth to a baby daughter, Gilliam, three years after Gabe had arrived. By then, the initial glow of having to be the perfect mother had worn off, and I was much more relaxed with Gilliam than I had been with Gabe. With two children, ages three and a new baby, my life was still pretty much occupied most of the time with the duties of motherhood.

The time spread between the birth of Gabe and Gilliam was not planned but was nothing short of amazing. The children were perfectly spaced, and they were both wonderful babies. By the time the two of them were in school, Hank's work became more stable, and his crew including managers were fully trained. This didn't mean he still wasn't working sixty to seventy hours a week, but it did allow a little more family time, and fewer hours were spent traveling at job sites and attending to office crisis and routines. It seemed like the timing could not have been more perfect for now I had time to be not only a great mom but also a more attentive and adoring wife.

I loved my children as children; now, as adults, I admire them and love them as friends. I think the true test with children is if you would choose to have them as friends even if they weren't your children. I would definitely opt to be with Gabe and Gilliam even if they were not the product of my own loving union with their father. I cannot imagine my life without these two precious people. I admire them and respect them as the wonderful adults they have become.

Gabe and Gilliam both went to college, married what I believe to be their God-chosen perfect mates; and between them, they have given me three grandchildren, so far. Gabe lives in Atlanta, and Gilliam lives in Charlotte. They are close enough that I get to see them often but not close enough to spend as much time with my grand babies as I would like.

Since the breakup with their father, they both want me to move. Gabe wants me to move closer to Atlanta, and Gilliam thinks I'd love Charlotte. It was, for a while, almost like a bidding war. First Gabe would send me links on the computer of condos and patio homes that weren't far from where he lived. Then Gilliam would mail me *Realtor* Magazines with places circled in red that she had found. Then each of them would send me information on local restaurants, entertainment, clubs, riding stables, and volunteer opportunities. Gabe even sent me the entire classified section of the Sunday paper, so I could see all the job opportunities.

At first it was interesting, and I may have even, for a brief moment, given it some consideration; but when it came right down to it, I declined any thought of leaving. This is my home. I like that I'm here, and our children and grandchildren have their home here on the island to come to for holidays and special occasions. Gabe and Gilliam love to vacation here on the island they grew up on when they can get breaks from work, and I know that they would miss this special place if I were to decide to move closer to either one of them.

Hank is a contractor. He is known for being one of the best and most reputable housing builders in the coastal tri-state areas of Florida, Georgia, and South Carolina. His business has grown, his relationship with sub-contractors is excellent, and his clients are seldom less than satisfied with their latch key investment. I was always proud to be married to Hank. His company isn't little. He has many crews with very capable site managers and he oversees the entire operation. He believed that it was and still is essential that he meet, personally, with every client on a rather routine basis assuring them that all is going as it should.

I think since Autumn entered his life that Hank is starting to turn a little more of the management and operational duties over to his second in command. I wonder sometimes if Autumn has demanded that Hank spend more time with her or whether the years are just starting to take their toll on Hank. It is more likely that he needs to back off to preserve his health and energy. It really doesn't matter what the impetus, Hank wouldn't do what he didn't want to do. Life does tend to get away from all of us, and when we realize we can't do it all anymore, that can be a rude awakening. Not all of us, however, chose to change our entire life over it but some do, like Hank.

Gabe has never had any interest in following his father's career path. He told his Dad when he went off to college that he would not be coming back to join him in the business. Gabe majored in history. His father was distraught but recovered quickly. Hanks business, *Rivers Construction Company*, would be *Rivers Construction Company* whether or not Gabe joined him. Hank had talked with me about Gabe joining him one day in the business. I knew he wanted it for the opportunity to grow closer to his son through the business, and so that he could pass it on and know that Rivers would remain a strong name in the industry.

Many fathers who have built a successful business look forward to sharing it with their son or in some cases, daughter. Hank, however, did not follow his father into his profession as a doctor, so he was, after the shock wore off, fairly understanding of where Gabe was coming from. The biggest worry for Hank was Gabe studying history. Hank is a very practical man, and he was aware that job opportunities for those who major in the field of history was, to his knowledge, fairly limited.

Gabe fell into some enormously good luck when a chemical company in Atlanta offered him a rather significant, albeit entry level position in their company upon his graduation. He graduated number three in his class. Regardless of one's major, that pretty much made you very desirable to most employers.

Gabe, while at college, had met Amy who is a very beautiful and sweet girl. When they graduated and he got the Atlanta job offer, they talked it over, and he scooped it up without significant concern. Amy, also being Georgia born and bred, was ecstatic that his job offer didn't come from Boston or Seattle. She loved the warm and sultry south, and anywhere under the Mason Dixon line would work for her.

Gabe and Amy's ninth wedding anniversary is already looming on the horizon, and Gabe is steadily moving up the corporate ladder. They are the very proud parents of two of my precious grandchildren, Jeffrey, who is seven, and Sean, who will soon be five. Of course, like their parents, in this grandmother's view, they are perfect babies.

Gilliam also met the man of her dreams while attending Georgia University. She and her handsome and devilish Mike married shortly after graduation and now live in Charlotte, North Carolina. The wedding was here on the island, on our property, and it was very beautiful.

After two years of marriage, Gilliam and Mike have just produced their first and hopefully not their last adorable baby. Christie is the sweetest little girl. At both Gilliam's and Mike's desperate cry for help, I arrived in Charlotte the day that Mike brought Gilliam and Christie home from the hospital. I loved every moment of the two weeks that I was able to spend helping them.

Gilliam and I spent a lot of time together talking while the baby was napping. It was a very good time for both of us. She asked a lot of questions about her dad and Autumn. I didn't even try to answer her questions. I just told her that she would be better served addressing everything she wanted to know directly to them.

Gilliam got very serious one afternoon and asked me if I was okay. I could tell from the waver in her voice that she was genuinely concerned about me. I did everything I could to reassure her that I would be fine. What new mother needs to be concerned about her own mother. New mommies should be allowed to place all their attention on their baby and the father.

"I'm not there yet, honey, but I'm doing a lot better than I was doing at the beginning. I'll be okay." I patted her hand and smiled, and she smiled back.

Being a parent for the first time can be scary, so having your mom there to lend a hand, some encouragement and a lot of much needed reassurance is helpful. It was great getting one-on-one time again with Gilliam. She is such a joy to be around.

Gilliam's husband, Mike, is an industrial engineer and spends a considerable amount of time with his head stuck in his computer.

Once Christie was tucked away for a few hours during nap time and early bed time, we girls got to talk like two sisters. If Mike was home, he'd hear us giggling and laughing and stick his head around the corner and say something silly like, "Is there a teenage pajama party going on in here?"

Gilliam and I spent one night just sharing stories about Gilliam's teen years. It was fun to watch Gilliam's look of surprise when she would tell me a secret story, and I would reveal that I knew about it all along.

"You did?" she would ask with wide eyes and an incredulous look.

I would respond, "What, you didn't think your old mom knew what you were up to when you were sneaking off to parties and telling me you were doing one thing while you were doing something entirely different?"

"Oh, Mom," she replied, "I wasn't that bad, but I really never thought you knew about that party I threw my freshman year in college when you and dad were on vacation."

I laughed and said, "Honey, you seem to have forgotten what a small place you are from. Don't forget, we have neighbors on Jekyll Island, and it is an island!"

Gilliam and Mike seemed very happy together, and I couldn't be happier for both of them. It was fun to watch them interact together like an old married couple, and it was even more amazing to watch the two of them taking of care of Christie together. Mike was going to be a good father, and Gilliam would be an amazing mom.

When the two weeks was over, it was difficult for me to leave the three of them and return home. I missed my home while I was gone, but the house seemed so quiet when I got back, and I felt so much lonelier.

I love this house, but this home was built to raise children in. I miss the sounds and the noises and the laughter. I hadn't realized how deafening the silence was until I spent those two weeks with the kids. It's too tranquil. Maybe I should sell this home to a young couple just starting a family and move to a smaller place. Oh, but then where would the kids stay? No, I'll just wait. God has a plan, a perfect plan, and it will work out exactly the way he desires.

I do have a wonderful family, and I'm painfully aware that it wasn't all because of me that they turned out so well and have such bright futures. Hank was a great father. He was a wonderful provider, and he never denied the kids things that they needed. Allowing the kids the opportunity to have a great education was uppermost in his thoughts, and because of his hard work we were able to send them to great schools. I know the significant part that Hank played in getting our family to where we all are now.

The kids know it too, but they still haven't gotten over what he did. Gabe and Gilliam are still hesitant to include their father in family gatherings. They both are grateful to their father, and they both love their father. They also have both met Autumn, and neither one of them like her. Of course, who is going to like the woman your father left your mother for? I don't know what role Autumn played in our breakup. I don't worry about whether or not it was Autumn's fault or whether our marriage was destined to failure even if she hadn't come on the scene. I suspect that if it hadn't been Autumn, it would have been someone else. If Hank was unhappy with our marriage, he wasn't going to live out the rest of his life that way. In the case of the kids, however, it's easier for them to blame Autumn than their father.

I have taken a rather nonchalant stance about throwing blame. I could blame myself, Hank, or Autumn; but around the kids, I just chalk it up to one of those things that can happen in this life. Of course, quietly and to myself, I am still not ready to let Hank off the hook very easily. I know that in time this will all work out, but right now, the family doesn't want to entertain Autumn in their homes, so that leaves Dad out too.

I did tell Hank in the heat of my anger that giving up his family was going to be part of his decision to leave me but actually, now, I feel very sorry for him. This is the time he needs to grow close to those little ones, and they need to know their grandfather. Space and time can restore all offenses, if, with God's help, we can only make it through until then.

It's a new day. I have pulled the shade down on thoughts of Hank and Autumn for the moment, and I am headed out for a wonderful day of riding my Blue and Grey. My car, a light blue Honda Accord, pulls into Victoria's Stable. Old Bill, the all-around stable man who was here before I came the first time thirty odd years ago, waves and yells "Good morning, Helena." As I drive past, I throw my usual salute greeting to him. I pull into the parking area where Blue and Grey are stabled and head in their direction.

Celeste, Victoria's daughter, is the co-owner of the stable. She comes over and walks alongside me as I approach the stalls that hold Blue and Grey. Like Old Bill, Celeste was also here when I first stabled Beauty. I have always admired her for her demeanor, but even more than that she is a pretty woman both inside and out. Celeste is about five and half feet tall. She is not overweight but is sturdy from all the years of working with the horses. Her shiny auburn hair is tucked into the blue baseball hat that she normally wears to keep the hair and sun out of her eyes and her long pony tail, as usual, escapes through the tightening hole in the back of the cap. Her skin is golden brown, no makeup necessary, from the hours she spends working outside. Her blue jeans are clean with a pressed front crease, and her plaid long sleeve shirt with the front darts clings perfectly to her rather tight and taut midsection. "How you doing today, Helena?" She smiles over at me as we walk.

"Oh, I'm fair to middling." I smile back at her. My dad always said that, and it always tickles me to say it. "How are my girls doing?"

"Well, that's why I'm strolling along with you and what I want to talk with you about. Blue appears to be having some trouble with her hind left leg. Early this morning, I called Mel. He has a very busy schedule today, but he told me that he's coming over to look at Blue as soon as he is able to break free from the clinic. He said if you came over for me to tell you not to ride her. He also said that if you have time to hang around, he'd like you to be here when he does the examination. That way you two can discuss what needs to be done if it should be anything serious."

"Hmmmmm." I didn't like thinking that anything could be seriously wrong with Blue. "Yes, of course, whatever Mel says.

You know, Blue seemed fine when I exercised her on Wednesday. She wasn't favoring the leg when we rode the dunes. I did take her down to the water, and we romped in the surf for a while. I wonder if a jelly fish was in the water?"

I continued on into the stable and entered the stall where Blue was standing. I rubbed her nose and gave her a carrot from my pocket. She nudged my shoulder in greeting as she usually did.

I moved to Blue's rear flank, talking slowly and softly to her. "Let me take a look at your leg, girl. What seems to be the problem?" My hand moved downward and softly yet firmly caressed and examined her left limb. She raised her head and snorted, and I knew I had found the spot that was causing the trouble. It was definitely tender to the touch. She let me know immediately when my hand palpated the spot that was giving her trouble. There was no visual injury that I could see. She acted almost like it might be a sprain or arthritis. Horses get arthritis in their bones just like humans.

I stopped and bent down to reexamine the leg. I saw Celeste nodding that she had done the same thing earlier. I looked up at her as I made my next comment. "I don't see any burn mark on her leg, and a jelly fish usually does leave a burn streak. I'm usually very careful watching for those long stringers of theirs, but I know that they can be easy to miss."

Celeste had stood watching as I did my inspection and then commented. "Helena, we both have checked that leg now and can see nothing, but Blue is certainly letting us know that something is wrong."

"Yes, Celeste, I agree. We'd best let Doc take a look. I am so grateful that you treat your residents like they are your own. Your scrutiny of them allows quick attention whenever anything isn't quite right. I take great comfort in knowing that you are always on top of things. I'll give Grey her exercise, and then I'll come back and wait around for a while. I don't have anything urgent on my schedule today, and I agree with Mel that I should be here when he does the exam. I can ask questions and what he has to say won't have to be relayed. If you aren't busy, I'd really like you to be here too."

Celeste nodded okay while saying, "You are the longest tenant we have, Helena, and we love taking care of your girls. They are great horses, and we wouldn't want anything to happen to them. Of course, I'll plan to be here when Mel shows up. Go have a good ride on Grey now. He's waiting. Old Bill has him all ready." That said she moved on to her next duty.

I would hate for anything to be really wrong with Blue. It nearly killed me when I had to have Beauty put down. She was old, and her body just gave out, but I loved that faithful friend so much that I grieved for months that she was no longer a part of my life.

Since Old Bill already had Grey all saddled up, I hopped on her back, and we had a wonderful ride. We rode down the trail, then past the dunes, and along the beach. Grey and Blue both loved to play in the water. We trotted through the low surf, just enough to toss some of the water up onto my boots and legs. I always keep my eyes open for anything in the grass or in the water. A jellyfish might have stung Blue, but truly, I would have been surprised if that had been the case. My blonde hair was streaming out behind me as we came at a gallop back to the stables almost two hours later. I rode Grey around for another ten minutes at a slow walk to cool her down and then slipped down off her back and returned her to the stables. I took off her saddle and blanket and brushed her down. Happy with her usual carrot treats, I patted Grey on her side while I whispered a sincere thank you into her ear, and then I moved on toward Blue.

When I arrived at the stall, Mel was there. Mel had been taking care of the horses at Victoria's since I first started coming here. At that time, thirty years ago, he had just taken the business over from his father and was right out of veterinary school. I think that put us at about the same age. Mel was a good man and an excellent vet. As I approached, he looked up and smiled. He was crouching near Blue's back leg. Mel was tall, lanky, and wiry, and it was easy for him to move around any animal to perform his medical inspections.

"I don't think it's anything serious," he said as I came closer. "I think she might have a bit of inflammation in the tendon back here, so I'm going to give her some anti-inflammatory medicine along with a little steroid, and I think we'll give her a week's rest."

He pulled a hypodermic needle, a rather large one, and filled it from two vials, and then gently inserted the needle into Blue's leg. "I'll check on her in a couple days. In the meantime, Helena, I don't think you should ride her. It would probably be good for her to be walked around the paddock, but don't walk her more than a half hour, and no riders."

Celeste who was standing off to the side nodded and said, "If you can't be here to walk her, Helena, we can do that."

Mel looked serious as he gave me the orders, like something was on his mind. It didn't take a brain surgeon to understand how much Mel loved his clients. He was an excellent veterinarian, and people from all over called on him to travel to see their pets including dogs, horses, and even hogs.

"Thanks, Mel," I smiled at him, nodding that I understood his directions. "I really appreciate what good care you take of my girls. They mean a lot to me, and it was so hard to put Beauty down that I don't look forward to ever having to go through that again. I am so relieved that this is nothing more serious."

Celeste, after inquiring if there was anything else she was needed for, excused herself and went on to take care of her other guests.

When she was gone, Mel looked up at me as he continued to caress Blue's leg where he had given her the shot, and he smiled. I always liked Mel, but I think this was the first time I realized what a great smile he had. I watched his hand rubbing Blue, and you could see his gentleness. He put his hand up over his eyes as if shading them from the sun and continued to peer up at me. "Helena, I know how hard it was for you to lose Beauty. I was so glad you got these two ladies to help you through that time. Blue and Grey are beautiful horses. These past three or four years have not been easy ones for you."

He bent his head down examining Blue's leg one last time and then standing up so that we were eye-to-eye, he said, "I don't know how appropriate my timing is, Helena, but do you have time to grab a cup of coffee at the diner? I'm starting to lag, and I need some caffeine to pick me up. And I'd like to talk with you."

I wasn't sure, when he referred to hard times if he was talking about my losing Beauty, my mom's and dad's deaths, my empty-nest condition, or Hank walking out on me. All of those things had been a part of what I had been going through the past three or four years. I also wasn't sure what he meant by appropriate timing. It was a little late in the day, and maybe he thought I needed to get home.

Figuring that he must want to talk to me some more about Blue, I said, "Sure, Mel, now is as good a time as any for me. Do you want me to meet you there?"

"Yeah, that sounds good." One more time, he flashed that gorgeous smile.

He led the way to the diner, which was only about a mile away, and I followed him in my car. I parked in the lot behind the diner and walked around to the front door.

When I got into the diner, Mel was sitting at a back table. Reaching the booth, I slid in to the long bench seat across from him. This was such a typical diner. The colors were red and chrome. It's kind of like going back to the fifties every time I come in, and I would never change a thing. It's almost an institution, it's been around so long, and it never changes. I like it when things don't change, but in this world that doesn't happen very often.

A song was playing on the jukebox. It was a slow country song, and it wasn't playing loud. There were two guys sitting up at the counter on the little round swivel stools that were upholstered in red plastic. The two men were hunched over eating pie and drinking coffee. They were talking and laughing in between bites, and their feet were tapping away on the foot rest, a two-inch chrome bar that ran the entire length of the counter. It was odd to hear the Morse code like staccato of rhythm that their feet made, particularly because there foot taps were not in sync with the beat of the music. Two young women were sitting in a booth about three in front of ours, so we had the back corner pretty much to ourselves.

We both ordered coffee, and after it arrived and the waitress went on to help someone else, he looked up at me. His hands were wrapped around his cup with his fingers tracing around the rim. "Helena, I doubt that this will come as much of a surprise, but I really like and admire you. I know it hasn't been that long since you've been on your own. It's been five years now for me, and I can appreciate that this has been a very difficult adjustment for you this past year or two." As his eyes looked up and met mine, he seemed to be very serious.

I smiled and kept my eyes focused on him, trying to figure out what this was leading to. "It hasn't been an easy time for me, but having been in a similar situation yourself, you know we just hang on and get through it. I sure don't need anything else piled on top of what I'm already handling though, so I'm hoping you don't have any bad news about Blue."

He looked at me somewhat puzzled, and then it was as if a light bulb lit above his head. "What? Oh, Helena, no. Blue is going to be fine. I asked you to come here for coffee because I wondered if you would consider going out to dinner with me this Saturday night."

I let my held breath expel, making a very unladylike gushing sound as it left my body. I didn't realize that I had been holding my breath until that moment. Then the invitation he just proposed hit me. I stuttered, "Like a date?"

I'm sure my face showed signs of my undisguised surprise. This man was certainly not one for small talk. He was a get right to it kind of guy. And here I thought he wanted to talk about Blue.

He laughed. His eyes crinkled up, and he let out a belly laugh that was absolutely enchanting. "Yes, Helena, exactly like a date." His smile broadened, and his eyes had a little twinkle I hadn't noticed before. "You must know that I've wanted to ask you out, but I've been trying to wait to give you time to adjust to single life. The problem is, I don't want to push you too soon, but I also don't want to wait too long in case someone else has the same idea."

I laughed back. Mel liked me. Whoa. This was amazing and something very unexpected. His blue eyes didn't just twinkle; they looked at me as though he had some secret knowledge of which I was not privy, and his dimples were more pronounced than I ever remembered. Of course, I had never sat across from him before, and so I had never studied his ruggedly handsome features.

I gulped and began, "Mel, I have to say, and apologize if I need to, but I guess I haven't been aware of your interest. I am, however, very flattered and very happy." I tugged at my ear and swallowed again. It was something I did when I was nervous. Hank had always laughed when I did it. I hoped that I didn't sound as stupid or inept as I felt. I have not dated in so long; I don't have any idea how to do this dance step anymore. Even as a teenager, I wasn't very good at flirtation.

"Hey, Helena, I don't want to put you on the spot, here, you can say, no thanks, I won't be offended. Disappointed for sure but not offended. We'll always be friends, but I was hoping maybe we might be more than that. Or, at least, explore whether or not we want to be more than friends."

I looked at him. I twisted the ring on the finger of my left hand. It wasn't a wedding ring. My wedding ring had left such a lasting mark on that finger after thirty-two years of wearing it that when I took it off, I began wearing an amethyst ring that Gilliam and Gabe had given me for Christmas years ago. "I'd love to go out with you Saturday night."

Mel expelled his breath as though he had also been holding it waiting for my answer. I truly was touched by his desire to take me out and by his sincerity in his approach. I could tell that this was not something casual to Mel; it appeared to be an occasion of considerable importance to him, and that made it very important to me. I think he might even have rehearsed it. Planning how he might approach me, asking me to the diner for coffee before actually asking me out on a date. This was so affirming to me; I was enjoying it immensely.

Mel had been married to a wonderful woman, Elaine, and he never had children. She was a rather frail person and actually seldom ever seemed to be in any great state of health. Robust would not be a word that would have been used in the same sentence with Elaine. No one in town knew anything about her leukemia until the last year of her life when her health declined so rapidly that it was obvious to everyone. She died about five years ago, and Mel, although devastated at first, seems to have adjusted to single life. I never thought of him as a man of interest. I don't know why. But of course, I haven't thought of anyone in that way. I'm still trying to figure out where my life is headed, and to think of heading there with somebody other than Hank hadn't yet crossed my mind.

Mel and I finished our coffee, he paid the bill, and we left the diner together. He walked me to my car, telling me he'd pick me up Saturday night. He told me to dress casual, and then he strolled back out front, with a little hitch in his step that I hadn't noticed before. I drove home singing along with the radio. It's interesting the little things we forget about when we're sad. I had forgotten how good it feels to sing along with the radio. I turned up the volume and sang at the top of my vocal reach. I was feeling good about myself again. Someone I liked and admired found me attractive. It hadn't really occurred to me until then just how totally unattractive I had been feeling lately.

As I sang the words of "Ain't No Mountain High Enough" along with Marvin Gaye and Tammi Terrell, I decided to claim this song for Mel and me even if our only date was the one we were going to share this coming Saturday. The chorus was filled with promise. This was a promise I hadn't realized—until today—that I needed.

> *There ain't no mountain high enough*
> *Ain't no valley low enough*
> *Ain't no river wide enough*
> *To keep me from getting to you, babe.*

I was singing now at the top of my lungs. My windows were down, and I was jiving to the music. I hadn't felt this alive in a long time. I was wanted. Someone wanted me. I wasn't old. I wasn't all used up. I was still attractive, and someone—not just any someone—Mel, wanted to go out with me. Yes. Yes. Yes. I kept singing.

The rest of my week was sweet. I got a pedicure and a manicure. This was something I hadn't done in years. I got my hair cut and had some highlights added. I didn't buy a new dress because Mel said casual, but I did actually buy a new lipstick and some eyeliner at the drugstore. I decided to wear my hair down, cascading over my shoulders, not up in my usual ponytail. I was feeling girly, and I was enjoying every minute of it. I don't think I have felt this excited about going out with a man since I was in college and first started dating Hank.

I stopped for a minute while my thoughts rushed back to all those years with Hank. Then, very intentionally, I shook off those thoughts, put Hank in a back drawer of my mind, and concentrated on Mel.

Saturday night came, and Mel picked me up right at seven. He and I both had chosen dress jeans, polished boots, and casual tops. He commented on how beautiful I looked and said, with appreciation in his eyes, that he liked my hair down. I felt like a teenager, and I couldn't stop smiling.

We drove to Savannah. For the hour it took to drive over and back, we enjoyed comfortable and easy conversation. We talked about Blue and Grey, his business, the weather, the marshes, our days at college, and a lot of easy subjects that were personal to just him and me. We didn't talk about children or spouses or family. That made it more like a date in a younger period of our lives. We had a wonderful dinner at a waterfront restaurant on the intercoastal waterway. We both had a crispy green salad and crab legs with lots of melted butter, and we spent the entire night talking as we slurped ice cold beer, licked our fingers, and laughed. I know that I tossed my head a lot and laughed more than I have laughed in a very long time.

Our first date was wonderful, and as it turned out, it was to be the first of many. He kissed me on the cheek at the door when he said good night and asked if he could call me again.

We were proceeding slowly. Neither Mel nor I was excessively needy, and therefore we didn't need to live in each other's pocket. That was good for both of us. I was used to a busy and independent man, and Mel fit both of those characteristics, so it wasn't one of those budding romances where people have to see each other every day or evening to exist. I don't think either one of us could have handled that kind of connection, at least not at this point in our relationship.

It was, however, definitely romance; and sometime during the day, we usually did hit base by phone. Our conversations were never long as they were usually stolen between Mel's clients. But it was nice to have someone want to inquire if all was well, and I loved to hear the smile in his voice.

Our first kiss at the end of our second date was very enlightening. The kiss was scary but wonderful. We both felt it. The "it" we felt was the "it" that everyone wants to feel when their lips touch someone else's for the first time. The kiss was tender and passionate and tasted good. We both had been around the block. In my case once and I didn't inquire nor did I want to know how many models that Mel had driven.

Some things are just better left unknown, and I'm happy that is one of them.

As my relationship continued to grow with Mel, I was even beginning to feel kinder toward Hank and Autumn.

God does have a plan. It's difficult to understand how God can use all things for good, but then when something significant happens, you begin to feel like you are having an epiphany. You know, feeling like God has let you have just a peek at what might be unfolding and reassuring you that in the background he is truly orchestrating and fulfilling his plan for a life that he designed just for you.

For a while after Hank left me, I moved away from God. I didn't really want to read his word, and I was too upset and broken to even pray, which had always been a part of my day, some days only a small part but it was still who I was.

Now I have begun reading from the Bible each morning and starting my day with a quiet prayer. I've been thinking more about how God works in all of our lives.

Way back when the world was just beginning, God gave Eve to Adam as a helper because God knew that being alone was not a normal human condition. That's why God created us, because he didn't want to be alone. I have absolutely no doubt that since God knows all things, he knew exactly what was going to happen in the garden of Eden. It was his desire that we would have free will. It's also his desire that we obey him, but he knows that it will not be easy for us to do that, and that we will fail. As difficult and disappointing as we are, he forgives us, and all he asks is that we love him and learn to love and forgive others. I'm slow, but I'm getting there.

Life was beginning to hold promise again. I was moving on. I was feeling better about me, which made it easier for me to feel better about other things.

Mel was good for me. I'm sure he didn't have any idea the impact he was having on me. He wasn't doing anything in particular except caring about me, and with his caring, I felt better about the person I was. I adored him, which was causing me some mixed feelings. Before Mel, I wasn't sure that I would ever be able to love and trust again. But Mel is not Hank, and living in fear of being hurt again is not living.

I haven't told Gabe and Gilliam that I'm dating again although, as I said before, I live on a small island, so it's possible if they've talked with their dad, that they know. Neither of them has said anything so I haven't either.

It's good. I like that for a while, I have a piece of my life that just belongs to me. It won't last long, I know that; and it's okay, but for now I'll just savor the feeling that I have a little piece of myself that's my secret.

The Thrill of Looking Back

> You gain strength, courage, and confidence by every experience in which you really stop to look fear in the face. You are able to say to yourself, 'I have lived through this horror. I can take the next thing that comes along…'
> You must do the thing you think you cannot do.
>
> —Eleanor Roosevelt

As good as things were beginning to go again in my life, I felt a twinge that something wasn't right. I didn't seem to have a purpose. I had no husband to take care of, the kids were raised, and my family was far away. I made knitted squares at night while watching TV for *Warm Up America*. The squares are made into blankets and distributed to the homeless, and others who need a cover for security or warmth or just to hold. Knitting, riding my girls, Blue and Grey, and cooking on the odd occasion for Mel were the almost total substance of my life. It wasn't enough.

Inside I was missing something life sustaining. What I needed was to be accomplishing something. I needed to do some good and not just exist. In church, I hear that God made us all for a purpose. Was my purpose fulfilled? Was I done? I could not accept that. I refuse to believe that God just puts us out to pasture. I'm healthy, I have a brain, and I have a heart; and all three things need exercise, and exercise means activity.

I had thought about getting more involved at church, but nothing there felt quite right. I had served on practically every committee there was to serve on. I'd helped out in the kitchen for years—setting up, cleaning up, and cooking for the family night dinners. I had served on the Christian education, evangelism, and mission's teams. I'd even been on several mission trips and helped to build a Habitat house in our city. I'd helped the worship team in preparing for the communion service. Working for the church was not the total answer. Serving the church is important, but serving God is more than serving the church.

God was being very quiet at the moment. He wasn't directing me. There was a hole burning in my heart. A vast empty space inside me needed to be filled.

Mel and I met for lunch every Wednesday at the diner. On this particular Wednesday when Mel headed back to his office, I ambled down Main Street and walked in to the old bookstore that Mr. Carlton had run for years. I found myself walking through the stacks of books and browsing the titles. Every once in a while, I'd pick up a book with an interesting title or cover, and I'd thumb through it.

Being in that bookstore, aimlessly searching through the books was rather like every day of my life lately. I was looking for something, but I had no idea what that something was? Have you ever wanted to look something up but didn't know what it was you were looking for? It's like when I was little asking my dad how to spell a word, and he'd tell me to look it up in the dictionary. I'd ask him, "If I don't know how to spell it, Dad, how can I look it up?" That's what I felt like now. I wanted to find something, but I didn't know how to look for it.

Maybe I'll get a book on Jekyll Island and find out, after all these years, if there is anything I've not seen or done. Maybe a couple day trips of exploring the island would be fun and fill a few of my idle hours. But again, it would just be filling hours, and that wasn't what I wanted. I wanted to do something that meant something.

"Mr. Carlton, where are the books on Jekyll Island?" I called to him as he sat behind the counter in the front of the store.

"There aren't any. Don't think any have ever been written." He called back to me.

No books were written about our island? That didn't sound right. I left the bookstore and went home. I turned on my computer and went to a book source to determine if I could buy a book about the island over the Internet. No books were available.

It was like a brick hitting me on my head. That was my purpose. A book needed to be written about Jekyll Island. I was no writer, but I had a camera. I had a pen and a notebook and a car, and I had time. I was going to write a book about Jekyll Island. That was going to be my new purpose.

What, I wondered, would I write, and for whom would I write it? I don't have a clue. What I do know is that for the first time in a very long time, except for my budding relationship with Mel, I felt truly excited about something.

That night, I pulled out my map of Jekyll thinking that I would begin driving around the island taking pictures and just pulling things out of the blue. After some further thought, I realized that the map was not a good starting place.

I needed to begin by researching the background of the island so that I could visit places of historical interest starting with the oldest places developed and then working my way to modern times. I would be very organized in my approach, and that way the book would follow a particular pattern and be interesting to read. I could see it now. The cover would be a dynamic picture of some point of interest that I had taken, and in bold letters across the front of the hard bound book would be the words "The Book About Jekyll Island" by Author and Photographer Helena Rivers. I loved that I had a purpose, at last.

What I liked most about my plan is it wouldn't be all about me. I would be writing something that would pass on not only to those in this generation but others in future generations. My grandchildren and their children would be able to benefit from the time I would put into researching my home. I was indeed excited, and I couldn't wait to tell Mel.

Turning on the computer that night, I typed in the name Jekyll, and I began exploring the amazing history of this incredible place. There was a lot of history available as I visited site after site. So much information about one tiny place and no one had ever put it all together into one book before now. I found photography of the island, poetry about the island, even stories about the island. I could camp on the information, explore the places, and write. Would I write a novel and incorporate all that I was learning, or would I write a history book intended also to be entertaining? I think I'll just let it develop itself and see where it goes.

The things I learned about Jekyll were astonishing. I didn't know that the island where I had lived the biggest portion of my life was named after Sir Joseph Jekyll who was born in England in 1663. From my research, I found that he was a barrister, that's the English term for *attorney*, who became a member of parliament, which is the equivalent of our congress and senate. By joining the parliament, he set his course to move through some rather spectacular ranks. I liked him already. He was a man after my own heart. He wanted to accomplish something.

Sir Joseph Jekyll held the position of chief justice of Chester and was master of the rolls. I'm assuming that would be like a sergeant of arms in our United States Congress. When he died in 1738, he was buried in Rolls Chapel. His story wasn't just interesting; it was fascinating. This was captivating stuff. I felt like my life was being infused with new blood, and I could not stop my searching or my reading. In his last will and testament, Sir Jekyll left 20,000 pounds to help pay off England's national debt. Can you imagine anyone today doing something like that? Twenty thousand pounds then would be like someone leaving a million dollars today to pay off the national debt of the United States. It was just a drop in the bucket, and his constituents thought that he was very foolish to have made such a gesture.

I thought it was wonderful. Just think. If people with money could give more back to the government voluntarily maybe we would not be so dependent on foreign loans. I think Sir Jekyll had the right idea.

As I kept reading, it just kept getting better. Now I knew who the island was named after, but I didn't know why it was named after this prestigious Englishman. Well it turns out, it was because he was a good friend of Oliver Cromwell. No, Oliver Cromwell isn't the one who named the island, James Oglethorp did. My challenge now is to find out how all these intersections cross.

I was getting completely caught up in this research, and the more I found, the more I could not believe that someone had not previously published this information in one book. I wonder if the school children on the island learn its history. Maybe that would be a purpose for my research, to incorporate this information into our current school curriculum. I made a mental note to talk with Beth, the local high school principal, about this. Beth and I had been friends for years, and maybe she could direct my research and make it meaningful from the standpoint of educating our young people who grow up here.

The deeper I dig into the facts, the more I know that I need to dig. This is going to require some major reconstruction to sort out this rather bizarre history in order to obtain the full picture. I am excited. In fact I am so enthusiastic that the first night I began this journey, I was still sitting at the computer reading when the sun rose the following morning.

I tumbled into bed at six and slept about four hours when Mel called wanting to know what I was up to. I told him that I had stayed up all night and what I was doing, and he simply said, "Good night, my dear, you need a little more shut eye. I'll talk with you later." When I hung up the phone, I rolled over and went directly back to sleep.

That day and the next day, I had to force myself to take a shower and do a few necessary chores around the house before I turned on my computer to continue my search for information about Jekyll.

It wasn't really surprising to find out that the island was a part of Guale, the Native American chiefdom of the Muskogian tribes of the Creek Nation who inhabited this part of coastal Georgia. I had studied the Creek Indians in school. I understood that these Indians were perfectly happy hunting, fishing, gathering the local nuts, berries and fruit, and growing pumpkins, beans, tobacco, sunflowers, and corn in the rich, dark soil of the island. They even made tea from parched holly leaves.

What did surprise me was that Spain, in the early 1500s had laid claim to this land calling it the White Whale. Then along comes the next surprise. Ponce de Leon, famed as the discoverer of the fountain of youth, was the governor and ruled this island for a period of time.

I was fascinated to discover that the French explorer Jean Ribault ignored that Spain was there and claimed the island for France. He thought the island was the most pleasant place in the entire world, and so he named it *Ille de la Somme*.

Unfortunately for this interesting French chap, he was forced to surrender the island to its original claimant, Spain. His execution, the result of his claiming the land for France and the Spanish taking it back, led to a war between the two countries. The skirmish took place along the Georgia and Florida coast and was swiftly won by Philip II of Spain. This was an eye-opener for the Spanish who realized that they needed to establish a colony on the island to thwart any future countries that may want to lay claim to her. Jean Ribault, although not intending to, really did a big favor for King Philip II.

I was mesmerized by the early stories of this land. It wasn't just interesting history; it was phenomenal to learn that Spain immediately established missions on the island, sending priests to the area to convert the Indians to Christianity.

The following Sunday, after discovering about the missions, I told my pastor and he too was surprised to learn of this. The priests that were sent over from Spain, not being accustomed to primitive living conditions or to living among heathens, were appalled at the Indians' behavior.

The Indians who were lifelong claimants of this land were likewise distraught that the priests were trying to stop their traditional bonfires, native dances, and celebratory banquets. These were an important part of their culture, and having someone tampering with these customs was not something the locals, who were our native American Indians, were prepared to tolerate.

In protest to these forced methods of conversion, the Indians retaliated by destroying the missions and slaying the priests. They felt they were given no choice, and they had never learned any other way to settle a dispute. For some reason, the Indians took Father Davila captive rather than killing him, and then they later released him in a prisoner exchange with the Spanish. It's my belief that Father Davila probably understood the Indians and their plight better than most of those who were sent to Jekyll. It is because of this that the Indians wanted to spare his life. In my mind, I could see Father Davila attempting to intercede with the other priests on behalf of the Indians.

I have, on a number of occasions during my short life, been very impressed by the power that love and compassion has on the behavior and ultimate outcome in a given situation. Having the will of someone else forced upon us only creates hostility. I believe that God gave us free will for just that reason. He, in his ultimate wisdom, knew that mankind would gravitate toward the desires of their own will. He quickly saw man's stubborn desire to please himself with the actions of Adam and Eve in the garden of Eden.

The Indians wanted to maintain their traditions. The priests tried to force their ways onto the natives. Each wanted their own will. Father Davila had compassion and love for the Indians and preferred a more loving approach. For this, Father Davila's life was spared.

If this Spanish and French involvement on Jekyll wasn't interesting enough, at this point in my research, I had traversed only a little more than one hundred and fifty years in time, and here comes the English. We already know a lot about the history of England and America and the Revolutionary War. At this time in history, the English had already established the Jamestown colony, and St. Augustine and they had decided to start establishing grants for land between the two areas.

Oops! That was their big mistake for right in the middle of these two areas was Jekyll Island! The English, being either very sly or very naïve, established relationships with the Cherokee, Creek, and Yuchi tribes and sent members of these tribes to attack both the Spanish and Indian settlements on Jekyll. Using English weapons, they were successful in driving out the Spanish.

Now James Oglethorpe, the one who established Georgia as an English colony, comes along. He is the one who named Jekyll Island after his good friend in parliament, Sir Joseph Jekyll. So how does Cromwell fit in?

My head is fairly whirling with all these facts. How could no one have wanted to put this all together before this? For the first time in months, I was so hyperstimulated that I didn't want to even stop to eat. I forgot to pick up my mail from the box at the end of the driveway for two days. I had to consider that maybe everyone didn't enjoy history like I did. Truth be known, I wasn't that big on history either, but this was history about the place I had called home for most of my life. To boot, it was interesting. To think that these people lived here, fought here, and died here was beyond belief. I understood, as I attempted to rationalize my compulsion for this project that my children were also conceived here and raised here, and one day I would die and be buried on this ground. I certainly would be joining some pretty influential people in a place that was also their burial site.

I loved to read about Louisiana and California and other places where not only hadn't I lived but so far have never even visited. Their early history was fascinating, but it wasn't personal. This was. Would people who didn't live here care about this history? Well time would tell because I wasn't about to quit digging, and I was even more convinced this story needed to be written and published.

The clock moves rapidly ahead for another one hundred years, and it is now the late 1730s. William Horton who was appointed by General Oglethorpe to set up a military post on St. Simon's Island was now a permanent resident on Jekyll Island. Horton had a prosperous plantation near DuBignon Creek. His plantation supplied beef, corn and ale to the population at Fort Frederica, the military post he commanded.

Hmmm, it's interesting to ponder what would have happened then if they had to live by today's standards since what William Horton was doing would certainly have been considered "conflict of interest." Remember that Horton was appointed by General Oglethorpe, so he had significant powerful protection. In the 1700s, it was just how things were done and how people became wealthy. No doubt the word kickback isn't all that new, and so Oglethorpe probably reaped some of the wealth.

Horton's plantation was attacked in 1742 by the Spanish and was burnt to the ground. Horton stubbornly rebuilt his home and began growing the "new" crops of barley and indigo. Burnt out a second time, he constructed his third home on that property out of lime, oyster shell, and water. It was an extremely tough building material that was called tabby, and the house is still standing today.

My research revealed that the Horton house is one of only two remaining colonial era structures in Georgia, two-story structures, that is. I stopped long enough to mark my map. This was one place I wasn't going to miss, and I marked beside the circled spot on my map—*Horton's plantation: Take Camera.*

Horton died shortly after he rebuilt his home for the third time. At the turn of the century, with the passing of fifty years, Christophe du Bignon took over the ownership of the entire island. The year was then 1792. I'm not planning on testing anyone on this history, but, for many people, it is important to know the year that something took place. If you are a true historian, which as I said before, I am not, it helps to establish what else was going on in the area or in the country at the same time that this history was being created. It's kind of like knowing where we were and what was going on when the Twin Towers came down in New York City. We remember much of history, even our own history, by other events of the day.

I remember after Gabe and Gilliam were both in school that I had begun teaching an adult Sunday school class. One Sunday, one of the class members brought up the subject of what was going on in the rest of the world when things were happening in the Bible. So many times when we read the Bible, we forget that it is the *greatest* history book of all time. We have a tendency to read it like it was disconnected from the rest of the world, but that is far from the actual truth.

I began investigating, and one of the more interesting facts, as it related to our current lives here in the United States, was that between the time when Isaac, Jacob, and Esau was born that Native Americans immigrated to North America from northern Asia. This was between AD 2066 and 2000. There were several other significant happenings that I remember from that investigation—one was that the Mexican Sun-Pyramid was built around the same time that Moses was born, in the early AD 1500s, and the Celts invaded Britain in AD 874, which was about the same time that Ahab became the king of Israel. Jonah was swallowed by the whale around the time of the first Olympic games in AD 776.

It may seem strange to you that I would care about this history, but if we thought we invented the Pony Express in the early days of our country, we need to think again because there was horseback postal service in the Persian empire in AD 540, and shortly after that, the Persians enjoyed playing Polo.

Many times I have wondered why those on the other side of our globe seem to resent Americans. I don't think that I, or we, have done anything to harm them. Then I think about sibling rivalry and how a new baby is often not welcomed by an older brother or sister. The United States is the baby.

The Great Wall of China was built in AD 215, which was more than one hundred years before Cleopatra became the last independent Egyptian ruler of the ancient world. We, as a country, are only slightly over two hundred years old. Think about the fact that almost two thousand years ago, in 75 BC, Rome began construction on the famous coliseum.

I do believe that in all things in this life, we need to look back at what happened before to understand what is happening now.

When I exhausted all the Internet search sites that I could find for information on Jekyll, I chained myself to a table at the library and continued my search. I spent so much time at the library researching that I had to pull myself away to do the ordinary things in my life that prior to this project had been my entire existence.

I had become like a woman possessed. I was so deeply engrossed in my research of the Island that doing things like cleaning, shopping, cooking, laundry, even riding Blue and Grey were simply nuisance distractions. The only thing that still held my interest more than my research was Mel. I couldn't wait for evenings when we could spend some time together, even if it was only on the phones, to tell him about my project and what I had discovered about the island.

I think Mel was interested. He appeared to be. But I also got the distinct feeling that he was concerned about the time I was putting into this project and what the outcome might be. I think he was afraid that no one would be interested in publishing a book about Jekyll Island, if I could even find a publisher. Mel, by this time, cared about me enough that he did not want to see me disappointed. I was, however, so enthusiastic that I was not going to be deterred.

Gabe and Gilliam seemed to humor me when I told them what I was doing. Last time I talked to Gabe, he said, "Yeah, Mom, that sounds like a real nice project to keep you busy." I got the impression it wasn't anything he thought was of the least importance, but if it gave me something to do, he was all for it. And Gilliam just came right out and said, "Mom, what on earth is motivating you to do such a thing? Maybe you need to come here for a couple weeks and let that project cool down, so you can get some perspective on it."

I tried to explain to her that I felt it was important that the islands' history be documented. Didn't she want to know? Didn't she think that someday her children would want to know? I told her, "We study everybody's history, don't you want to know what went on here before you lived here?"

She laughed. "No, not really, Mom. I really don't care who owned the island before. Will it change the future? Mom, I think you need to quit looking back and start looking forward." She told me about my precious granddaughter and what she and Mike were up to, and then we gave each other our love, and she hung up.

I sat there thinking. Was what I was doing stupid? No, I didn't think so. I thought it was very important, and I was still excited to continue learning everything I could about Jekyll. Monday morning, after my routine annual visit to Dr. Shirley, I went back to the library.

Here I was in 1792 again. Christophe du Bignon came to Jekyll to get away from the devastation perpetrated against the provincial families like his own that was caused by the French Revolution. I pictured him looking a little bit like Napoleon, without his hand resting on his chest woven through the space between his jacket buttons. In my imagination, I see him with a full head of black curly hair, a rather prominent nose, and steely blue eyes. He would be a commanding figure of a man who expected much from the people around him. His Jekyll Island plantation was prosperous. Cotton was his main crop. Christophe introduced slavery to the island in 1808. His son, Henri Charles du Bignon, who I conjured as being like a relative twin of his father in both looks and carriage, took over the plantation in 1825 upon Christophe's death.

I was blown away by the next bit of information that I managed to dig out of the old records of the island. Only fifty years after the importing of slaves to the United States was made legal, the next-to-last shipment left Africa. In November of 1858, four hundred and sixty-five slaves were delivered to this island in the bowels of the ship *The Wanderer*.

The Wanderer. What an apt name. My mind moves off into a field full of thoughts fertilized by my compassionate heart. Fifty years is nothing more than a wink of God's eye.

Not historically but personally, think of it, only one more time would these desperate souls be rounded up and placed into bondage. I wonder if some of those making that long watery voyage to this country did so voluntarily and with great expectations of leaving behind a worse life for a better one. Was what they paid in servitude worth the price of their passage? They had no idea what was ahead.

There are so many ways to look at slavery, which existed even in Biblical times. God was aware of slavery and told the masters to be kind to their slaves and the slaves to obey their masters. There is and has always been slavery throughout the entire world. Think of Moses leading his people out of the slavery that they endured in Egypt. During those forty years when they wandered through the desert, they looked back. For some, slavery can be a predictable force that may be preferable to the unknown elements that come with freedom. We see that today with battered spouses, harangued workers, dependent family members who hesitate to move on even though moving on could mean an improved life.

Today there are probably more slaves than existed before. Children, women, men used for various purposes against their will, not free to live the life they were meant by God to live, rather living a life under the duress and power of another. I pray the extraordinarily outrageous prayer every day for the release of slaves throughout our world.

As my mind drifts, I ponder all that was happening here in 1858. It is difficult to accept that this was going on only about one hundred years before my birth. Approximately one lifetime ago, these things unfolded on the very soil where I now stand and live. I wonder what it will be like one hundred years from now.

Every bit of history that I was unearthing in my search of discovery was like a shining jewel. This wasn't just about Jekyll Island; this was the history of America. This was a significant and important piece of our history, and I had never heard it before. I had never studied about it in school. I never knew it existed.

I wished that I had Mel there to share each discovery with. Sometimes I would take out my cell phone and text him. When he got the time, he would text me back. I liked that about him.

He was attentive to my needs. I wonder if I was giving him back as much as he was giving to me. I stopped for a moment when that thought entered my mind and said, "Dear, God, please don't let me fail Mel like I believe I must have failed Hank. I care about both of these men. Help me be a good mate to this man who is so very dear. Amen."

I forced my head back into the research book that was currently spread out before me on the table. The island remained in the du Bignon family; however, in 1886 an investment plan was hatched to sell the island to the wealthy, and they would use it as a winter retreat.

As with all new endeavors today and apparently true even then, you first have to start with the clubhouse. So the clubhouse was completed in 1888, and fifty-three investors put in six hundred dollars each to form the Jekyll Island Club. It was the initial desire and intent that this club would remain exclusive. The initial investment strategy was to allow only one hundred members.

The world's wealthiest were attracted to the Jekyll Island Club where, due to the mild winter weather, even in the coldest months in the north, they could visit to hunt, ride horses, bike, play tennis, and even sun bathe on the beaches. It was a true tropical environment for those who resided in the colder parts of the north eastern United States.

Many of the members built their own mansions adjacent to the club house desiring to reside and entertain in only the greatest lap of luxury. Those mansions are still on the island today. Pulling out my map I circled that area and made another notation, *Jekyll Island Club: Take Camera.*

World War II played havoc with the winsome and playful environment heralded as the club's biggest attraction to owners and guests.

After the big one was over, in 1947, the state of Georgia condemned the island and paid the members who remained a total of six hundred and seventy-five thousand dollars for all the buildings and land. It was robbery.

My head was throbbing, and I realized I had been sitting here mesmerized for hours, forgetting to not just get up and stretch occasionally, but I hadn't even bothered to eat lunch or to get a sip of cool water from the fountain. I left the dimly lit library and entered a bright sunshiny day. The sun was so brilliant that it actually caused pain in my eyes. I slipped my dark glasses off the top of my head and snuggled them onto my nose.

I strolled down to Molly's diner and got a tall glass of sweet tea and a chicken salad. Molly has a reputation in town for the best chicken salad, and it doesn't ever fail to satisfy. Molly cooks her own chickens each morning, cools them, chunks the meat, and adds fresh grapes, walnuts, chopped celery, and real Duke's mayo. Yum. Then she makes fresh banana or cranberry bread to serve with it.

Oh, Baby!

Let no man value at little price
a virtuous woman's counsel.

—George Chapman.

As I sat there in the diner's coolness sipping my tea and munching on the cold, fresh salad, Hank walked in. He was alone. He saw me, and our eyes met. I thought he would probably sit at the bar like he usually did, but instead he strolled toward me. "Mind if I join you?"

"Nope, I don't mind," I said not very excitedly, "have a seat."

I put another fork full of salad into my mouth and chewed slowly. Hank looked like he wasn't feeling well or had something significant on his mind. I've seen that look before. He just didn't look right. Maybe upset was the better word to describe his demeanor. All I had wanted when I got here to the diner was to sit in my favorite back booth where Mel and I had met the first time for coffee, eat, and think about my research and Mel.

In the midst of my plan enters Hank. This would not be the quietly ruminating lunch that I had desired. But for my entire life, whenever Hank was around, it was always all about Hank. It always had been, and I guess, even when I am no longer married to him, it always would be.

Hank sat in the seat across from me picked up the menu and pretended to look through the offerings. I say pretended because he knew what he was going to order before he walked in the door. It's the same for the waitress, Sally, who came over and took his order. She probably had it written on her pad before she got to the table. Good old Hank, any one in town could have ordered for him. For thirty years, he's been ordering the same thing, so it wasn't unusual to hear him ask for a cheeseburger, medium, with cooked onions, and a Coke. I wanted to ask him if it was true that Autumn was a vegetarian, but I decided this wouldn't be the right time to do that.

Sally gave me a cute little smile, which I think behind it was saying, "*What are you two doing together?*"

"What cha up to?" Hank asked as Sally left to put his order in with the cook.

"I've been at the library doing research." I put another fork full of chicken salad in my mouth as I ended my response and chewed slowly as I looked over at him.

"Yeah, the kids told me you're off on some kick, digging up the history of the island to write a book or something." He looked at me, but it was like he was looking right through me. It wasn't me that he wanted to be sitting here with, that was obvious, and he didn't look or act very happy.

"Yep, that's what I'm doing." I felt kind of resentful by his words for a number of reasons. The kids and he were talking and not just talking. They were apparently talking about me. That did not make me happy although when I talk with the kids, I talk about Hank, so maybe fair is fair. I was also peeved that Hank apparently didn't take what I was doing any more seriously than the kids did. Well I was determined to prove them all wrong and I would.

Shaking off the irritation, I politely ask, "Are you okay?"

Sounding sincere and feeling sincere are two different things. I really didn't care if he was okay or not. Actually, that's only partially true. Part of me will always care, but part of me wishes that Hank would move to Savannah and leave me on this little island without having to run into him like this. I think I'm all through with the past, that I have moved on, and then I see Hank and Autumn or run into one of them, and it's all right back in my face again. Sitting here at the table with Hank now, in my mind, once again I go to my creator and I ask, "God, will I never ever be able to put the past truly behind me, even with your help?"

I had lost myself so deeply in my thoughts that I almost jumped when Hank answered, "No, Helena, I'm not okay. I'm fifty-seven damn years old, and Autumn told me last night that she's pregnant." He looked thoroughly disgusted. With whom, I'm not sure. His food hadn't arrived yet, and he was sitting with the knife spinning it around in his two hands. It was plain to see how agitated he was.

"Wow." I let the wow drag out until the first *W* was lost, and it almost sounded like someone who has caught his thumb in the car door. I should have stopped there, but sometimes the devil does want his due. The opening presented itself, and I took it, "I would have thought you two kids would have known how to prevent that. I guess we should have had "the talk.""

It was definitely not the right thing to say. Hank was hurting, and I was rubbing it in. But, boy did it feel like the right thing to me; sometimes paybacks just feel so good.

Then to rub more salt in the wound, I continued, "I wonder how Gabe and Gilliam are going to feel about having a little brother or sister."

Hank shook his head and looked at me as if I were a traitor. "Thanks for understanding, Helena." Our eyes met, and I could see water forming in the corners of his eyes. Hank had never cried in all the years I'd known him.

He started to slide out of the booth we shared, "I think I'd better go sit somewhere else."

I instinctively reached out my hand and laid it on his. "No, Hank, don't go. I'll try to behave myself, but honestly, Hank, it's not easy for me either. I know you're hurting. Believe me, I understand hurting. What I still am having a problem with is 'accidents'."

I looked up at him and rolled my eyes. I could feel the tears welling up, and I was working hard not to show my emotion or let it be heard in my voice. I wanted my words to be supportive, and yet deep inside I still felt the hurt of Hank's betrayal. "You seem to be rather accident prone these days. First, you accidentally fall in love with another woman, and now she accidentally gets pregnant. It almost seems like some kind of poetic justice, except it's not, it's life."

I was talking to Hank like he was Gabe or Gilliam, and I knew it and so did he. "And, Hank, you are just going to have to make the most of it. If you truly love Autumn, and you have to or you wouldn't have left me for her, then you'll both be okay. And the baby couldn't ask for a better father. You raised two great kids so far…now you can raise a third one."

"No, that isn't true Helena." Hank shook his head.

I held my breath as I waited for him to explain which part wasn't true.

Hank continued, "I did not raise two great children. You did. I was busy making a living. I get no credit for Gabe or Gilliam. I wish I did. They are two great people, and I love them both. Even if I could take any of the credit for them turning out so good, I was thirty plus years younger than I am now. Do you know, Helena, that when this little one gets ready to go to college, I'll be in my seventies! What am I doing?"

His voice was shaking, and except for the time in our bedroom, almost two years ago, when he told me he was leaving, I don't think I had ever seen him look so scared. The life that Hank had thought he wanted had played a dirty trick on him. Life does that when we least expect it.

"Hank," I put on my in-charge voice, "I'm going to give it to you like I'd give it to Gabe or Gilliam sitting here with me in a similar situation. I'm going tell you what you're going to do. If you're smart, which I know you are, when I'm done you'll do what I've told you. I know I'm not your mother, but I'm a pretty smart woman."

He looked at me with pleading eyes, similar to what I would have seen on a child's face, and I continued, "You're going to eat your cheeseburger, and then you're going to go find Autumn, and the two of you are going to act like grownups and start planning your wedding. Neither one of you will want your child to be born a bastard." As the word rolled off my tongue, I saw Hank flinch.

"I'm sorry, Hank, I know that's a cruel way to put it, but that's exactly what it is if you don't get hitched and soon." My voice cracked. I was telling the man that I had been married to and had children with to marry another woman. How insane am I?

"Wait a minute, Helena." Hank started to talk, and I held up my hand to silence him as I continued.

"I'm not done yet, Hank. When I am, it will be your turn, but I suggest you think about what I'm saying before you start refuting it. Since you don't need to go on a honeymoon," I rolled my eyes for emphasis, "I suggest you take the money you would have spent on one and open a trust fund for that little one. If you aren't around when that precious child goes to college, because you're worried about how old you will be when he or she reaches that stage in their life, then you'll want to at least have planned for his or her future." I nodded my head as I put my fork down, which I still held in my hand and slid back in my seat.

"I know you think I just acted like someone who has a right to talk to you like that, and I do. It's true, I am no longer your wife but, Hank, I am your friend." I almost stopped when the word friend tumbled out of my mouth so easily. I was Hank's friend. It was almost an epiphany. I knew right then that I always would be Hank's friend. I did still love this man not any longer as a husband but as a friend, and I do deeply care what happens to him.

In addition to being a friend, Hank is also the father of my children and a grandfather to my grandchildren. We still have a lot in this life that we share and being friends will make that sharing a lot easier. Autumn is pregnant with Gabe and Gilliam's brother or sister. Extended families can be difficult, but I already knew that I was not going to be the one that prevented us all from being a family.

I looked Hank directly in the eyes and said, "Hank, right now I think you need some good friendly advice. Actually, maybe it's motherly advice because if your mom or my mom was still here, I think what I just said is exactly what either one of them would have said to you."

I leaned over in the seat and picked up my purse and the book that I had brought in with me from the library to read but never got to open. "I'll leave you to pay my bill; I'm heading back to the library to work on my new endeavor. And, Hank, I'd appreciate if you would support me in my new life like I will support you in yours." I slid out of the booth, patted Hank's hand, kissed him on the cheek, and left.

I know this isn't nice, but I think I actually may have had a little skip in my step. I couldn't wait to tell Mel. I looked upward. *I know, God, this is not the kind of behavior you expect from me; but just this once, I'm going to enjoy the moment, before common sense and good values take over, and I ask your forgiveness.*

I didn't go back to the library; instead I slid into my very hot car. Putting the windows down to expel the heat, I pulled out into the street. I decided to take a drive to the historic district of the island. I wanted to visit the Jekyll Island Club area, and I knew that after my encounter with Hank, I wouldn't be able to sit at a table in the library and quietly concentrate on research.

The Jekyll Island Club, when I reached the area, was a remarkable two hundred and forty acres in the mid-section of the river side of the island.

The enormous two-winged club's hotel is the centerpiece of the district. There are currently more than thirty cottages the size of mansions that surround the hotel, which is still operational.

I went inside the hotel where I obtained an informational brochure about the Jekyll Island Club that explained that the three-story turret on the front of the club's hotel contained the presidential suite, which was one of several rental suites in the hotel. Some of the cottages also have rooms for rent, and some have been converted to museums, art galleries, and bookstores.

Leaving the hotel, I notice that there is a plaque that says the district and the hotel were designated in 1978 as National Historic Landmarks. Thirty-one years after Georgia took the land from the original owners, claiming the land and buildings to be condemned, it became recognized as a national treasure. I made a mental note to do some additional research on how this all came about.

Driving around to observe as much of the area as was possible, I parked at the museum on Stable Road and noticed a sign that read, "Tram tour guides needed." I walked inside and inquired.

Leaving the museum about thirty minutes later, I leave as Jekyll Islands' newest tour guide and museum docent. My obligation as tour guide will start next week with a schedule to work two days a week.

When this day started, it seemed like every other day; but a lot had happened, and I decided that I would circle this on my calendar as a day to never forget.

Just a half hour ago, when Mr. Parker, a stately white-haired gentleman of significant years, started the interview by asking me what I knew about the island, I think I blew him away. I noticed the look of surprise on his face as I started recalling all that I had learned in the past weeks of my research.

I could tell instantly by the expression on his face that he was significantly impressed, and even more than that, he was excited to find a kindred spirit who shared his love for the history of this island. He didn't hesitate even a moment before he offered me the job. I felt like he had been waiting his entire life for me to open that door and walk in.

I could not wait to share with Mel the adventures of this wonderful day. What happened since arriving at the Jekyll Island Club shadowed the previous news Hank shared with me about him and Autumn. I could hardly believe that only several hours had passed since I had made my mother speech to Hank.

Some days are just meant for wondrous things to happen. The amazing thing about my inquiry about the tram tour job and meeting Mr. Parker was that Mr. Parker also told me they were looking for a docent at the museum. He said he thought I would fit that bill nicely.

I asked him who I should talk to about the docent position, and he, with a mischievous smile on his face, responded, "Me." In addition to my two days as tram guide, I have also been scheduled to work two afternoons from one-thirty to four-thirty as docent. That's four days a week where I will have a real purpose. God does answer prayers; we just have no idea how or when.

I'm not done yet. During the course of our conversation about the tram tours and the docent position, Mr. Parker asked me how I had come to know so much history about the island. I told him I had gone to the library looking for a book on Jekyll Island and found that there was no comprehensive book about this wonderful place that I have called home for over thirty years.

When I told him I was researching to write a book about the history of the island, he was very enthusiastic. He thought the museum might be interested in underwriting my efforts and helping to get it published. He knew they would want to offer such a book in their museum shop, and if offering to help underwrite it helped to get it in the shop, they would probably agree to do that. He told me he intended to approach the board at their next meeting.

As I went back to my car, I realized that even with my two new jobs, I would still have ample time to ride the girls, continue my research, and do whatever else I wanted. Even though Mel put no such restriction on me, I found that I tried to keep most of my evenings open in case his schedule made it possible for us to spend some of that time together.

When I look back at the last several months, I realize that by stepping out in faith and moving in a new direction, I have truly taken strides toward affecting a new purpose in my life.

I have progressed from wife and mother to tour guide and docent, all because I wasn't afraid to believe in myself and meander outside the restrictive barrier that limited the order of my "previous" life.

I want to finish my research and write the book about our island. I want to be a good companion for Mel. Today I learned that it's possible now that I can be a friend to Hank. I love the idea that I will have a job where I will be helping others to understand a little more about the history of this area and how it has impacted our country. And I still have my horses.

I have no idea what tomorrow holds in any area of my life, and I don't feel a great need to know. I just appreciate that right now, I feel alive, enthusiastic, and focused on the exciting years that lay ahead of me. It's been a long time since I've felt excited about my future. For a long time, I didn't think I had a future; but now I know I do, and it's looking good.

Taking It with You

> The world is full of poetry. The air is living with its spirit;
> and the waves *dance* to the music of its melodies,
> and sparkle in its brightness.
>
> —Percival

Sidney Lanier, American musician and poet, made his impact all over Georgia.

One day that I had dedicated to my research on Jekyll Island, I came across some information about Lanier. I was introduced to the works of Lanier when I was a Sophomore in college, but I never knew that he had been born in Macon, Georgia, which is not far from my own hometown. I wondered at the time how I could not have been aware of that. We southerners love to celebrate each other and our successes.

I was absolutely delighted to find out that we also shared a birthday—the month and day only, but that was a good thing since if I had been born in 1842, as Sidney was, it would definitely explain why some days I feel really old.

Actually since Sidney and I share February third as our common birthday, I feel like I'm entitled to call him by his first name. He probably wasn't as attached to being born in February as I am. I love February because I always think of it as the love month. It's kind of like when I read my Bible, I relish turning to First Corinthians the thirteenth chapter because that is the book that Paul wrote about love. But, of course, I digress.

Traveling straight north out of Atlanta, you reach the sixty square mile Lake Lanier, named after Sidney. The reservoir was created in 1956 when the Buford Dam was built to hold back the waters of the Chattahoochee River. The Chestatee River also feeds the reservoir, which is a source of fresh water for the ever burgeoning and overpopulated Atlanta region.

On the coast of Georgia, we also took claim of the important man with the two-hundred-and-three-foot tall Lanier suspension bridge over Hwy 17. As people cross over that immense structure, they get an inspiring view of the marshes that I have loved ever since I moved here; and apparently, from his body of work, so did Sidney.

I cherish what I believe to be one of the most profound poems that Lanier ever wrote. I have dabbled in writing poetry since I was very young and have strived to allow words to flow from my heart into rivers of pure joy. I can't do it. Sidney did. I have basked for years in his *Hymns of the Marshes*, "Sunrise."

Like the marshes themselves that change and yet are forever constant, this poem seems to fit me no matter at what age or situation I find myself. It is a masterful piece of writing that reaches into my soul. This poem begs you to know the man as he shares his heart and soul. Writers do that. People read their words and move on, but the author leaves a piece of him or herself forever on the page, vulnerable to critique, brave in their endeavor.

When I read these words, a light comes on in the center of my being, and I am there with him. I can close my eyes, and I can see the marshes, the swallows, the sunlight. I understand his vision and his heart.

The tide's at full: the marsh with flooded streams
Glimmers, a limpid labyrinth of dreams.

With those words, he paints so perfectly the picture of my marshes. I can see the waters filling the tidal basins and engorging themselves around the wild rice and sea grasses. The glimmer of the rising sun feels like one giant glass mirror reflecting God's light all around us. Even if you have never seen the marshes, his words make them come alive. If you had lived in a cave all your life and never even seen the sun glimmering on water, you could close your eyes and see the scene unfold in front of you.

> *Oh, what if a sound should be made!*
> *Oh what if a bound should be laid*
> *To this bow-and-string tension of beauty and silence a—*
> *Spring,—*

Beauty. Silence. I love how he uses the tautness of the string on a bow to describe how just one noise, one chirp of a bird, one splash of a fish tail against the water would break the beautiful breath holding moment that stretches before him.

> *Yon dome of too-tenuous tissues of space and night,*
> *Over-weighted with stars, over-freighted with light,*
> *Over-sated with beauty and silence*

He begs us to search for that one moment where it seems the earth has stood still, and even the rotation of the world has for a brief moment stopped.

> *In the leaves? in the air?*
> *In my heart? is a motion made:*

My sensitive and sentimental core has bonded with his through his words; I share his feelings in wanting to find the very things in nature and in our life that truly matter. What gives harmony to our existence are those things that stir our hearts.

> *And invisible wings, fast fleeting, fast fleeting,*
> *Are beating*
> *The dark overhead as my heart beats,—and steady and*
> *Free*
> *Is the ebb-tide flowing from the marsh to the sea*

Sidney's words allow my heart to unburden itself of its tethers—no longer to be in bondage to whatever it has been chained to today. I can see the ducks gliding noiselessly on the shimmering water. I can see the tall and willowy wild rice bending in the slight breeze of dawn. I don't need to hear the little swallows and wrens as they make their way through the tall grasses stopping occasionally to hang precariously on a fragile blade. Just knowing they are there is enough. Night is lifting, and dawn is breaking, and the water that was once trapped in the marshes frees itself and moves back out to the sea from where it came. With his precious words, Sidney Lanier captures the lingering fragrance of life on my beautiful Jekyll Island.

That poem is so real I can smell the marshes.

Someday, after I finish the book on Jekyll, perhaps I will write a book on Sidney Lanier. Since we share a birthday, it's almost like we're family. When I first discovered Sidney's poetry years ago, I began building a folder on the Lanier heritage.

The family background that I've currently uncovered goes back to Jerome Lanier who was a Huguenot refugee and probably served as a musician or poet in service to the court of Queen Elizabeth I, the daughter of Henry VIII and Anne Boleyn.

Jerome was the beginning of the bloodline of musicians, poets, and orators who served the rulers of England, Scotland, and Wales, including James I, Charles I, and Charles II.

Thomas Lanier, from another branch of the Lanier tribe, traveled across the big ocean to the United States in 1716 along with numerous others of the Lanier ancestors. Thomas settled in Richmond, Virginia and seeming to like to cavort with royalty and people of influence, it wasn't difficult to believe that a Thomas Lanier married an aunt of George Washington and their offspring became widely scattered in the southern states.

My Sidney's father was Robert S. Lanier who was a lawyer in Macon, Georgia. His mother, Mary Anderson, from Scottish descendants who also settled in Virginia, hailed from a family gifted in poetry, music, and oratory. Sidney came upon his talents honestly receiving his gifts from God as they were passed down to him from both the paternal and maternal sides of his family.

As I study Sidney's genealogy, I have taken complete ownership of the dear man. He has a history far more fascinating than my own. He was a child prodigy in that he could play almost any instrument he picked up, but he was enamored with the flute.

When Sidney was fourteen, he entered Oglethorpe College, near Midway, Georgia not as a freshman but as a sophomore. Oglethorpe was a Presbyterian institution, which, with his mother's Scottish heritage, was a true fit. He graduated at age eighteen in 1860. A year later, regardless of his genius or talent, war broke out, and he was summoned to serve in the Confederate Army with the Macon Volunteers of the Second Georgia Battalion. He refused promotions during the war for the sole purpose of remaining with his younger brother who was his devoted companion in arms.

During the war, my Sidney was overtaken by consumption, which killed so many soldiers. His flute playing, having made his lungs strong, is what is believed to have spared his life. He played first flute some years later for the Peabody Symphony Orchestra in Baltimore, Maryland. Sidney had a colorful and variegated history.

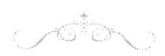

I force myself to refocus back to documenting the history of my beautiful Jekyll Island of which I have also now taken complete ownership. I only hope to be a proper mistress and authority to this beautiful place.

My Jekyll is a barrier island with its entrance achieved when one comes across the paved causeway. The island is fraught with acres of western shore tidal marshlands. The small yet poignant short lines of the poem "Sunset" reveals in full color all that those marshlands are and will always be. The marshes are also protection from hurricanes and other storms. Without them, the Georgia shoreline would be a lot farther west than it is currently.

It is from the vantage point of those flat roads, which loom beside the marshes that the Lanier Bridge stands out as an amazing behemoth of a landmark.

Most of the settlement of the islands' communities and golf courses lie on the north end while until 1964 when Title VII was passed requiring integration, the southern end of the island had been the sole facilities of the African-Americans. Now the island is settled in its entirety, and hopefully, any segregation for any reason is self-inflicted.

It is part of the human condition that everyone has wanted to accumulate wealth and power in one manner or another with the goal to retain it into infinity. As one person put it so aptly, "shrouds don't have pockets," which is what keeps lawyers busy writing and administering our last will and testament.

I have moved in the direction of assets and money because at one time a party of our nation's greatest bankers, brokers and money men stealthily and secretly, under cloak of night, stole away to Jekyll for a week of secret planning. For seven days and nights these busy and powerful men virtually hid away from busy eyes and ears, covertly talking and designing something that presumably was of great importance.

Those twentieth century clandestine meetings held here in 1910 resulted in, what many believe to be, the impetus for our Federal Reserve System. The men who met right here on Jekyll

Island represented about one-fourth of the entire world's wealth at that time.

It raises the hair on my arms just to think what might have been argued and discussed as these powerful men smoked cigars and drank brandy. These debates determined the future of our country's monetary policy and the banking and currency system that has existed now for more than one hundred years. The planners are gone, with their shrouds empty, but their ideas live on, and many of their families still live off their accumulated wealth.

Even though I moved here after Hank and I were married, this island is home. As such, it is easy to take it for granted. I never had the sense that it was anything amazing or unusual, but during my research, I realized that this is indeed a very special place with a royal and amazing history. I imagine that anyone, who took the time, could discover that where they live also has a history rich in characters and happenings that have brought it to where it is today.

My tenacious digging has allowed me to learn about the overtaking, overthrowing, segregation, secrecy, deaths, and all that has occurred on these few acres of land. It really is just a few acres of land in comparison to the size of our entire amazing country and all the rich history that abides everywhere.

This rare and involved look at Jekyll that I have been afforded has made me take stock of my own life. That's what history does. It makes you look at your history, savor it, learn from it, and not repeat personal mistakes.

My kids would come home from school when they were young and say, "I don't understand what good history is ever going to do for me." Of course, Gabe soon outgrew that and fell in love with history. Perhaps he got that from me even though I am a late bloomer. I think if Gabe knew what I was really doing with my research, he'd be very proud of me. When this book is published, it will be a great and proud moment for me to hand one of the first copies to Gabe. It will be a time when we both will be able to share our joint appreciation for what came before us.

Looking back at my own life, I have a new appreciation of the unfolding details of my years. I have gained insight, and I now understand that the significance of the tiny trials that have confronted me in the few years that I have been on this earth is nothing. When I compare the happenings in my life to those immense sacrifices that have been made by those who have been the forefathers of this country, I just want to thank them for the easy life that I live today.

I feel that same way when I open my Bible. I read about Moses. He was scared to death to lead his people out of Egypt to the promised land. But he did it. I think of Abraham who, because God asked, was willing to show his faithfulness by sacrificing his own son on the altar. I think of Job who endured so much and never stopped believing in his Creator. I think of John the Baptist, who, before he was beheaded prepared the way for the people to understand who Jesus was. I think of all the disciples and in particular of Paul and John. Paul endured so much and never quit working to build the church for God. John died an old man, alone, on the island of Patmos after having the revelation from God and writing it down for us.

I am grateful for a God who understands what a weak human I am and loves me anyway.

I love looking back—from the garden of Eden to the clandestine meetings on Jekyll—and feel true gratitude to those who left to us their rich, rich history of sacrifice and achievement, sinners and saints alike. I'm humbled by and delighted with the legacy they left for us to inspire us to pick up where they left off and leave our mark on this world.

Someday I hope that some great, great grandchild of mine will pick up what I wrote in *The Story of Jekyll Island* and get a glimpse of the person that I am, not great but inquisitive and one who truly cares about the past and the future.

I gulp for air as I pull the car off the road. Tears are streaming down my face as I think of Hank and me. I think of Gabe and Gilliam. I think of Autumn and the new baby. I think of Mel. What legacy am I leaving?

When my grandchildren and great grandchildren and great great grandchildren find information about me, will it be information that tells them I made a difference? Will their life be better because of my influence? I don't desire fame; what I want is to do more than just barely make a mark for the time I spent on this earth.

Will being a wife, a mother, a horse owner, a tour guide, a docent, and an author make that difference? I close my eyes and pray. "Dear, God, am I fulfilling your plan for me? Please give me your eyes to see others with your mercy, strength, wisdom, compassion, and kindness to pass on to others. Help me, Lord, to feel your peace. I don't need to understand. Just use me. I love you, God. Amen."

I sit in the car, staring out at my beautiful marshes. The sun is setting, and the light is shining; and I know, with all my heart that God's purpose for me is simply to trust that he is walking beside me as I allow him to lead. My purpose is that simple.

Once more, my mind travels to the poetry of Sidney Lanier. He wrote a poem in 1878 while he was in Baltimore. It was after the war. He was older and more settled and understanding of the human condition. You could hear it in his words.

Pass, kinsman Cloud, now fair and mild;
Discharge the will that's not thine own.
I work in freedom wild,
But work, as plays a little child,
Sure of the Father, Self, Love, alone.

I put the car in gear, and I drive home.

The marsh passes. Then I travel down the street with the diner. I come to my road, and I veer off onto it as it takes me home. Pulling into the drive and going past the large trees, my heart quiets. Parking the car, I get out and climb the seven wide brick steps that take me to my massive front door. It's never locked. I turn the brass knob, push the door open, and walk inside.

Laying my purse on the chair inside the door, I continue through the house toward the large French doors that lead out to the back patio. The sun is shining across the polished floor, and the gardens are blooming with summer flowers. I stand there looking out on all that beauty.

It's been a strange two years beginning with the day that Hank told me he was leaving. My emotions during that time have plummeted, and they have soared.

My saving grace has been that God has walked every day with me. He has shown me that, like the last word in Lanier's poem, I will never be alone. I, for the first time, now understand that it's okay if I'm alone on this earth. When I'm sure of my Father, of myself, and of the love that I am capable of giving and receiving, I will never be alone. I can take with me, everyday, everyplace I go, all the love that I could ever have and ever give, sheathed in my heart and in my memories.

No matter where tomorrow takes me, I feel at peace that the only valuable element of my life that is worth keeping is love.

Plan B

> None of us knows what the next change is going to be, what unexpected opportunity is just around the corner, waiting to change all the tenor of our lives.
>
> —Kathleen Norris

I met Mel that night. He came over to the house, which he was becoming more accustomed to doing on a fairly routine basis. We don't see each other every night, but about three or four times a week, we actually get to have one-on-one, face-to-face conversations. It was so much better than the phone, and both of us hate texting, although we do it. It's easier for Mel to get a text during the day and answer it when he has free time between patients. With my days becoming more involved, we will probably be doing even less of that.

As we sit with our wonderful glasses of crisp, icy cold Chardonnay, me twirling mine in my glass between sips, I tell him about all that had happened that day. I had prepared a small plate of crunchy, sweet Fuji apple slices and some heavenly sharp cheddar wedges with crisp rye crackers. I loved this time when we could enjoy sharing our day with each other and having just enough little finger foods to stave off the hunger that is always induced when I drink wine.

I hesitated for only a moment before sharing with Mel the epiphany I had in the marshes. He listened as we sat on the couch, his arm around me, and my head leaning lightly on his broad shoulder. Mel's boots were left at the door, as he always did—not by invitation but by personal habit—and his feet were now crossed and resting comfortably on the coffee table. During our first evening together, I had encouraged him to put his feet up on the table. I told him it was something I didn't mind since the huge wooden table was built to be used, and over the years, my kids had climbed on it, hammered on it, and many feet had been propped on it. I believe that Mel feels comfortable here, as comfortable as I have always wanted my house to feel to anyone who entered. It wasn't a show place it was a home.

I noticed as we sat there that he had a small hole in the toe of his brown socks. I'll have to put socks on my list for when I go shopping, however, if Mel is like most men, he probably has drawers full of new socks. Without a wife for the past five years, he most likely washes and replaces everything in his dresser without looking for holes, rips, stains, or significant evidence of wear. I've always considered that one of the wife's most important duties in this life is to keep holey and threadbare underwear from returning to a man's dresser drawers. I say that tongue in cheek, but honestly, looking at Mel's socks, it probably is true.

My foot was tapping back and forth against his foot as I recounted all the many and varied incidents that had occurred during my day. It was the farthest thing from a routine day that I have experienced in a very long time. Nothing was hum drum or particularly mundane starting with lunch and ending in the marshes.

Mel did his "hmmmm" at all the right spots, verifying to my ears that he was listening and indicating in his inevitably sweet way to continue. What I wasn't sure of was his level of interest.

There was something a little "out of the norm" about Mel tonight. He seemed anxious maybe or impatient. I couldn't really put my finger on it, but he didn't appear to be as relaxed as he usually is. Maybe it was me and not him. But still…

He had his eyes closed as I recited the poetry from Lanier. I had never asked Mel if he liked poetry or not. It's always been such a big part of my life that I just assume everyone feels as I do.

I know better than that. I can't stand hard rock or rap music, so it stands to reason that some might not enjoy the symphony or the classical compositions that speak to my soul. I love ballet, but street dancing is very difficult for me to appreciate. Ah, but Jazz. Who can't appreciate good jazz?

Looking over at Mel even with his eyes closed, there was still a slight strain in the lines of his jaw and around his mouth that spoke to me. I wasn't sure what it was that my eyes were sensing. "Mel, are you listening?" I asked.

He didn't open his eyes, but his voice was soft when he spoke. "Yes, my dear Helena, I am listening." His arm didn't move from behind my neck, but his hand came up and ruffled my hair. It was a sweet, tender, and endearing move. That's what made me so enamored with Mel. He could give a horse, a dog, or me just that sweet loving touch, and you knew just how much he cared.

Mel's voice had a bit of drowsiness in it when he said, "You've had a very busy day. My head is frazzled just thinking about it."

Then he opened his eyes, and looking down into my eyes, I knew that he intended his next words to be confirming to me. "I was hung up for a while on your meeting with Hank over your chicken salad. I can't imagine Autumn being pregnant and Hank not knowing what to do. It's pretty much a given. The advice you gave him was solid and good, and I'm proud that you found the voice and courage to speak it to him."

He gave me a little hug around my shoulder. "I'll be anxious to see what direction Hank takes from here. I think once he gets accustomed to the idea, Hank will just adjust like you did when he left you. What I don't understand is why he sought you out to share his troubles with?"

Mel paused for a moment, and when I didn't respond, he continued. "Or maybe he didn't seek you out. Maybe it was just fate that you two would end up in the diner today at the same time."

Mel's words kind of faded out, and I could tell he was thinking. I put my arm around his chest and gave him a little squeeze of affection encouraging him to continue.

He did have more to say. "After all the hurt and pain that Hank caused you to now want to share this personal and intimate detail of the life he has with Autumn could almost be considered cruel." He hesitated when he felt the reaction of my body's slight stiffening. "But I think in Hank's case today, it was just fifty-seven-year-old male terror, and he needed a friend's shoulder to cry on." He looked at me to see how I took those words, and as my body once again relaxed, I shook my head that I agreed with his assessment. I was constantly amazed at the always kind and generous insights that Mel formed about people and situations.

Somehow I have never put significant stock in people being perceptive about themselves or those around them. With Mel, it was different. He seemed to be able to look right into the core of a person and define the values and principles that made them tick. Maybe that's also what made him so wonderful with animals. He didn't need the human language to tell him what was going on. Mel senses things that never remotely occur to the majority of people in everyday situations.

His next words pulled me back from my thoughts that had strayed away. "You are an amazing woman, Helena. Every day I am more amazed at your strength and grace in all situations. For many years, I have admired you from afar; but now as we are growing closer and closer, I find you are a truly fascinating person with a very good heart and an even more generous and loving spirit." There was a slight hesitation, and he finished with, "And you're spunky too!"

He stopped, and I just sat there like a little Cheshire cat looking at him and smiling. It was so satisfying to have a man think I was something special. I have always been an *in the shadows* kind of person, so to actually stand out in the sunlight for someone was an entirely new experience. I felt good. I heard his voice, and as

I tuned away from my self-serving thoughts, I caught his words in mid-sentence.

"...to getting not one but two jobs. I could not be more excited for you. I don't know if I would have had the guts to try for the tram guide job but then to talk to that man who you described as 'dashing' about the docent position. By the way, should I be concerned here? I believe your exact words when you described him to me were 'tall, stately, and distinguished with a full head of wavy white hair and an endearing smile.'"

I laughed throwing my head back and then pouncing forward and throwing my arms around him, this time I gave him a huge hug. "Thank you, Mel, for pretending jealousy. That is so flattering. Except for you, I'm not really into older men."

Mel turned quickly when he caught my words and threw me back on the couch and said, "Older man, huh? I'll show you older man." His lips came down on mine, and I was swallowed up in a momentary feeling of pure animal lust. Stopping the kiss as abruptly as it started, he sat up pulling me up with him. He bounced me up squaring my seated position on the couch and came at me with, "So who's pretending jealousy? I am jealous. Trust me when I tell you this, Helena, it tears my heart apart to hear you describe another man in a manner that indicates your appreciation of him so fully." As the words tumbled from his mouth, I needed to see his eyes twinkling to know that he was teasing. His arms went around me in another sweet embrace, and his hug was generously reciprocated until his fingers found my ribs and began a little ticklish dance. I giggled and pushed back against him to make him stop.

"Helena, you working as a docent at the Jekyll Island Club Museum is so fantastic. You will be able to continue your research for your book, and I'm sure you are going to find the information at the museum as fascinating as what you will bring to it from your recent research. Things are just fitting so in place. I am amazed and very happy for you. Today may be a day that goes down in history as one of the best days of your life. At least, I hope that it does."

"Mel, you are so easy to share things with. I love that you care, and your encouragement has meant so much that I could never express it to you. I am finally feeling like I am actually growing into the woman that I was always meant to be." I stopped, pausing for a moment not knowing whether or not to share the next thing with Mel. I knew that we had expressed to each other our love, and so I hated to hold back anything from someone to whom my love was certainly growing.

"Mel, I didn't think a couple of years ago that I would ever look on Hank's leaving me as a good thing. I can remember when he walked out on me wondering how God was ever going to use that for good. Today, I believe I actually do know the answer to that painfully asked question. I needed to be loosed from those bonds that had been holding me for so long. I needed to find who I was beyond being Hank's wife. I never had my own identity. I was a wife, and I was Gabe and Gilliam's mother. Now, for the first time in my life, I'm Helena Rivers, and I'm excited about her future.

I looked up at him and smiled. I felt energized and in control of who I am. "It's scary as all get out, Mel, but I needed to reach this point so that I could see the full scope of what God had planned all along. I truly do believe that he has a plan for each of us, and that he knew that plan even before he created the heavens and the earth. It's amazing to watch how he works to bring his plans to fruition."

Mel took my hand and gave it a squeeze. The look in his eyes was clouded again, and yet his words were reassuring. "Helena, I grew up in the church. I believe in God, and I know who Jesus is; but when Elaine died, I blamed God for taking her from me. I pretty much turned my back on him because he didn't give me what I wanted. In fact, not only didn't he give me what I wanted, he took away from me what I had."

I squeezed his hand back. Mel had never talked about Elaine or his relationship with God, at least not to me. I wanted him to continue if he wanted to, but I didn't want to say anything just yet. Squeezing his hand was the best that I could do to give him the go ahead to stop or continue as he felt led.

He continued, "I know you're too polite to ask, but the one thing I wanted more than anything else, or at least I thought I did, was a son. That Elaine and I weren't able to have children was something we both mourned during the years of our marriage. We eventually got over it and accepted it as God's plan. But then when he took Elaine from me, leaving me all alone I was confused. Why would God do this to me?"

Mel was sharing things that were so honest and so painful. Looking down at his hand holding mine, I moved it just enough to intertwine my fingers with his. I wanted him to understand the gesture. I wanted him to see and feel all the love I felt.

"These past months with you, Helena, have helped me to sort out so many things about my life. I have listened to how you relate to God, and it's like he's your best friend. You seem to have a friendship with this unseen entity that at first puzzled me, but now I'm beginning to understand. God is the reason for your existence. I get that he actually does come first in your life. And that doesn't bother me. I also get, for the very first time in my life that because he comes first, all the rest is somehow better. I'm working to achieve that same kind of peace and understanding that you have. I want that better life not because God gives me everything I want but because I love him, like you love him."

I was overwhelmed at Mel's insight and understanding of who I was inside, in my heart, and I couldn't stop myself from doing what I did next. I raised my head to his as it rested on the back of the couch, and I kissed him fully and completely on the mouth. This was not a kiss of lust; this was a kiss of love and of promise. It was the best kiss I had ever shared with anyone. I did truly love this man. Several years ago, I didn't think that I would ever be able to love again. This was such a tender, intimate, and revealing moment for me.

Mel kissed me back. I could tell he was feeling the same thing that I was. It's a moment in time that might never be repeated, and that might not ever occur in some people's lives. It never had before in mine, and I think it probably never had before in Mel's.

He cleared his throat. "Helena, I love you so much. We have lost complete track of where my original thoughts were headed. I want to finish those thoughts before we go on to anything else. I was touched when you told me about pulling over on the side of the road in the marshes today and having a good cry, talking with God and hearing his answer. It is just so who you are."

I smiled at Mel and simply said, "Thank you for listening to me, for understanding, and for caring. That's what I love about you, my darling Mel."

"What you couldn't possibly know about me, Helena, and this is what makes it so much more amazing is that in my office at my clinic where I know you have not yet been—"

I interrupted him, "Yeah, why haven't I ever been in your office at the clinic? Is there something deeply sinister and secret in there?"

He laughed. "No, Helena, what is in there is a framed piece from a poem. I loved these words so much that I had someone write them out in calligraphy for me years ago, and I had them matted and framed, and they hang over my desk. Those words have nothing to do with animals or me; they have to do with this island that I have always loved."

"Really," I asked, "what are the words?"

"'Jekyll, a Limpid Labyrinth of Dreams.' You know, Helena, the words you recited to me today from Sidney Lanier's *Hymns of the Marshes*—"Sunrise."

He winked at me, which he sometimes did. I have discovered that Mel, as we have grown closer and gotten to know each other better, has a flirty little way about him that is very endearing. I never knew before that it existed, and that in itself is comforting because it means he doesn't flirt with everyone. He flirts with me.

I put my hands to my cheeks and barely squeaked out, "Really, you love that poem? You love my Sidney Lanier like I do? You and I truly share the love of the beautiful marshes? I am touched beyond anything...I don't even know what to say. Where have you been all my life somehow seems appropriate."

Mel laughed that wonderful laugh. "It's very difficult for me to imagine you in any situation where you wouldn't know what to say, Helena." He laughed. "Don't you see, my dear, God's hand has been at work all along, for years he has known that this day would eventually come."

"I do. I really do see God in so many things and amazingly in us finding each other at this stage in our lives. It is such a God thing. I do have one question, however." I stopped and looked at Mel.

"Well, go ahead, what's the question?"

"Why those specific words? Why, 'Jekyll, a Limpid Labyrinth of Dreams'?"

He paused for a moment before he answered. He picked up his glass of wine and sipped from the contents, which were no longer cold but room temperature. He sat the glass down and picked up a piece of cheese. His hesitation or nonchalance in answering me was driving me a little crazy. Didn't he want to tell me?

Finally he looked at me, and his words chilled me to the bone. "I have loved Jekyll all my life, and I never wanted to live anywhere else. I always felt that a much greater power than me put me here. I believe I am here for a very specific reason. I believe this is where all of my dreams will come to fruition. A labyrinth takes you in all kinds of directions, there are turns and curves and dead ends; but eventually you reach the finish and come out into the open, and the confusion of the labyrinth is behind you. That's why I've never left here and why I never will. I'm still waiting."

I sat there looking at Mel, and tears welled up in my eyes. I was so overcome with emotion that I wasn't sure if I could maintain my composure, but I knew that I had to. It took me a moment to know that I could speak, and then I said, "So far as you have shared with me, Mel, you're only unfulfilled dream is to have a son. It's a little late for that, isn't it? Unless you're thinking of marrying a younger woman, like Hank did, and starting all over. But you've kind of told me that doing that isn't for you. And you've been widowed for five years. If that's what you're planning, you need to get going on that dream. Is that your dream?"

I knew when I said those words that if that was his dream then that meant I was out of his life. I felt tense and somewhat sick to my stomach as I waited for his answer. I even said a prayer in my heart, "Please, dear God, don't let that be his dream." I knew when I prayed that silent little prayer that it was totally selfish. I should care enough about Mel that I want him to be happy. But I really loved this man, and I wanted to share that happiness with him.

His next words were a bit puzzling. "I don't think that my day was half as interesting or as enlightening as yours was, my dear."

As he continued, I knew he wasn't going to answer my question. Why not? "I did do one thing today that I'd like to run past you however. I have taken in every word you've said, and I understand your question, which right now I don't intend to answer. But I have a question for you. It may be a bit much on top of all the other things that have happened to you today, and maybe I should wait." He paused so I jumped in.

"Wait, no, you don't have to wait for anything, Mel. You have been wonderful letting me share my day with you, please tell me what you did today. I want to know how your day went and what you did. Please don't let tonight be all about me. I'm ready to listen, and I'll answer whatever you want to know. Go ahead and ask me anything you want. I may not be able to give you a good answer, but I certainly will try." I wanted that tenseness that I was feeling to pass, so I laid my head back on his shoulder in the same place where I had laid it after that wonderful and passionate kiss. I turned my face so that I was looking up at him, encouraging him to go on. His eyes were looking down into mine.

He didn't move. Our eyes were locked. His lips touched my forehead, and he kissed me lightly, saying, "Helena, you know, or at least I think you know that I love you."

With those words, I felt a bit more relaxed about his wanting a younger woman, but I still was concerned as to why he hadn't answered me when I had directly asked if wanting a son was his unfulfilled dream.

"I think you are truly an astonishing woman. I like how you handled your husband leaving you. It was crushing, and yet you kept your shoulders back and at least to the world you carried on." He paused for a moment to let his words sink in.

"I like the kind of mother that I have seen you be over the years. Gabe is a fine man, and Gilliam a wonderful daughter. You have raised two remarkably well balanced people who are very much, from what I know, like their mother. They are smart and kind and generous of spirit just like you."

There was another pause. "I like the way you take care of your horses." At last the vet in Mel came out. I chuckled.

"You know how important exercise is for Blue and Grey, and you never miss riding them. You curry them, pet them, talk to them, bring them treats, and care for or get care for their injuries. You have no idea how many horse owners don't do half of what you do for your animals. I have watched you and Blue and Grey, and I know that they are more than just animals to you. They are your family."

He picked up the wine glass and emptied it of the now warm liquid.

"I like that you don't let grass grow under your feet, and today certainly proved that. You haven't laid back and felt sorry for yourself like many women do when they have been betrayed by unappreciative husbands. You also didn't rely on other people to provide you with comfort and give purpose to your life. Instead you've gone to work researching to write a book. You haven't had the slightest idea of where all your effort would lead, but you have enjoyed the journey. I like all those things about you." He smiled and kissed me again on my forehead.

I sat up and pulled my legs up on the couch so that I was sitting with my knees on the cushions, my feet tucked beneath me, and my body facing his. I swallowed hard because I was feeling so much emotion at the moment. His words had touched me in a way that he could not possibly imagine. That he could see all of that in me and care so strongly about who I was and what I was and what I was doing was overwhelming. I didn't deserve a man as caring as Mel, and yet I wanted him more than anything I have wanted in many, many years.

"Mel, I love you too. You are such a wise, talented, intelligent, caring, and loving man; how could I, or anyone else, not love you? For heaven's sake, Mel, the whole town loves you. The whole island loves you."

His eyes momentarily hooded. I caught that look, even though it was in his eyes for just an instant I wondered what I had said that he didn't like.

His voice was soft and slow, and his words were kind but spoken a little more forcefully and with an inflection that was unusual for Mel. "I'm glad the whole town and the whole island love me, Helena. Is that how you love me? Like the town and the island loves me?"

I wasn't exactly sure how to answer that question. It was kind of a catch twenty-two. I was going to be damned if I did or damned if I didn't answer this with words that he was looking for. "Well, yes and no. Of course I love you like the whole town and the whole island loves you."

His eyes were guarded, and he was alert and obviously waiting for me to continue so I did. "But, Mel, I also love that we're building a relationship together, just the two of us. At least, I think we are. Those last few kisses sure said we were building something. At least to me they did. I know I'm very out of practice, and I haven't spent time with any other man except Hank in the past thirty years, but those kisses and our time together doesn't seem like a casual friendship kind of thing to me. If I'm wrong, you need to tell me pretty soon because I'm sinking fast. I don't think you've been spending time with other women since we've been dating or have you? Please tell me you haven't. I may be writing more into this than you intended, but I thought we were building something; well, not just something, something really significant together. Am I wrong?"

Mel laughed. The guarded look in his eyes was gone, and they actually went from guarded to twinkling in just a nanosecond. The laughter gurgled up from deep inside Mel and erupted from between his closed lips. He turned and put both of his arms around me and hugged me tighter than I have been hugged in years.

"Helena, Helena, Helena that is exactly what I love about you. You are so honest and sincere, and I never need to worry what you are thinking. You have no ulterior motives, no agendas, and no secrets. But unfortunately, I do."

"What?" I cried out as I pushed him forcefully back wiping the smile from his face. "Mel, I don't believe you. You are not a Hank. You are not leading me on. If you are playing me, Mel, then I'm swearing off men forever. Here I am, wearing my heart like a pendant dangling at the end of a gold chain, and you have some secret ulterior motive. No, I refuse to accept that." As my last words left my mouth, I could feel the tears building behind my eyes. I sucked it up as much as I could and prayed that Mel didn't see my fear of yet another possible rejection.

Mel dropped his head onto his chest. "Helena, forgive me, my darling. I told you that I had done something today that I wanted to run past you. What I did was, I drove to Savannah.

You aren't the only one who spends time doing research. I have been looking for something that is very important to me, and I finally found it, in Savannah. I bought something, and I'd like to see your reaction to it. It means a lot to me, and I'm hoping that it might mean something important to you also."

I was feeling somewhat relieved, and I could feel the hurt evaporating from my body. He bought something. Well, at least it wasn't another woman that he accidently had fallen in love with. The tenseness that I had been feeling once again seemed to dissipate, and I let out my breath in one great exhalation.

This entire day had been like being on a rollercoaster ride. When was it going to stop, and when could I get off? I looked at Mel and realized that he was looking back at me very intently; apparently that gush of air rushing from my lungs had let him know that I was feeling more than just a little uptight. I was having a difficult time not thinking about his dream and his waiting for it to come true. I needed to break this tension, and so I put a lilt in my voice and answered as breezily as I could.

"Well, goodness, that sounds very interesting, Mel." I wondered if my recent outburst had only served to make me look like a fool.

"I'm sorry I wasn't available, or maybe you would have wanted me to come along to Savannah with you."

"No, Helena, I actually wanted to go by myself this time. The drive over gave me a lot of time to just think about some important things that I haven't really taken the time to think about as clearly or as thoroughly as I have been wanting to."

He seemed somewhat pensive for Mel, and his thoughts appeared to be very inwardly focused.

"My business is so busy, and our time together is so precious that most nights when I get home, I just fall into bed exhausted, and then I get up the next morning and start the whole crazy and busy schedule all over again. This thing that I bought is terribly important to me. This wasn't something that I purchased on the spur of the moment. A lot of thought has gone into it. It's expensive, or it ultimately could be and maintaining it throughout the years will require a lot of my time and effort. It's also going to require a lot of devotion, and so it isn't a decision that I've made lightly. The commitment that this will necessitate, if I do it right, will not just be for a little while but for many years. It's a scary proposition, but I really think it's worth it."

I could not imagine what he was talking about.

"I'm hoping when you see it that you'll understand why it's so important to me, especially at this stage in my life, and agree with my reason for procuring it. Hopefully, you'll want to help me with it and be a part of using it."

Why couldn't he just come right out and tell me what it was. If he wanted me to be a part of it then it wasn't something detrimental to our relationship. Was it so expensive, or would it be so time consuming, which he hinted at both things, that it meant not moving forward with our relationship?

Finally I blurted out, "I'm sure it will be important to you, and I'm sure I'll understand, but I don't know why you would think it's important for you to have my approval. Did you buy a horse? Some medical equipment? Another practice? A house in Savannah? What? Is it something you brought home with you? Can we just go see it." I put my feet on the floor and was ready to get up.

Mel put his hand on my arm pulling me back. "Its right here, Helena. I've got it right here." He looked into my eyes and opened his hand.

"Will you marry me, Helena?" I looked down and saw the ring. It was a beautiful chocolate diamond solitaire surrounded by a circle of sparkling clear diamonds. It was set in platinum and was dazzling as the lights shone off of it. I looked up and saw the love and hope in Mel's eyes. My heart was pounding, I actually felt dizzy. I was not expecting this.

The air escaped from my lungs like air escapes from an untied balloon. "Ahhhhhh." My eyes looked at the ring, at Mel's eyes, and then away.

"Darn, I was really hoping you weren't going to say no." His voice sounded disappointed and lost, like sounds you would hear from a rejected teenager.

"Mel, I'm not saying no." My eyes looked at his, and I expelled the second breath I'd been holding. "I'm not saying no. I...I need some time. We need to talk. We need to find out a few things before I say yes." I looked at him, and I knew he loved me. "Mel, I don't even know what to say. You've completely taken me by surprise. I...I need to digest this." I saw a flicker pass through Mel's eyes. "Not alone, Mel, with you. We need to talk about our future together. What we both want and what we both expect. You haven't even hinted, I don't think, about marrying me; and I don't think I've hinted it to you, yet. Until tonight. Tonight has been the most serious we have ever been together. I do want to marry you, but I don't want to say yes tonight. There are a lot of things that we just need to talk about before I say yes."

"Okay." Mel said. "Do we begin that talking now or when?"

"No, Mel, not now. Put the ring away, and let's explore the possibilities collectively over the next several times that we're together. Let's talk about what being married would mean to us. There are a lot of questions, Mel. Where would we live? What would we expect from each other as marriage partners? Let's talk about those next steps. Mel, I know that we love each other. That's all that really matters at this moment. But I loved Hank too, and look where that led. I couldn't go through that again. I have no doubt that we will get married, but I need to talk about things before I say 'yes' to your proposal. That's not an insult to you in any way. It's because I do love you so very much that I care what happens to both of us. It's just something I need to do. Both of us, we really need to think a lot of things through together."

Mel slipped the ring into his pocket. He put his arms around me and pulled me to him, and I hugged him. He kissed me long and hard. There was no doubt in either of our minds that the kiss spoke of our love.

"I can handle this, Helena, in fact I think you're right. We do need to understand a few more things about each other and our future together before we make a lasting commitment. For some reason, I had a premonition that you might react as you have, and so I prepared for that with my Plan B."

"Plan B? What can be a Plan B to a wedding proposal and a request to wait while we talk some things over?" I was truly puzzled, but it was pretty much par for the course for this entire day.

Mel reached in his jacket pocket and pulled out a slightly larger box. It was still a jeweler's box, so I had no idea what his Plan B could be. He looked at the box in his hand and then at me. He reached out and took my hand, moved it so my palm was up, and placed the box in my palm.

"I want you to wear my ring. This one won't fit your finger, which is where I want my ring to be, always, but its round like the diamond, like a wedding ring, indicating a love that has no end. And it has diamonds. Please accept this, and wear it until you wear the other ring."

I found that my hands were shaking slightly as I opened the box. Inside the box, lying on the deep maroon silk was a round tennis bracelet—each link of the chain was shaped in a heart, and each heart was holding a small cut diamond.

"Oh, Mel, this is so beautiful and so extravagant."

He reached into the box, took out the bracelet, and snapped it around my left wrist. Then he kissed the palm of each hand and simply said, "I love you, Helena."

"I love you too, Mel. Can I ask another question?"

"Of course, my dear, but I'll answer it before you ask it. I would have given it to you right after I placed the ring on your finger if you had immediately said yes. Was that the question?"

I looked into his laughing and happy eyes. "Yes."

He stood up, pulling me to my feet beside him, and said, "Let's go for a walk." We left the house, hand in hand, and we walked.

The bracelet dangled from my wrist, touching his hand that held mine as we walked. We didn't say much. We just walked. I love that about Mel. He understood that I had not rejected him, and this walking time was his way of letting me know that. Doing something conventional, and comfortable said he understood. He also wasn't going to push me. He was willing to wait, and I think he understood and maybe even was glad for the way I was approaching his proposal. He obviously thought I might do what I did, or he probably wouldn't have also purchased that beautiful diamond bracelet that was extremely extravagant but was also completely filled with love. When we got back home, he kissed me at the door and told me he'd talk with me in the morning.

I went to bed that night with my head swimming, and my heart was lurching. I took the bracelet off and laid it on my nightstand. I would put it on again in the morning, and I would wear it every day. Mel would not see me without it on. I didn't really sleep very well. I loved that Mel wanted to spend the rest of his life with me, but I was scared too. I wanted it to be the rest of our lives. I didn't want to say "I do" to anyone who wasn't all in. I thought of all the words he said leading up to his proposal. He understood working at a relationship. I think that's what he was telling me. He understood that my saying yes would be costly in time and effort, and he was willing to do whatever it took. My head kept replaying the tape until I finally drifted off to sleep.

The next morning was a beautiful day. The sun was shining brightly, and I felt like I was eighteen again. I had a job, well, actually two jobs. I had someone interested in my book, but most importantly, I had a man who loved me so much he wanted to marry me. When I pack a day, I really pack a day.

Grey Streak

> Our bravest lessons are not learned through success, but misadventure.
>
> —Alcott

It was a perfect day for spending time at the stables. It was summer, and my girls were putting on a few pounds. A natural occurrence for horses, to gain some weight in the hot summer months. Blue and Grey are fed perfectly to maintain their health and keep them resistant to disease, about four pounds at a feeding. The proteins in their food are carefully monitored to prevent stress that might lead to behavior problems. Blue and Grey are in perfect health. I love to be a part of their exercise and grooming schedules, and Celeste watches all her horses carefully. When I say her horses, I'm referring to those that she boards, which include my two.

When I got there, the girls were just finishing their morning feed, so I knew I'd need to wait at least an hour before I could ride. It's rather like not going swimming right after one eats. Our body uses a lot of energy digesting our intake, and so it's best to let our organs do what they need to do first before requiring them to do what we'd like them to do.

I talked to the girls, patted them on their head, and then got the hose, and filled their water troughs. The receptacles weren't dry, but just like humans, horses require lots of fresh water for good food digestion and hydration. God gave to all his creation good instincts for how to take care of ourselves. We, his human creation, are the only ones who seem to ignore what we should do in favor of what feels good or tastes good. Although domesticated dogs come in at a pretty close second to humans in their eating habits.

I liked spending time with my horses. That's probably also what Mel loves about being with his patients. They are good listeners. I told Blue and Grey all about my day yesterday. I told them about Hank and Autumn. As I brushed and ran my hands over their silky flanks, I told them about my new jobs, reassuring them, in case they were worried, that I would still have plenty of time for them. I told them about Mel, who they both already knew. They liked Mel. He brought them apples. Horses do love carrots and apples. They like the sweet taste, I'm imagining, and the crunch in those big teeth. When I told Blue that I had not said *yes* right away to Mel's question, she threw back her head and did a high pitched whiney. Her reaction was quite amusing. If one didn't know better, it would be hard to believe that they actually don't completely understand our English language. When she did her little act showing her annoyance with me, I took her big gentle face in both my hands and told her that it wasn't a permanent delay; and Mel understood, so I thought she should too.

When you stand in front of a horse rubbing their nose and talking with them straight on, they can feel your touch and hear your voice; but since their eyes are set on the sides of their beautiful heads, you need to stand to the side, so they can see you. I did that now. I stood slightly to Blue's right side and told her I was sorry that she wasn't happy with my decision to wait just a while before I said the ultimate yes to Mel, but that I would make it up to her, eventually.

All the horses at Victoria's are strapped at night to keep up their circulation and encourage muscle tone. Strapping is a series of rhythmic thumps with a pad on the shoulders, quarters and neck. Because my girls are stabled as opposed to being kept out in a pasture, I know they are brushed frequently, not just to keep them looking good, but to encourage and allow sweating for the excretion of waste matter. All animals, even human ones, need to sweat. A genteel lady from the southern states would say "glow or glisten," but sweat is sweat. I always brush them after their morning exercise when they are warm, and their pores are open.

I really love being part of my girl's lives, and although I don't like most of the stable duties, I do like doing little things for my Blue and Grey that I know they enjoy or that are immensely important to their good health.

I picked up Blue's front hoof to see if it needed cleaning. I ran my fingertips over the clinches, checked for foreign objects, like a small rock, and looked for any bruising and for thrush. The hoof had been recently picked and dressed. I wasn't surprised since Celeste and the crew here takes extremely good care of all their guests. By the time I had checked all of Blue's and Grey's hooves, it was time for me to ride.

I rode Blue first for about an hour. I curried her down and led her back to her stall. It was good to be back on Blue again, and I was glad that the inflamed tendon had healed well and was no longer bothering her. I could tell when we rode that she was not favoring that left leg. We raced full out for a short time, which both of my girls like to do. I would just slacken up on the reins and tell them to go, and I would get the ride of my life. Both Blue and Grey love to run free, and even if I'm on their back, along with the saddle, I can tell they feel some of the wildness that once most assuredly was part of their ancestry.

I threw the blanket over Grey's back, then the saddle, and tightened the straps under her girth. Grey and I left the stable in the distance, and we took the normal path down to the water. Grey kept flicking her head off to the left like she really wanted to go off the path and run free, so finally I loosed the reins and telling her to go she flew across the open meadow. My hair was flying out behind me, and Grey's mane matched my own as it flew loosely in the wind. Finally, I slowed her down to a reduced pace, and we trotted off to the far end of the field that would eventually lead down to the surf and our last piece of fun for this day.

Suddenly Grey stopped. She reared up slightly unto her hind legs and then began a backward dance. Somewhere there was danger. I fully understood her behavior, and I knew something wasn't right. I looked down into the grass along both sides of where we were. My eyes then searched the area in front of us and then darted to the horizon. My entire body swiveled in the saddle as my shoulders turned first right and then left, and my neck followed allowing me a three hundred and sixty degree range of vision of my surroundings. Horses will react to smoke, which they smell long before our human noses can detect its presence. I didn't see any hint of plumes rising in the sky, and Grey was now backing up more aggressively and prancing from her right to left legs. It wasn't fire, and it wasn't an impending storm since the sky was clear and blue.

Something had to be in the grass. I was sure that was where the danger lie, but I couldn't see anything. Then I saw it. I knew from its distinctive markings that it was a copperhead. I could feel the panic and bile rising in my throat. There wasn't much that frightened me more than the bite of a poisonous snake. With some bites, you usually had ample time to secure required treatment. I knew with the copperhead, there usually was time; but if treatment wasn't quickly sought, it could mean death. Surviving a copperhead bite didn't mean you were home scot free for the aftermath usually included necrosis of the tissue around the wound. You might live, but the cells in an organ or the tissue surrounding the bite would not.

Before I could turn Grey to retreat, I saw the copper color on the head and the chestnut color on his back as he struck. What happened next seemed as if it was occurring in slow motion as the snake lunged forward and sunk his fangs into Grey's leg midway between his hoof and the knee joint. Grey reared up shaking her legs and flipping the snake into the air. I had prepared for the reaction and was holding tightly to the reins and the saddle horn as I squeezed my legs as hard as I could against Grey's sides to maintain my position in the saddle.

I knew I had no time to delay. I had to get Grey back to the stables now and get the antidote for the bite. It would only be a short time before the venom would, upon entering the blood stream travel the full distance to the heart and other vital organs. I urged Grey forward quickly but not at a full run, which would only have made the venom travel faster through her blood. When I got back to the stables, which only took about five minutes traveling at the steady pace I established, I jumped off Grey and ran looking for Celeste. I found her immediately in one of the nearby barns, and as I screamed to her what had happened, she ran for her snake kit before I had even reached her.

When I saw her action, I immediately turned and headed back to Grey. I wanted to keep her calm, and I led her into her stall cooing to her that she would be okay. Celeste was there in what seemed like seconds. She administered the shot. I knew now there was nothing else we could do except wait. I prayed for a long period of waiting which meant she would survive. There was no walking Grey today to cool her down, but I did remove the saddle and blanket and began to curry her as I talked softly in her ear.

"You're going to be okay, girl. I know you're going to be okay. You can't die. I love you so much, and I refuse to let you die." I continued my mantra into her ear more for myself than for her. "I lost Beauty, girl. I will not lose you too. The medicine will work. We got here in time. I know we did. You are going to be okay."

Within ten minutes, Mel came screaming into the yard in a cloud of dust; and running from his truck, with his door left wide open, he moved quickly into the stall. Barely greeting me with just a passing bit of eye contact, he gave Grey his full attention.

Celeste must have called him, and apparently when I told her that it was a copperhead, Mel must have been concerned enough to know to treat this like the life-threatening emergency that it could be. That scared me.

Was Grey in that much danger? *Oh, my dear God, please don't let Grey die.* I stood aside, back as far as I could in the rear corner of the stall, and just watched Mel as he examined the bite. Reaching into his bag, he pulled out a sharp metal scalpel and a long hose with a bulb on one end and something metal on the other. I could see his hands working feverishly as he began to cut into the horses flesh where the bite had occurred. He then attached a small suction apparatus and began pumping with the attached bulb. I could see that fluid was being extracted from the site along with blood. He pumped until only blood came from the site, and then he applied a salve and bandaged the wound.

All the time that he worked on Grey, he talked soothingly to her. I believe his words were also meant for my ears and to sooth my anxious heart. I could hear him tell her that she was going to be okay, and he told her that he would do everything he could for her. He patted her and calmed her then I saw him coaxing her and taking her into a laying down position. Once she was down on the straw filled floor of the stall, he kneeled beside her and continued his cooing and soft words of reassurance. Now he pulled a small vial from the worn old doctor's valise and a large needle, and filling the needle, he inserted it into Blue's flesh.

I was mesmerized as I watched Mel. He loved this horse. Not because she was mine, but because he loved Grey. Mel had so much heart and so much love. This was the man who wanted to spend the rest of his life with me and who had reassured me that I and the success of our relationship would be his priority.

I couldn't believe now that I had had the audacity when he asked me to marry him to tell him we needed to wait until we had talked. What was I thinking? Any woman would be blessed to have Mel want to be her husband and I had told him he would have to wait for my specific answer until we had talked.

The amazing thing, which I hadn't even thought about until now, was that he had already thought I might do that, and he was prepared with his Plan B. If I wasn't going to put that ring on my finger the night he asked he wanted me to wear a round endless circle of diamonds on my body, specifically on my left wrist, closer to my heart than even my ring finger would be, to let me know each time I glanced at it or felt it against my skin that his love was the unending kind. He also felt it was very important for me to understand that he would wait until I finally wore his ring and make that true and complete commitment to him. He wasn't walking away.

Finally Mel got up, put his arms around me, and held me close.

"Helena, I'm not sure if the poison has taken hold of Grey or not. I can't do anything more for her right now. I really feel with your quick return to the stable and Celeste getting the antidote into her as soon as you arrived at the paddock that Grey is going to be fine. Celeste told me that you didn't run Grey after the bite, that was very good thinking, and that the antidote was given within ten minutes of the bite. Both of those things are crucial for survival. Those two acts most likely saved her.

I'm thinking that since she had the poison in her system less than ten minutes before treatment that she has better than a seventy percent chance not only of survival but of having no life-threatening organ damage. I evacuated the rest of the sac of venom so that no more could seep into her system, and I gave her a super dose of antibiotic, which I'll repeat every twelve hours for the next couple of days. Now unfortunately, we have no choice but to just wait."

Mel stopped talking and I leaned in to him as his arms tightened around me.

His cheek, rough with a mid-day growth of whiskers rubbed against the soft skin of my face. It felt good. For once I didn't mind the sandpaper feel. It made me feel alive.

"Thank you, Mel, for coming so quickly. I don't know if I can handle losing Grey right now."

He pulled me back, and looking into my face, he said, "Honey, I don't know if she's out of danger or not; but hang in there, have faith and pray. You're stronger than you think you are, Helena. I've seen that strength, and I know it's there. So is your faith. Believe in yourself. Believe in God. He is with you always, even when I want to be with you and I cannot, I know that you are not alone."

Once again, words so beautifully written by my Sidney Lanier came full circle to touch my heart.

> *Pass, kinsman Cloud, now fair and mild;*
> *Discharge the will that's not thine own.*
> *I work in freedom wild,*
> *But work, as plays a little child,*
> *Sure of the Father, Self, Love, alone.*

"I will," I whispered.

"Helena, I can't do anything more here now, and I really need to get to my patients at the clinic. They are stacked up, and I just ran out the back door when Celeste called. They might not even realize yet that I'm gone, so I do need to get right back."

"It's okay, Mel, you go, and I'll stay right here with Grey if I have to sleep here all night. Is there anything I should be watching for that might indicate everything worked or didn't work?" As I said those last few words, my voice caught.

Mel gave me a few instructions and then he took off after giving me a sweet and supportive kiss.

I got the hose and filled the water trough. Then I took the horse blanket and threw it in the straw beside Grey. I sat down beside her reclining into her warm underside with my arm thrown up over her back. I nuzzled my head into her and began to pray.

I was still in that position when Celeste stopped by about thirty minutes later. She came over and put her hand on my shoulder.

"Are you okay, Helena?"

"Yes, Celeste, it's not me I'm concerned about. I just want Grey to make it through this."

Celeste looked at me, and her eyes were very serious. "I'd love to tell you that she will be fine, but honestly, Helena, it could be touch and go at this moment. I've seen copperhead bites go both ways. Even though we both acted quickly it might not have been quickly enough. The time may have been too long before the antidote was administered. I'm not trying to scare you, but I think you do need to be prepared."

She looked thoughtful for a moment and then continued. "Grey is young and strong and in good health, so she may survive this with no residual problems. Her future is in the hands of someone far greater than ours."

I sobbed when she said that and hugged Grey even tighter. I had never heard Celeste talk about God before, and that both reassured me and scared me at the same time.

Celeste continued with words that I feared but didn't want to hear. "If Grey does survive the bite, she may have some problems that may necessitate that we put her down. You will have to call on that iron will and determination of yours if that happens, Helena. Some horses have gone blind or deaf from the venom, and with some, it has significantly weakened their heart or other vital organs. If she makes it through the first twenty-four hours, she will live, but it may be weeks before we know the extent of damage that may have been done by the venom coursing through her veins. From the way you described the snake, it wasn't a baby it was a full grown adult, which means the venom could be stronger."

She came over and put her hand on my shoulder again. "Helena, let's both of us hang on to the strong possibility that she'll come through this with no damage, and she'll be fine. I've also seen that many times."

I looked up at Celeste when she was done talking, and my words choked out as tears rolled down my face. "Thank you for telling me all this, Celeste. I didn't really want to hear it, but I do need to know what may happen. I just have to believe, right now, that she's going to be fine. She is such a brave girl. I think she's sleeping right now."

"Actually, Selena, she will sleep for some time. Mel told me that he gave Grey a sedative mixed in with the antibiotic. He wants her to sleep. The quieter she is, the less chance the venom has to travel through her system. She needs to be as calm and quiet as we can keep her. That's why he laid her down. He needed to do that before he administered the sedative or her legs would have just buckled, and then she might have broken a leg."

"Okay. He didn't explain all that to me, but it does make sense. I'm going to stay here beside her. Is that okay?"

Celeste smiled, and reaching out, she squeezed my hand. "You can do whatever you need to do, Helena. I'll be checking in frequently to see how Grey is doing, and I'll check on you to see if you need anything. Do you have your cell phone with you?"

"Yes, Celeste. Oh my goodness, I should have called you when that snake bit Grey, shouldn't I?" I was horrified that I may have jeopardized Grey by not doing something I should have done.

"No, no, Helena. I wouldn't have wanted you to take the time to call. You did exactly the right thing just getting here as quickly as you could. Doing that probably saved her life. We'll just have to wait and see. I was going to suggest that if anything happens with Grey or you need anything, just call me on your cell phone. It's the closest thing we have to an intercom. You do have my number keyed into your phone, right?"

"Yes, of course I do. That's a good idea, Celeste. My phone is fully charged, and I'll call if anything happens." I smiled up at her.

"Or if you need anything. Don't forget that. Call me for anything, Helena. Either Old Bill or I will check on you frequently." Celeste turned and left, and I snuggled back into my sleeping Grey. As I lay against her, I could feel the gentle expansion and contraction of her lungs. Her breathing was slow and even and steady. I took that as a good sign. The slow in and out motion that Grey made with every breath was like being rocked in a small boat on a quiet lake.

I drifted off to sleep. Excitement, anxiety, and fear are powerful adrenaline enhancers, and the ordeal had left me exhausted. When I woke, Mel was standing over me. I don't think he had touched me. I believe I just sensed his presence. My eyes opened, and he was just standing there looking down at me. The look in his eyes was tender and caring.

"Hi, beautiful. Took a little nap, did you?" He smiled.

I sat up and rotated my neck and head, moving my arms and shoulders, and doing a little stretch. I felt stiff from being in one position too long.

"What time is it, Mel?" I asked.

"Well, my work day is done, and I've brought you some coffee. I also picked up a couple fish sandwiches and some fries. It's not exactly a gourmet meal, but I thought you might be hungry."

"I need to run to the facilities." I stood up and left to splash some water on my face and wash my hands.

When I got back, Mel was on his haunches examining Grey. He had his stethoscope hooked into his ears, and he was listening to Grey's heartbeat.

Looking up as I came nearer, he said, "It's regular and strong—that's a good sign. And she doesn't have any fever; I've already checked that. Right now, Helena, I'd say all the signs are very positive that she's going to survive this. The only thing we won't know is if there has been any serious organ damage. If there is, she still may need to be put down. I'm sorry to have to tell you that, but I know you would want to know. If she makes it through to morning and all is well, we'll do some tests on her organs in about two weeks, and then we'll know for sure." His eyes were filled with pure regret.

"Mel, Celeste has already filled me in on a lot of what you just said, so I've had a little time to think about it and to accept and adjust to what might happen. Thank you for caring so much about Grey and about me."

As I looked at Mel I added, "Mel, I love you so very much. You are such a good man."

"I love you too, Helena. I love you more than I ever thought I'd be able to love again. After Elaine died, I just sort of shut down, and you've woken me up again. I wish you didn't have to go through this, and that somehow I could have prevented it. I know that I couldn't, so in lieu of that, I'm glad I'm here to go through it with you."

Mel and I ate our sandwiches and drank our coffee sitting on the blanket with our backs leaning against the stall wall and our knees that were bent up in front of us touching each other's. When we were finished we stretched our legs out and sat quietly, holding hands and talking in soft whispery voices.

Mel told me about his day, and I listened and truly cared about what he was telling me. Finally he said, "Helena you should go home and take a shower and get a good rest in your bed. There is nothing you can do here."

"Oh, honey, I don't want to leave Grey alone."

"She won't be alone. I'm going to stay right here all night in case something happens, and she needs me." Mel squeezed my shoulder as he finished his words.

"Do you need to stay? Do you think she's going to die?" I asked.

"No, I'm about ninety-nine percent sure she is not going to die. I think, from what I can see right now, that she's going to be okay. I don't know about the organ damage, but I feel pretty certain she'll still be here to see you in the morning. So I do think you should go home. There really is nothing you can do here, and I promise I will not leave this stall until morning."

"Okay," I responded slowly. "I'll go home, but I'm coming back at five; and I'll bring you breakfast, and then you can go home and grab a shower before you have to go to the clinic. Is there anything else I can do for you? Is breakfast at five okay, or would you like me to come earlier or later?"

"Helena, breakfast at five sounds wonderful. Now you run along and try to get some rest. I have my bedroll in my truck, and I'm just going to spread it out here on the straw and sleep beside this beautiful woman. I'm used to this, dear. Actually, I probably shouldn't tell this to the lady I want desperately to marry, but I sleep over many nights with other women, like Grey." He smiled, and I returned his grin with a big one of my own.

"As long as the women you sleep with have four legs, my dear, you are forgiven in advance."

"Thank you, my queen. This knight, hopefully in shining armor, appreciates your pardon, and I do solemnly promise no sleeping with any women who don't have four legs with one exception. But that exception will have to wait until you say *yes* and *I do*."

I bent down and kissed him solidly on the lips. He gave my behind a little spank as I turned, and then I walked to my car and drove off knowing that Grey was in great hands and so was I.

Getting into my car, I picked up my cell phone. Driving out through the stable gates, I dialed his number. He answered. "Good night, my darling. Thank you for staying with Grey. I love you."

"No problem. I love sleeping with fast and wild women. I'm going to turn off my phone for a few hours, so I can get some sleep. I'll see you at five, and if all goes well, can I take you out to dinner tomorrow night?"

"Okay, hon. Sleep well, and yes I'd love to go to dinner."

I heard a faint and sleepy good night, and then he hung up.

In the morning, I got up at four, baked fresh scones and grabbed a jar of lemon curd from my cupboard. I brewed fresh coffee and filled my stainless steel thermos. I threw in some sugar and creamer, two cups, little plates, and napkins, and headed to Victoria's and to the man I loved.

Grey had survived the night and was beginning to come out of the stupor that she had been in from the tranquilizer Mel had given her. She was standing when I got there, and Mel had just come from washing up and shaving. I guess he was used to sleeping over since he came prepared for doing just that.

We had dinner that night. The first thing Mel told me, which I thought was extremely interesting, was that he and Celeste had talked sometime in the morning before I arrived. Together they had decided to make up small antidote kits that a rider could pick up before beginning a ride. Celeste would keep them prepared in her cooler, and they would be in a small padded pouch that could be slid into the rider's pocket or hooked on their belt. If something happened like happened to Grey the rider could administer the antidote within minutes of the bite, preventing the possibility of death or organ damage. Instructions would be inside the pouch with portions to be given according to pounds, and it could even be used on the rider if they should be the victim of the bite. Mel said that Celeste and he both couldn't figure out why they hadn't thought of this solution before this incident with Grey. The island had dangers, and they felt responsible, even when the horse and rider were away from the stable, to protect them.

I was thrilled to hear that. Perhaps, if Grey has no organ damage and survives, there was a purpose for what happened. This happening to us could possibly prevent the anguish of those hours, days, and weeks occurring for someone else. I always appreciated good things coming from bad.

Throughout the dinner, we used the time to begin talking about a future life together. It was easy and sweet, and our plans were very compatible. I needed this pleasant diversion after so many hours of anguish. It seemed like I was doomed to go through these ups and downs. With Mel by my side, I was no longer going through them alone. Now it was the three of us. God, me, and Mel.

The Follow Up to Plan B

All changes, even the most longed for,
have their melancholy; for what we leave
behind us is a part of ourselves; we must die
to one life before we can enter another.

—Anatole France

Two weeks after Grey had been bitten by the copperhead during our ride, Mel ran tests on her. After the completion of the body scans, x-rays, ultrasound, and the blood tests, Mel reported that as far as he could tell, Grey had not experienced any major organ damage. He had a huge smile on his face when he gave me the news. I know that he had been waiting for the results of the testing with almost as much fear as I had.

It had been difficult to move forward with plans for ourselves with that looming over us, and so we both agreed, without words, to table discussions until we knew how Grey was. That behind us we now were free to begin determining the direction our lives would take from here.

It had been a month since Mel asked me to marry him. It had been a difficult month for both of us.

My riding was a lot more restrained now. Before when I had felt free to let the girls have their way and gallop wherever they wanted now, with Grey's experience, I was more than a little hesitant about riding off the paths. With Blue's inflamed tendon and then Grey's experience with the snake, I was a little fragile when it came to my girls. I was nervous about the danger to which just an ordinary ride could expose them.

After a lovely dinner together on the Saturday night following the good news about Grey, I asked Mel to please pose the big question to me, again. He did, and, without even a moment of hesitation, I said a resounding "yes." Much to my surprise, he had the ring in his pocket. Whether he had anticipated that tonight would be the night or whether he just carried the ring always in his pocket, I didn't know. I didn't ask.

Mel and I had thoroughly talked through everything about our future lives together before that time when I requested that he once again ask me the big question. We had covered a lot of territory, and we both felt that the time we spent going over those very important aspects of our life together would put us on a strong footing for building a long and lasting marriage.

The first thing of great importance that we discussed was where we would live. I had been in this house for more than thirty years. It was home, and I couldn't imagine selling it. I also didn't think for a moment that Mel would be comfortable here.

It took a number of nights of discussion, and we even made a list of pros and cons, good and bad, advantages and disadvantages for moving either into my home, his home, or selling both, and moving into our home.

In the end, we decided on Mel's house as the place where we would begin our life together.

We decided, however, that he would first move out of the house for the three months prior to our marriage and allow me to make some changes that we would both agree on in advance. When I brought up that idea, Mel was in total agreement that changing his house into that place where our dreams could be lived out was an excellent idea. He even suggested that when I was done with the house, I could begin on his clinic. He had a small apartment attached to the clinic, since his work required more than an occasional stay over. It was both Mel's obligation and pleasure to keep a close watch on an animal following surgery or who was in critical condition from an illness or injury. I told him I would love to do that and would make it a priority even before the house.

One thing he very self-consciously asked was if, when redesigning and redecorating the small apartment attached to his clinic, I could remove the twin bed and put in something that would accommodate the two of us. He asked if I would mind, on occasion, staying there with him rather than both of us sleeping alone in two different places. I loved the question, and I acquiesced immediately to his request.

We agreed to eliminate some of his furnishings at his house and replace them with some of mine and to add some new pieces as necessary. We both decided the one thing we needed was a brand-new master bedroom suite. We planned on shopping for that together. I agreed that I did not want to begin our life with three of us in the bed. If he kept his bedroom suite, Elaine's presence would surely be felt; and if we used my bedroom furniture, then I knew we'd sense the lingering essence of Hank. Neither of us wanted any part of that. This was a new life for Mel and Helena, and although our mates would continue to live in our memories and our hearts, they didn't need to be ghosts between us as our marriage, and life together began.

Being traditional and also needing time for planning, coordinating, and redecorating, we set our wedding date for September 7, which was five months away.

After we made the decision to live in Hank's house, we talked about what realtor to use to sell my house and property and the timing for doing that. Should we list it before the wedding or after? Should I ask the kids if it was okay with them if I sold the house? What if they said no? They would have some anxious feelings that the home they grew up in would not be there anymore when they visited. Mel assured me that they would learn to be comfortable in his home, our home, and we could even move their old bedroom furniture into his spare bedrooms to give them that special feeling. We were, after all, still on Jekyll and only a few miles away from where they grew up. There were so many questions, and each of them was important and emotional.

I remember the night we decided to call Hank and let him in on some of our plans. Mel was with me. We were on the speaker phone when I rang Hank's number, and he answered.

"Hi, Hank. It's Helena. Mel and I are calling you on our speaker phone."

"Hi, Helena. Wassup?"

Oh my, I thought, *Hank is turning into a yuppie. Wassup? He must be learning that from Autumn.* I laughed to myself and continued.

"Mel and I wanted to tell you that we are getting married. We've set the date for a month before you and Autumn will have your new baby. The date is September 7.

Hank congratulated me, and then realizing that Mel was with me and we were on speaker phone, he congratulated Mel too. He had the audacity to tell him what a great wife I was. When those words rolled out of Hank's mouth, Mel and I caught each other's look, and we were both rolling our eyes. It was hard not to laugh out loud.

"Hank, Mel and I have decided to live in Mel's house after we do some modest remodeling and redecorating. I'm going to be taking some of my special pieces from my house, but most of the furniture will just stay here." Hank listened patiently probably wondering why I felt it necessary to fill him in on all of our plans.

Finally, I said, "Mel and I have discussed this thoroughly, and we wanted to know if you and Autumn would like to have my house?"

Hank was blown away by the offer.

"Hank, Mel and I really believe that this is the right thing to do. However, there are no strings and no hooks. If you and Autumn don't want the house, we will put it on the market, but we wanted to make this offer to you before we considered anything else."

Hank and I both knew that it had been a wonderful home to raise Gabe and Gilliam in.

Hank, being the sound business person that he was, came out with the question that both Mel and I had anticipated. "So how much do you guys want for the house?"

I knew that Mel didn't want to speak. This was my house and my ex-husband. Mel told me before I dialed the phone that we would do this together, but he wanted me to do the talking. After all, it was my house. I had lived in it for over thirty years. I had raised my children here. I had earned it.

"Hank," I said. "Mel has a similar home in size and age, and it also has a stable and a paddock. He suggested we move Blue and Grey there, but we have finally agreed that it is more practical for both of us, at least for the time being, to keep them at Victoria's. We don't need two houses, and we want you to have this house. You can consider it whatever you want, a gift, a returned gift, a way to keep the house in the family for Gabe and Gilliam, whatever. We know you could build a home anywhere you want for Autumn and you and the baby, but this is such a perfect house, and I do hate to sell it to a stranger. There are too many years of family history here. You can remodel it and redecorate it like Mel and I plan to do with his place and make it Autumn's and your home. Like I said, no strings."

I think Hank was truly puzzled and overwhelmed that we would make this generous offer to him and to Autumn. An ex-wife giving back the divorce settlement was pretty much unheard of.

Hank called me the next day after he had discussed with Autumn about moving into the big house. He said that he and Autumn had talked it over, and although she was excited about raising the baby in that house, she would only feel comfortable accepting the offer under one condition.

"A condition," I said, "Autumn has a condition for accepting my giving you two this house?" I was puzzled and almost ready to be a little peeved.

Hank said, "Wait a second, Helena, till you hear the condition before you get your nose out of joint. Autumn and I believe that since you received the house in the divorce settlement, it is only fair that we either buy the house from you paying you the fair market value or with my contracting business that we trade the value of the house for doing the remodeling that you had planned to do at Mel's. You mentioned that Mel wanted to also remodel his clinic, so I'm sure that would be part of the deal too. Maybe even a new dog kennel." He laughed. He thought he was being cute and funny, but actually Mel had talked about building a larger kennel for the dogs he treated. Hank went on. "We can work it out at my cost, which will give you a lot more value for the dollar."

Mel and I felt very comfortable with taking the value of the house out in trade. Together we would figure out what we wanted, and then we planned to approach Hank with our expansion desires for both the clinic and the house. Hank was very good natured about doing whatever we wanted to satisfy the trade. Mel had wanted to make some additions and changes to his clinic for some time.

The four of us met at the diner, which caused some local eyebrows to raise, and when we left, it was decided that the house remodeling we wanted done and the clinic remodeling would be a wonderful way to transact a fair and appropriate deal for the house. I actually was beginning to like Autumn. I think I understood what attracted Hank to her in the first place. And now that I had Mel, I didn't have that "what's wrong with me" feeling anymore. My self-confidence, thanks to Mel, was strongly back in place, and so accepting Autumn became much easier.

Mel and I moved forward with the plans for joining our two lives together, and we were able to agree on almost everything we discussed regarding our wedding, our honeymoon, and our future life together.

Once things calmed down, I began to have a little consistent rhythm once again to my daily routine. I had started my two new jobs, and I had also begun drafting out the book, which I had originally wanted to call *The Book About Jekyll Island* but had ultimately decided on *Jekyll, a Limpid Labyrinth of Dreams*, from the Sidney Lanier poem.

The book is taking on a life of its own. It's not just going to be the history of Jekyll, it's going to be a history of the people who shaped it, including me. Mr. Parker from the library is overseeing the project as I write. He is so encouraging and enthusiastic that I can't wait each week to share my progress with him.

Hank and Mel are not just being cordial with each other; they are developing something akin to a friendship. Not best friends but a friendship. Autumn and I have the same kind of thing happening. It's going to make it so much easier on Gabe and Gilliam when they come to visit their mom and dad, step parents, and step sibling on the island.

Hank and Mel have moved some of Mel's pieces out of his house that he is ready to let go of. They took the old bedroom suite to the Salvation Army who was delighted to receive it. The big master suite at his house now stood empty as did the living room and dining room. Mel had decided that we needed to replace all the furniture in the rooms that we would inhabit the most together, and I fully agreed with him. When Mel was at his house, he never used the living room or dining room; and he slept in one of the guest rooms, which suited him just fine. Soon he would be vacating the house when the full remodeling crew began their activities. Mel had moved a few more of his clothes and personal things to the clinic since he was also staying there a little more often even when he didn't have a patient to care for during the night. I think it was cozier and easier for him than being in the half empty house alone.

I have been marking some very special pieces that I want to move over to Mel's place, but I'm not ready to do that until the remodeling and redecorating is complete. I'm not taking very many pieces, but there are some things that evoke wonderful memories of raising my children and even the good years with Hank that I don't really want to leave behind.

Gabe and Gilliam were here with their children recently, and they have taken a few pieces to their homes. I encouraged them to inquire about anything that might be an asset to their homes, and if I didn't plan on keeping it, Hank already said to give them whatever they wanted.

When Hank and I told Gabe and Gilliam about our arrangement for their dad and Autumn to take over the house when I married Mel, they were thrilled. I knew it would be an arrangement that they would approve. Having something relatively similar, even if redecorated and with some new furniture, to return to would make accepting a new stepmother a lot easier. They always had liked Mel growing up. When they would go to the stable with me and help me with Beauty, they had gotten to know Mel; so when I told them we were dating, they instantly approved.

When Mel and I called them to announce our wedding plans, you could hear the whooping and hollering, which made us both ecstatic with joy at their happiness for us and for themselves. Instant approval is not a difficult thing to accept. Mel was smiling from ear to ear the night we told Gabe, and he was feeling pretty much the same way when Gilliam asked him if she would be allowed to call him dad.

By now, both Gabe and Gilliam had forgiven their father. So had I. And the kids were learning to appreciate that Autumn did have some redeeming features, the biggest one being that she really did love their father. Soon they would have two parents, married to two new partners. To add to the mix, they would also have a new brother or sister, younger than their own current children.

I think it took Gabe and Gilliam a little by surprise the first time they realized that their father's new child would be an aunt or uncle to their own youngsters. I would imagine that not a lot of aunts and uncles have nieces and nephews older than they are, but this is a new world; and extended families come in all shapes, sizes, and ages. Actually, Autumn, the stepmother, was only eight years older than her new stepson, Gabe. That might have taken some getting used to in the past, but today it's the new normal.

Adjusting to their parent's new partners and a new sibling would continue to provide some challenges for Gabe and Gilliam. The fact that they could still vacation and visit in the house they were raised plus have a new house that Mel and I would inhabit seemed to provide double compensation for the pain they had been forced to endure during the past several years.

Everything that the four of us are doing has been a healing thing. Hank and Autumn have been married for several months now. It was a small wedding at the church with just Autumn's immediate family, Hank's, and my children, several of Hank's closest friends, and Mel and me. We had dinner after the wedding at a restaurant in Savannah, and having listened to the advice I had originally given to Mel that day in the diner, they put the money that they might have spent on a lavish honeymoon into a trust fund for the soon-to-be-arriving baby. Their child will be born about a month after Mel and I are married. Hank has adjusted to the idea of the baby and appears to even be looking forward to another chance at being a better dad than he thinks he was to his first two. Autumn is excited about motherhood for the first time. Mel and I are just glad it's not us.

We decided together that the perfect place for our wedding to be held was at Mel's home, soon to be our home. He has a wonderful back garden and patio area that will hold the approximately one hundred guests. Gilliam is going to be my maid of honor, and Gabe is going to be Mel's best man. The town is buzzing about our plans. Hank and Mel and Autumn and I have kept this little burg buzzing for almost two years now. After Mel and I get married, I wonder what they'll find to talk about then.

The entire town appears to be truly puzzling over the fact that Hank and Autumn and Mel and I appear to be friendly with each other. Maybe we can be the poster children for how Jesus asked us to forgive and love one another.

I feel so genuinely affectionate about Jekyll Island and this town I live in. I am truly fond of our friends and the town folk. Even when I know we may be the subject of some tantalizing conjecture, I also know it's not malicious. That's what is nice about small towns; everyone knows everyone, but everyone also cares about everyone. If there is a crisis, the entire town starts making casseroles and doing whatever is needed to help out. It's America at its best. In many ways, it's like turning the clock back to the kinder and gentler times that the first President Bush used to talk about. It's like those thousand points of light. It's like Ozzie and Harriet. It's like the Amish and the Mennonites getting together for a barn raising for a neighbor who needs help or a start. I hold these people so preciously in my heart; I don't ever want to leave them or this place.

Before the Special Day

> It is not the strongest of the species that survive, nor the most intelligent, but the one most responsive to change.
> —Charles Darwin

Mel and I have been working diligently at ticking off items on our combined list of things to do before the wedding. Although we pledged to each other to keep everything simple and easy, putting together even our modest wedding, we discover, still requires a lot of planning.

Mel volunteered to take on securing the music for our wedding and reception. One of Mel's patients, well actually the owner of one of his patient's, Alicia, has a brother who is the lead singer in a very popular band who plays in Jacksonville. She contacted her brother for us, and his band agreed to provide our music and make all the announcements at the reception. When he told me that it was all worked out, I gave Mel a gentle love hit in his upper arm followed by a high five and a sweet thank you kiss.

Today the box of invitations we ordered arrived in the mail. We decided to have white lettering on heavy charcoal vellum with a light gray watermark print in the background of Blue and Grey in their stables at Victoria's.

Almost everyone who is on our invitation list knows us well and will understand the connection between Mel's career and my horses. Our marriage is a reflection of our mutual interests and another bond, besides love, that links us together. The wording was meant to be serious and yet light and fun.

> Blue Blue and Grey Streak
> are pleased to
> announce the upcoming nuptials
> of their veterinarian
> Dr. Melvin Anthony Daniels
> and
> their owner
> Helena Andrea Marchant Rivers
>
> They invite you to join them
> in the outside gardens at
> The Daniel's residence
> on Sea Crest Road
> On September 7, 2013
> At 4 p.m.
> to observe and celebrate,
> in the sight of God, family, and friends,
> the joining together for life,
> of Mel and Helena.
>
> Reception will follow with dancing and horseback riding.

Holding the invitation out at nearly my entire arm's length, I admire the effect and smile with pleasure. I lay the box of invitations on my desk. I can't wait to show them to Mel tonight when he comes over for dinner.

One of the things that Gabe and Gilliam requested was that we serve my "Helena Canapés" at the wedding reception. I went over to my recipe box and pulled out the instructions for the canapés so that I could provide it to the caterer. Until now, I had not ever given this recipe to anyone, not even my children or my closest friends. As far as my kids are concerned, you'd think that serving my canapés was more important than all the rest of the wedding.

I sat there for a moment looking over the directions that were typed out on the 3" × 5" recipe card.

Helena's Secret Recipe for Fruit Topped Canapés

1 (8 ounce) package cream cheese, softened
1 teaspoon grated orange rind
lemon zest to taste
2 tablespoons orange juice
½ teaspoon ground ginger

Remove the crust from a loaf of thin sliced white bread, cut each slice in half on the diagonal, and bake the triangular bread pieces on a cookie sheet in the oven at 350 degrees until crisp but not brown.

¼ medium honeydew melon
8 fresh strawberries
1 or 2 kiwifruit
1 ½ cups fresh pineapple wedges, drained
¾ cup seedless red grapes
¾ cup seedless green grapes
½ cup mandarin orange sections, drained
½ cup fresh blueberries
small fresh mint leaves

Using an electric mixer, beat cream cheese at medium speed until smooth. Add orange rind, orange juice, and ground ginger, mixing well. Spoon mixture into a decorating bag fitted with tip No. 18, and pipe mixture around the edges of the triangular bread croutons. Set aside. Cut fruit into various shapes, and decorate toasted triangle centers as desired with fruit and mint leaves.

The difficult thing about this recipe is that you could mix and cut in advance, but they had to be assembled right before serving, or the toasted bread would become soggy. That would make it a nightmare for the caterer, but I would request one tray of these canapés and be sure they were served immediately to my children. That, hopefully, would be enough to satisfy them.

The rest of the menu was pretty normal stuff. It would be a buffet of very heavy hors d'oeuvre to include finger sandwiches. Mel and I had already discussed with the caterer the need to provide some manly types of foods for those with a heartier appetite and some delicate morsels for the lighter or more discriminating guests.

We agreed with almost everything the caterer suggested including seeded rye rolls layered with thinly sliced pieces of medium rare roast beef and horseradish sauce, sour dough bread heaped with fresh ham and cheese, crust less soft white bread oozing pimento cheese, and delicate tea sandwiches with sliced cucumber and cream cheese.

After the sandwich menu was decided on, the caterer moved on to salads and suggested we include the usual macaroni, potato, broccoli, field greens, and molded gelatin salads. We okayed everything with the exception of the macaroni and potato salads. We eliminated the two salads that contained mayonnaise in favor of a German potato salad.

Attention then turned to platters of various cheeses with an assortment of crackers, along with mountains of fresh fruit and crisp veggies topped off with the perennial favorite at every reception, sausage bites and meat balls; and he told us, with this menu none of our guests would be unhappy.

I had added the Helena's canapés, and Mel had requested a platter of fresh slivered Icelandic salmon with capers and mountains of cleaned steamed shrimp. Something for every taste and appetite. That pretty much rounded out the food, and we were both happy.

The next and last discussion was beverages, which we agreed would include chilled Champagne that would flow freely along with wine and beer, a fountain of unspiked punch, soft drinks, and ice tea. That meant we would need to have a drink bar set up in a convenient location along with at least two people serving.

We were in the midst of having sessions with my officiating pastor, and it was a pleasure sitting with him and Mel every week as we discussed our values and beliefs.

Since Mel was generously taking on the music without my assistance, I agreed to arrange for the wedding cake and the flowers, and I had not yet made decisions on either. I knew I was pushing it, but I felt confident that neither would be a problem.

We were moving methodically forward, one step at a time as the date moved closer, and we were doing it without unnecessary stress.

I had purchased my dress. It was a simple sleeveless pale pink, floor length sheath with a matching full-length long-sleeved coat in the same material, with a frog closure across the bodice. In September, it would be perfect if the day was warm and the evening cooler. I felt elegant in the simple dress that hugged my still slender body beautifully. I felt like a bride when I tried it on.

It was about a week later, and Mel was sitting on the couch after dinner with his head resting on the back, his eyes closed, and his arm around me. It was storming outside, and we were listening to the crack of the thunder and watching the flashes of lightening as they streaked across the sky. We hadn't had a good storm in a long time.

In recent nights, our conversation was about the wedding, but tonight we were fairly quiet as both of us thought about the animals. Most animals don't like storms. At Victoria's, we knew that Celeste would be in the barn moving from stall to stall, reassuring her guests that all would be well. Mel had called the clinic about twenty minutes ago and felt confident that all was well with one of his staff looking after the few guests, which currently were staying overnight.

Mel's phone rang. When I heard it, I just said a quick prayer that I hoped an animal wasn't in trouble, and he'd have to go out in this torrential rain to tend the poor thing. He reached into his pocket and flipped it open. I heard him say in his usual business like voice, "This is Mel."

Then he listened, and immediately his body sat erect, his feet came down onto the floor. He had already moved to the door and was slipping on his boots as he was listening.

"I'll be right there," he said, and hanging up, he said to me, "Our house is on fire. It's been struck by lightning."

He grabbed his coat and headed to the door.

"I'll be right behind you." I yelled as he opened the door and slammed it behind him.

I ran to get my shoes, a sweater, and my rain coat; and hurrying as fast as I could, I ran out the door, into my car, and began driving quickly toward Mel's.

I remember praying to God on the way. "Dear, God, please, please, please don't let this fire be too bad. Don't let any animals be involved. Don't let any firemen be hurt. Don't let Mel get hurt. Keep everyone safe. Don't let anyone be involved in an accident getting to this fire, including me. We can always rebuild the house, but we can't rebuild the people. Thank you, Lord."

I could hardly see out of the windshield. The front glass was fogging over, and the wipers were swishing back and forth as fast as they could go. I tried to find the buttons to turn on the defroster, but my hands were shaking, and looking where I was going took all my attention. Finally I pulled over onto the side of the road and found the knobs I needed. Pulling back onto the road, I continued as fast as I could in the direction of Mel's home.

As I rounded the last bend before I got to his house, I could see the red glow of the fire. The blaze was reaching upward, significantly higher than the roof line, and it looked like the entire structure was engulfed in flames. I didn't really know whether to pull in closer to the house or park my car on the road and walk the rest of the way. I didn't want my vehicle in the way where fire trucks or emergency vehicles needed to be.

I finally decided to park just outside the gate. Getting out of the car, I ran through the mud toward Mel's house. It was slick and slippery, and I almost fell twice, yet somehow I was able to correct my slides. I was relieved not to have my progress impeded by being propelled unto my face in the muck. There was more than one fire truck there, and with the flames lighting up the night scene like a Broadway stage, I could see a multitude of men scurrying and working diligently in teams to aim the hoses onto the spitting and flickering fire. It didn't take long before I realized the flashes of light seemed to be getting dimmer. I spotted Mel, but I stayed back. He was talking to some of the men, pointing at something; and it didn't look, right now, like he needed me to be another worry for him. I just stood there. Soon I felt an arm go around me on one side, and one go across my shoulders on the other. Looking up, I saw Hank and Autumn, one on each side of me like little tin soldiers, protecting me and holding me up.

"We heard the call on the scanner, and when they said it was Mel's house, we came right over." Hank gently said the words as he squeezed my shoulder.

"Thank you, guys, for coming. I just can't believe this. We were getting ready to start the remodeling next week. You probably have the plans drawn up for the changes and the crews all ready to go. This just doesn't seem real or fair."

Autumn squeezed my waist and said as I looked over at her. "Don't worry, Helena, Mel and Hank will take care of everything. Hank and his crew will rebuild the entire house if they need to. It will be okay. We promise you, we'll do everything we can to help you and Mel."

When I realized that I was shaking from the rain and cold, I also realized that Autumn was soaked through to the skin. I turned to Hank. "Hank, as much as I love that you guys are here, you have a very pregnant wife, and she should not be standing out here soaking wet. You need to get her back home and dry her off and get her warm."

Hank looked at me, nodded, and looked over at Autumn whose teeth were beginning to chatter. Hank bent down and kissed me on the cheek. "Will you be okay?"

"Yes. As soon as Mel gets free, I'll go over to him, but I'm just trying to stay out of the way for the moment. You two really do need to go. I will be okay. You coming has meant a lot to me, and I know when I tell Mel that it will mean a lot to him too. Thank you."

They left, but I felt like neither one of them really wanted to leave me. There was real concern coming from both of them, and it made me feel good in the midst of all the bad. Love does make a difference, and it sometimes comes from the most inconceivable sources. Who would have ever guessed that day in the bedroom when Hank told me he was leaving me for a woman he had accidentally fallen in love with that this would now be happening. Who would have guessed that I would be watching Hank and his very pregnant accidental love walking away after coming to be with me. Two people I may have spent my entire life hating cared about me, and I cared about them.

My attention turned back to Mel and the house. The flames were gone, and now the scene was dark except for the lights from the trucks and those on stands that had been set up to allow the crew to see what they were doing. I spotted Mel standing by himself, and I headed in his direction.

Approaching him, I reached down and let my hand slip into his. He turned and looked down at me.

"Well this certainly is something, Helena. What a way to start a new life with you. It looks like what's left of the house won't be saved. We'll know in the morning when the sun rises, and we get a better look. What are we going to do now?" His voice, for the first time I ever remember, sounded weary and tired.

"Mel, I am so sorry. Hank and Autumn were here. I just sent them home. Autumn was soaked and shivering. But they came to tell us that they'll do whatever we need. They'll build a whole new house for us. They just wanted us to know that." I squeezed his hand, and he squeezed mine back, but he didn't turn his head toward me he just kept watching the house and the men still working to make sure there were no embers still burning.

The rain had subsided, and although we could still hear the low rumbling of thunder and see some far off flashes from the lightening, it was moving away and was now out over the ocean.

We watched as one of the crews began gathering their gear, and while conferring with the men from the other truck, it was obvious they were preparing to exit the scene and return to the firehouse.

I rubbed my cheek against Mel's arm. His jacket was soaked through, and my cheek was numb with the wet and cold, but it felt comforting. I was still holding his hand, and I gave it a squeeze as I said, "Mel, this isn't the first crisis we've gone through together, and it won't be the last. The amazing thing is, you and I are both here, holding each other up, and we always will do that. I know the house meant a lot to you, and what is in it is certainly important to you and has been a big part of your life for many years, but you are far more important to me than the house ever could be."

"I know, Helena, and I agree. It's just that things were going so well, and I just hate that this might put our wedding on hold."

"Oh, Mel. This is not going to put our wedding on hold. We can live anywhere. I'll live in the clinic with you. Or we'll pitch a tent. Or sleep out under the stars. I don't care. Wherever we are together, that will be our home. And it doesn't matter where we get married. Getting married in your garden was idyllic, but anywhere we get married will be the perfect place."

Mel bent down and gave me a sweet and gentle kiss on my lips. "Thank you."

We stood there, I have no idea how long, just holding hands and watching the activity around the house. Finally the chief came up to Mel and said, "Mel, we're pretty sure that everything is cold. We really can't do much more here tonight, but we can leave the truck and a partial crew here all night if you want in case something starts up again. It looks like not much is going to be saved, but I'm not real sure of that in this light."

"Thanks, chief," Mel said, "You guys go ahead and go home. I don't think you need to leave the truck and a partial crew, but I'm going to leave that call up to you. If you think you should, then by all means do it. I'm going to go over to the clinic for the night. I'll see you here in the morning. I probably don't really want to see it in daylight, but I don't see as I have much of an option."

"Mel, your home obviously took a lightning strike. We'll verify that tomorrow when the fire inspector comes. If you get here before we do, please don't try to enter the house, if there is anything to enter. The inspector needs to do an examination of everything before anyone starts moving things around."

"Sure, chief. I understand. I won't go near the place but is it okay if I walk around on the outside just to observe what I can?" You could tell that Mel was working hard to maintain control. I could feel the slight tremble in his hands from the rawness of his nerves.

"Absolutely, Mel. We don't want to make it any harder on you, but we also want to make sure that whatever structure is left is safe for someone to start crawling around. We don't need to add personal injury to what is already a tragedy."

The chief patted Mel's shoulder. You could tell he had compassion and was really feeling badly about this. It must be difficult to go through this time and time again with family after family. Firefighters really are heroes. Unheralded most of the time but their jobs are not easy. Besides putting themselves constantly in harm's way for people they may not even know, there was the emotional impact of what they did. It wasn't easy to watch someone lose everything, even if it is just stuff. Amid that stuff, however, is the evidence of a life: pictures, mementos, holiday ornaments, dining room tables where families shared meals, and beds where babies were conceived and people had pleasant dreams, and couches where people sat and made memories. Firemen also deal with lives that have been snuffed out by smoke and fumes and bodies that have been burned beyond recognition. Sometimes the victims survive, but more often than not, they don't, and sometimes those victims are fellow firemen.

As I stood there looking at the house, I was even more grateful that the lightning struck Mel's house while he was with me and not inside that burning inferno. I could handle almost anything, but losing Mel right now was beyond my capacity for any possible recovery. I realized at that moment that I would give up everything I owned as long as God didn't ask me to give up Mel.

"Mel, will you come home and spend the night in my house? I just want to know you're safe, and I'll feel so much better tonight if we are both under the same roof." I said it softly.

"Yes. I'd like that. Can I just lay with you and hold you tonight, Helena. I understand your need for security and comfort, and I have the same need."

We both drove home, and when we got there, Mel went into the guest bathroom and took a long hot shower while I did the same thing in my bedroom. He had pulled his bag out of the back of the truck and carried it into the house with him. I knew he had the things he needed in there when he had to spend the night with an animal in critical condition like Grey was the night the snake bit her.

When he entered my bedroom, he was in clean jeans and a tee shirt, and his face was freshly shaved, and his hair was still wet and hung in damp waves. I had put on a pair of warm pajamas, and I had already pulled the bedding back.

"What side do you sleep on, hon?"

Moving to the right side, I said, "I usually like the right side, but I'll take either."

He moved to the left side as he answered. "No, I'm a left side sleeper, so this is perfect."

He laid down in the bed facing the right side, and I slipped into his arms. He switched off the lamp on his side of the bed and pulled the covers up over us settling under our chins. His arm went around me, and I snuggled into his shoulder.

"I'm so tired, Helena. Right now, I'm more tired than I ever remember being." His hand reached up and tucked my head under his chin.

"Me too." I closed my eyes enjoying his arms, his warmth, and his smell. I listened as his breathing became steady and light, and I knew that he was sleeping, and I fell into a deep, sound sleep.

It seemed like only moments when I heard Mel stirring. Opening my eyes, I could see the light coming through the windows; and glancing at the clock, I was amazed that it was now seven in the morning.

"Good morning, my Sleeping Beauty." Mel smiled over at me and softly kissed my lips.

"Good morning, my handsome prince," I responded when our lips parted.

We both pulled apart, stretched, and sitting up, we got up on our respective sides of the bed.

"Well I didn't think we'd sleep together before our wedding but *sleep* is definitely the word to use for this one. The next night we spend together, Helena, you will not get quite as much sleep." Mel sounded like Mel again, and I loved that he had a little teasing quality to his voice and his words.

"Mel, if on our wedding night we repeat tonight, I might have to rethink my decision to marry you." I threw him a kiss and headed toward my bathroom.

Turning, I gave him a flirty little eyebrow lifting smile and closed the door.

After washing, brushing my teeth, and getting ready to dress for the morning, I opened the door, and he was gone. I hurried into my jeans, sweater, and boots; and skipping down the stairs, I was delighted to find that Mel had made a pot of coffee and was getting cups down from the cupboard.

"I love a handy and self-sufficient man," I said as I went over and put my arms around his waist and hugged him as tightly as I could.

"And I love a woman who wakes up looking as beautiful as you do."

I quickly fixed us some fried eggs and toast, a glass of cold orange juice, and a sliced banana. We downed our breakfast quickly. With the dishes rinsed and sitting in the sink, we both ran out to our cars; and after a brief kiss in the driveway, we each, in our own vehicles, headed toward his house.

A Change in Plans

> Life has taught us that love does not consist of gazing at each other, but in looking together in the same direction.
>
> —Antoine de Saint-Exupery

When we arrived at Mel's house, the fire chief and the fire inspector were already there. Much to the surprise of both of us, Hank was also there conferring with the two men, and he had brought one of his best foremen with him. I think Hank was anticipating beginning the rebuilding process as soon as he was given the clearance by the fire marshall and Mel to begin.

I hung back slightly while the guys conferred, and then I walked around to the back side of the house. Looking up at the garden and patio side of the house, it hardly looked like the house had been touched by the flames, while the front appeared to be totally devastated.

My heart was sad. I cannot imagine if this had been my house that caught on fire, how I would feel about all the years spent there being wiped out in just a few hours of hot burning flames. My heart ached for Mel, but he seemed to be doing pretty good this morning. Better than I expected him to be.

As I rounded the front of the house again, I heard the fire inspector say, "This looks very suspicious. The fire began in the upstairs front bedroom and burned down through to the living room and dining room. I walked those rooms this morning, and there appears to have been no furniture in them while the rest of the house is crowded with furniture, pictures, and evidence of a full life. It's like someone planned to burn the front of the house. I really do suspect arson."

My heart stopped for just a second even though I fully understood the reason for the house being the way it was. I also understood how suspicious this would appear.

Mel, with his hands in his pocket responded immediately. "I certainly understand your questions, but I think we can clear them up for you in a matter of moments."

Hank shook his head in agreement, and even the fire chief put his arm on the inspector's shoulder and said, "Yes, Clive, it won't take us long to fill you in on the change that's about to occur in Mel's life."

Clive had driven in that morning from Savannah. Once it was explained that Mel was about to get married, after five years of being a widower, and that we were preparing to remodel the home and bring in some of my furnishings, the inspector seemed to relax.

By the end of the day, we had been given clearance to do whatever we planned to do with the house. Of course, it was a very long day since half the town drove by or stopped with condolences and food, and the insurance man came to also make his inspection and report.

Mel had cancelled all routine appointments at the clinic and arranged with another vet from a nearby town to be on call for any emergency. The vets had ongoing close relationships with each other and had previously treated many of each other's clients. Gene, the doctor who was filling in at Mel's clinic today, would also be covering for us during the week we planned to honeymoon in Aruba.

That night, Mel stopped by the clinic to check on a few of his recuperating friends and then came to the house. I had some pork chops in the freezer that I defrosted and grilled. Not feeling particularly hungry or excited about cooking for very obvious reasons, I threw a couple scrubbed sweet potatoes in the microwave. While they became more tender, I cut up some salad greens and drizzled on some balsamic vinaigrette dressing.

It wasn't a great meal, but tonight it would have to do. We could finish the bottle of white wine that was half full and chilling in the frig.

As I had suspected, neither Mel nor I was particularly hungry. We were emotionally and physically exhausted, and we were both quiet over dinner, lost in our own somber thoughts. We had spent the day together and talked over things about the house as they came up. There wasn't much left to talk about that we hadn't already conferred on during the day.

I commented on the thought of arson and the insurance man and Hank being there with his foreman. Then Mel told me that Hank was coming over in the morning around eight with his lead foreman with some ideas for how to proceed from here.

I asked Mel to please spend the night again. The two of us were drained. All of our physical reserves and emotional energy was spent, still we needed the comfort of each other, of arms and the physical warmth of our bodies beside each other.

We both slept like we were among the living dead. We got up at six, our usual time for rising, and had just finished breakfast when Hank and Jim arrived. Hank had long rolls of architectural paper under his arm. With a brief salute, he made his way into the dining room as the rest of us followed, and he began to spread out on the table the evidence of an obvious very long and busy night.

Mel and I were quite frankly blown away when we saw what Hank, and obviously some old and trusted members of his staff, had been able to accomplish in one evening.

"We already had a start on this with the ideas that you two had given to us regarding the changes you originally wanted." He looked up and made eye contact with both of us as we stood beside the table. Both Mel and I were leaning on the table looking toward the drawings and my left hand, with the dangling tennis bracelet and the chocolate diamond ring, was intertwined on the table with Mel's right hand.

"Jim and I talked for quite a while with both the fire inspector and the insurance man, and we won't need to rip down the entire house, just the front part. I feel really comfortable, Helena," and then he turned toward Mel, "and Mel, that we can rip the burned part down, cart it away, and rebuild the house, and you will never know that it ever burned." Mel and I both sighed at the same time, and turning our faces to each other, we smiled, and Mel leaned in and kissed me lightly on the lips.

"How long do you think all of this will take, Hank?" Mel was still fearful of having to postpone the wedding or move it to another site.

"Jim and I have discussed this, and we've both been on the phone last night and again this morning. We've talked with all of our existing building clients and their foreman, and everyone has agreed to a month long delay in their jobs in order to help you start your lives together, on time." Hank was beaming. I could tell that this really mattered to him, and at that moment, I truly loved him for it.

Mel turned to Hank and hugged him. Hank hugged him back. Then I went over and hugged both Hank and Jim.

Looking up at Hank, I asked, "You think you can be done and out of there in one month? That in only four weeks, we can be back to where the house was before the lightning strike?"

"Yes, Helena, I have five crews starting today, and their only concentration is this job. Each crew has a specific part of the building. Four of them are already ordering material. One crew is, right now as we speak, beginning the tear down and clean up at the site. Jim and I stopped over there before we got here. They started working at sun up."

"Hank," Mel said with a voice that was reflecting relief, gratitude, and astonishment, "Helena and I just will never be able to repay you for what you are doing. Last night, it seemed like we would have to postpone our wedding."

"Well, buddy," Hank slapped him on the back, "we can't let that happen. Don't forget Autumn and I are moving in the week you guys are on your honeymoon. We have a schedule to keep. You might have been able to postpone your wedding, but I don't think there is any way that little Devon Shane Rivers is not going to be born in August."

"It's a boy! When did you find that out?" I cried.

"We had the sonogram done yesterday to make sure that all the toes and fingers and everything was developing as it should be, and Autumn and I decided while we were there that we wanted to know. We were going to come over today with the news and a very important question for you two."

Mel fairly beamed at Hank. "Congratulations, Hank. You already have one fine son, and I'm sure Devon will grow up to make you just as proud."

"I'm sure he will, Mel. I know you mentioned to me one day while we were moving some furniture that your only unfulfilled dream was to have a son. Well, once you and Helena get married, you will have a son, the best, in Gabe." He winked.

"Autumn and I have talked, and we think that we'd also like you to be in Devon's life. We'd like both you and Helena to be part of our boy's life. Would the two of you consent to be Devon's godparents? We'd also like to put you in our will as his custodian if anything should happen to us. I know you think I'm going to be in trouble for asking without Autumn here, but she told me to ask you this morning. She thought it might be kind of consoling for your aching hearts right now and allow you to be a part of sharing in our joy. We are both hopeful that you will say yes."

Mel and I looked at each other, looked back at Mel, and in unison said, "Yes."

This time it was Hank who let out the breath he had been holding. This was really important to him; we could see that. It wasn't a decision that was made on the spur of the moment, and

I hadn't thought about Gabe being the son that Mel had always yearned for. But of course, he would be. And now, Devon too!

Hank cleared his throat and rather brusquely, not wanting to let emotions carry us all away, stated, "We need to get back to work. My crew is also going to pull out all the electrical from the entire house, plus the heating and cooling ducts and the water pipes. Everything will be top of the line and brand-new. We'll also do the kitchen remodeling that you wanted and expand the laundry room, and while we're at it, we're going to add on a small addition and build a downstairs master bedroom suite and a guest room and bath. You two aren't getting any younger, and as long as we're building, we'd like to set you up for any circumstance that might come along. This will be the best age-in-place house you can imagine. You can use the addition for anything you want, but it will be set up so that you'll be able to live all on one floor if you ever want to."

Again, I was amazed at the foresight and thoughtfulness that was going in to this rebuild and remodel, and I could not be happier.

Hank continued with one last thing. "Jim and I are going to get over to the house and see how the crews are doing on all their respective responsibilities to this site. What you two need to do is look over these plans, and if you have any changes, let me know before the week is out. Even after we get started if you need something added, moved, deleted, whatever, we'll just do it as you want it."

Hank glanced at the drawings, and you could almost see his thoughts moving through his head. "You may want some additional skylights or different room layouts, doors in different places, walls angled in a manner we haven't thought about, so just mark the drawings; and when you are done, give me a call, and we'll go over it. I also have Jim's numbers on the bottom of the plans; he will actually be overseeing everything and conferring with me when he has a need. You can call him or me; we'll be working closely together until this is done. And, Mel, we'll get those plans to you that we have for your clinic too. Is everything okay for now?"

Hank stood up straight and indicated he was about to move on. I smiled, and he smiled back at me. Mel began to move with him toward the door. He put his arm up on Hank's shoulder, and I heard him say, "I feel really good with this in your hands, Hank," turning, he looked at Jim, "and you, Jim. Thank you both for all you are doing for Helena and me."

I heard the door shut, and Mel came back. He moved toward me and wrapped his arms around me. "What a night and a morning, Helena. You were so right when we were worrying our way through until Grey was declared all right. That wasn't our first crisis, and it wouldn't be our last. You know what, darling, I feel like God is really looking out for us. As difficult as all this is, I am amazed at the angels God is sending to help us. I feel at peace, and I know that we are meant to spend the rest of our lives together."

"I do too, Mel. There are no mistakes. We have been put together for a reason, and I don't know about you; but I'm willing to wait to find out what that reason, or those reasons if there are more than one, is."

Plans Continue

> It is best to be with those in this time,
> that we hope to be with in eternity.
>
> —Fuller

Hank, Jim, and their crews were accomplishing major things at the house every day. Just stopping by in the morning and again before the end of the day was like watching one of those time accelerated films of a flower as it starts from a seed and then within minutes, grows and blooms.

We didn't make many changes to the plans that Hank had provided to us. We both liked the idea of the addition on the first floor with the extra bedroom and baths.

We have both known couples who only had sleeping and bathing facilities upstairs and when something happened like a broken leg or hip, they were left at a huge disadvantage. I'd rather not someday need to put a bed in our living room and bathe in the tiny half-bath sink. I grimaced as I thought of my Aunt Patty when she was in her seventies. Following a car accident, they moved a hospital bed into the living area of their small condo, and that's where she spent her first six weeks of recovery. After that, she moved up and down the stairs on her behind until her broken leg healed enough to allow her to put weight on it.

I think that having our master bedroom downstairs, in an entirely new section of the house, would be kind of like having our own little hide away that was built just for us, which, of course, it was. Mel felt the same way and suggested that we put our new bedroom suite directly into the downstairs suite when it was delivered and take up residence there the night of our wedding.

We both felt that the upstairs could essentially be shut down from everyday use and be set aside for guest quarters. We asked Hank if it would be possible to put in a small dormitory style kitchenette on the second floor with a small sink, a little microwave, and an under the counter refrigerator in a large storage closet at the end of the center hallway. Hank loved the idea and after looking at the space suggested that he could also add a small stack washer and dryer and overhead cupboards. He explained that since it was next to the bath, it would be very easy to tap into the water and drains. We loved the idea. It would be like a short-term separate living quarters, and I was sure our kids, when they stayed with us, would appreciate the convenience.

Mel was getting more and more excited about the house as it began to all come together, and his initial depression over the fire was rapidly dissipating.

What was amazing to both of us was Hank. Maybe he was trying to make up for his betrayal to me, and I'm sure that was part of what we saw, but we both were blown away by the way he and his men worked so closely in unison on everything. There was none of the right hand not knowing what the left hand was doing. It was no wonder that Hank's business was so successful. He was all about pleasing his clients, and everything he did proved that. He listened. That was the amazing thing.

How was it that I lived with this man for so many years and never realized what an amazing person he really is? It gave me cause to more closely examine how much of my time and devotion I had really given to Hank. During the years of our marriage, I saw myself as a supermom and prided myself on being all about keeping a clean house, being a great cook, and being an amazing mother. What I hadn't done was put Hank at the top of that list.

Observing Hank and Autumn when we are all together, it becomes obvious that Hank needs a woman who admires him, listens to him, and puts him first. I pray that Autumn will continue to provide that for Hank even after the baby arrives. Hank is a good man, and I feel, for the first time, that I also am responsible for sending him into the arms of another woman.

It's not easy to closely examine yourself with honest eyes. I would have to be blind not to see the look of appreciation in Autumn's eyes when she looks at Hank. I know he never saw that look in my eyes in all the years we were married. I really had just taken everything Hank was and did for granted. Now, for the first time, I saw how truly amazing Hank is. I don't want him back as a husband; we have both moved on and found new loves. I don't wish to change things, but I wish for the first time in my life that I could have a do-over. I was wrong, and someday, when it's the right time, I'll let Hank know that.

I told Mel that night about my thoughts, and he sat quietly and listened. He told me he thought that maybe I was being too hard on myself. He said that all the years he had known Hank and me, he saw me only as a very devoted wife. Maybe Mel's right, maybe I am being too hard on myself; but to be painfully truthful I know how I felt, and I never felt truly enamored with Hank. I know in my heart that I loved him, but he was just Hank, and he was always there. Even when my Mom and I had that one very serious talk, I wouldn't listen because Hank was just Hank, and I never, for even a second, thought that he needed more than I was giving him.

Mel said something interesting during our discussion, and I may be thinking about this for some time in regard to all my relationships. He said that when we marry very young, we aren't yet who we will grow into. To help me understand the point he wanted to express, he talked about parents who never see the extraordinary people their children become because they still see them as children, growing—not grown. Mel looked into my eyes, not jealous, not criticizing, simply loving the woman he was about to marry, as he said, "Maybe Hank was always that man who was just starting out in life with you, and in your mind, you never saw what he had become, until now."

I didn't answer. I nodded that I understood, and I think there is much truth in Mel's words.

Three weeks into the project everything on the outside of the house was done. Mel's home looked exactly as it had before the fire. The crews had been very careful not to cause any more lawn or shrub damage than necessary, and Hank had even moved in a crew that was replanting and putting down new sod.

The roof over the entire house had been replaced, and true to his word, Hank had the wires pulled throughout the entire house and replaced them along with water lines and all the duct work. He had also had a fumigator come in to clean and disinfect all the rooms. He pulled up floors if the cleanup crew wasn't able to bring the floors back to their original state or if there was any lingering smoke odor.

The entire house needed to be painted or repainted, and there were those workers at the house now along with the group that was doing the kitchen and laundry room remodeling. Hank assured us that everything was moving not on schedule but actually ahead of schedule.

One afternoon as Mel and Hank and I were together at the house, I asked Hank, "Do you think it would be appropriate for Mel and me to send a personal letter of thanks to those wonderful people who agreed to delay their jobs so that your crews could all work on our home?"

Hank didn't hesitate a moment before answering, "Helena, you have always had a grateful heart. I think my clients would love a personal note from you and Mel. Very few people think to show their gratitude. I'll have Autumn get their mailing information for you."

Mel and I decided that I would write the notes, and that we would include a picture of our fire-damaged house and an after picture of the outside, showing all that was accomplished thanks to their sacrifice. Mel would include his business card with an offer of his services, and I would add Jekyll Island Club tram tour and museum tickets. We also decided to enclose a wedding invitation.

These fine people were making our wedding possible on the day we originally planned. We didn't know if any of them would want to come to a wedding of virtual strangers, but if for no other reason than to meet us and see the progress that was accomplished on our home, they might. They were, after all a very important part of our very special day.

Over the next few days, I wrote the notes of gratitude. Both Mel and I signed them, and we put them in the mail. I mailed all the invitations that same day. Our day, thanks to Hank and all his generous clients, would continue as planned.

After lunch one day, Mel and I did an unannounced stop at our church. Our pastor was in and assured us that he fully understood why Mel and I had not been able to continue our scheduled pre-marital counseling with him. He laughed. "It isn't like you are youngsters and don't know what you're getting into!" He told us with a hand on both of our backs as he walked us out that he felt very comfortable that God was blessing our union.

Part of the original remodeling plans for Mel's house was to include covering the back porch and deck. When we stopped by last week, we walked around to the back of the house and were astonished with how the roof lines had been worked into the house roof so that it looked as if they had always been covered. The effect was spectacular and with that addition, we decided we really had no need for tents for the wedding. All the food, the band, and if need be, the guests would now fit under that covered area that stretched twenty feet out from the house and almost seventy feet from one corner of our house to the other.

From the inside, the additional roofing seemed to darken only slightly the kitchen, dining room, and back family room; and since that was the setting sun side of the house, the roof would serve as an awning on hot summer days to keep the entire house cooler.

The flowers were the next to the last thing we needed to plan. The wedding cake also needed to be attended to, and my original plan for both had fallen through because I had, with my mind on the house remodeling, forgotten to schedule and order them. Now I had no idea what to do about either, but I imagine that people have gotten married without flowers and without a cake, and if that's what it meant then so be it. My happiness and Mel's would not be affected by the lack of flowers or a wedding cake.

I hadn't gone to work since the fire, three weeks ago. I talked with Mr. Parker last night, thanking him for the extended time off. I asked him if I could return tomorrow, and he was delighted. He had been filling in both places for me, and he was ready for a little down time.

He was quick, however, to assure me that if I needed more time, he was up to continuing for a while longer. I pledged that I was ready to resume my post and reminded him that I still needed time off for my honeymoon.

I loved hearing the sound of Mr. Parker's laugh when I reminded him. He responded in such a manner that it reminded me of how Ashley Wilkes might have spoken in *Gone with the Wind*, "You are such an asset and a treasure, my dear Helena, that we here at the museum will acquiesce to whatever you require just to have you here when you can spare the time."

I put on my best southern belle demeanor as I responded, "Mr. Parker, I dare say you make me feel like Scarlett O'Hara. If I had a fan, I'd wave it in front of my face and bat my eyes at this very moment."

I love that our friendship has grown so close that we can tease in such an easy and relaxed manner with each other. We both laugh at the thought, and I tell him that I will see him tomorrow.

Driving through the marshes the next day on my way to the Jekyll Island Club, I revel in the deep cerulean blue of the sky. It is a different kind of blue, a cross between azure and sapphire, almost unreal in its deep vividness. It is stunning against the yellowish brown of the wild rice and the green of the wetland grasses. If an artist were to mix that color on their palette and flow it across the top of their canvas, no one would believe that the area between earth and heaven could in reality be that color. Yet here it is.

God's glorious landscapes move my heart and take my breath away. His projected beauty is one of the reasons I love riding Blue and Grey. As we romp together through the woods, in the fields, on the beach, splashing in the Atlantic, I am treated to the most amazing gallery show of artistic perfection.

For some reason, everything this morning seems to be more clear. It is almost as if I had spent my entire life looking at the world through dirty glasses, and now it is vibrantly sharp and pure. I had experienced that only once before, and it was in Labrador at the very top of the St. Lawrence Seaway. I had never been to Alaska, but when I commented on the clearness to a friend, she told me it was the same way in Alaska. She said the reason is that there is less industry, less cars, and less pollution. Jekyll felt that way today.

There was a steady breeze blowing in from the Atlantic, perhaps it was moving crystal ventilation onto the land and clearing away any hint of man's sullied existence from the air leaving everything it wafted past fresh and alluring. Whatever the reason it was wonderful, and I was enjoying every inhaled breath of it. The sun was also casting a beautiful bright yellow sheen on everything it touched. The temperature was in the high seventies, but the air was not heavy like it normally is this time of year.

When I arrived at the Jekyll Island Club, it was about a half hour before my first tram tour. Before running into the museum to check in, I verified that the tram and horses were ready. The driver, Ben, waved to me as I scurried up the sidewalk and ascended the steps.

I noticed that a young couple was sitting on the benches indicating that they were waiting for the tram ride to begin. So far they were the only ones lingering outside, but people don't usually begin gathering until about fifteen to twenty minutes before departure. I have learned that many who are taking the tour are spending every available minute browsing the museum or the gift shop. People today want to shove everything they can into their vacation hours. As long as they have purchased their tickets beforehand, they know they won't miss the tram.

I stole one additional glance back at the waiting couple before opening the museum door. It was apparent that they were very much in love, and that their vacation time was being spent on what they believed to be the most important thing—each other. Their body language indicated that they had some secret that they and they alone shared. Their shoulders were touching, and their heads were together. I could see lips moving as they talked and heard some light laughter. It was fun to observe them. I wondered if Mel and I looked like that. I hoped we did. All of a sudden, I realized that having them on the tour this morning was going to make this a very special day for me.

The two beautiful chestnut horses were, for the most part, standing at the ready except that on occasion their tails would swish like a fly swatter attempting to chase away the insects that annoy even horses. Ben had the carriage hooked up and was sitting in the seat in his white slacks and light blue long sleeve shirt ready to depart. His uniform and mine matched. We both also had on white straw derbies that were comfortable and kept the sun from our eyes and off our faces.

The carriage held sixteen people plus the driver and, of course, me. The hansom we rode in was more like the one that we sing about in the song from the musical Oklahoma, "The surrey with the fringe on top." It was made of white wood, rather ornate with light blue trim, and it had a white top that had a white canvas awning hanging down about six inches with light blue tasseled trim. It was just enough to offer the riders a little shade when the sun was sweltering and yet allow a full view for all the passengers of all that we passed.

The seats of the landau were white leather, and there were four rows of two seats on each side with a narrow walking isle down the middle. My seat was in the center, right behind the driver. I was the only person whose seat faced the back of the carriage; everyone else sat looking forward. I had a public address system so that I could be heard by everyone without shouting, and the driver and I had a coordinated route so that I could explain everything while looking at the patrons, and they could look all around them as I discussed what they were seeing.

We had twelve tourists on the tram this morning, filling up the three rows closest to me, and we were making the final preparations to leave. I looked at my watch and scanned to see if anyone else was approaching. I turned and asked Ben if he knew the count, and he told me that everyone was loaded. We nodded to each other, and he gave the signal to the horses to begin their paces.

As I reached to turn on my microphone, the woman who looked like she was on her honeymoon introduced herself to me. They were sitting in row one on my right. "Hi," she said, "my name is Paige, and this is my husband, Victor."

Victor reached over and shook my hand and said, "We're from Baton Rouge, Louisiana. We're on our honeymoon. This is a gorgeous place. Do you live here on the island?"

I smiled at them. So they were on their honeymoon. I should have guessed that. "Yes, I have lived here for most of my life. It is a beautiful place. I hope that you'll enjoy the tour this morning. I'll do my best to fill you in with everything I know." As an afterthought, I added, "I'm getting married in just a few weeks too."

The young woman grabbed my hand and smiled. "I hope you marry someone as wonderful as I have, and that the two of you have a wonderful life together."

"Thank you. I think we will. Now, I need to start telling you what we're passing, so none of you miss anything important." I loved hearing the horse's hooves as they clopped on the cobblestone roadways that had been in place for more than a century.

I nodded to the passengers as I introduced myself. I asked where everyone was from, and after a moment or two of introductions, I began explaining about the Jekyll Island Club and all the significant history of the buildings and places they were viewing from their carriage seats.

We stopped twice while everyone disembarked, and we did a short walking tour of several places that could not be reached by tram. Once everyone was back on board, we resumed our horse paced ride. I loved doing this. It felt so very natural and comfortable. Sometimes a passenger would ask a question I couldn't answer, and I would suggest that if they wanted to stay when the tour was complete that I would attempt to get that answer before they moved on to something else.

Today, when the tour ended, Paige and Victor hung back to speak some more with me. As soon as I had said good-bye to the other ten who had been on board, I turned my attention to them. "Did you enjoy the tour?" I asked.

Paige smiled broadly as she said, "I enjoyed the tour very much. You must have been doing this for quite some time. You are extremely knowledgeable about this history." She appeared to be truly enthralled with what she was seeing and learning about Jekyll.

"Victor and I are going to find out if there is anything like this available in our hometown. If there isn't, there should be."

She paused for only a moment and then continued, "We are both chefs. We own a restaurant in Baton Rouge called Durant's Cajun Eatery. We wanted to invite you and your new husband to our restaurant if you're ever in our town." Paige handed me her business card and then gave me an opportunity to digest her comments and respond. She was quite the little spitfire.

I hoped that my response showed how touched and flattered I was by her comments and her invitation, "How very thoughtful of you to extend us that invitation. I will certainly pass it on to Mel. Right now our plans are to honeymoon in Aruba, but we've had some recent difficulties, so that might be up in the air at the moment."

"I'm so sorry," Paige's voice showed genuine compassion and caring.

"Mel is my future husband. His house was struck by lightning about a month ago, and that's where we planned to have the wedding and to live after the wedding. It's in the process of being rebuilt right now, and it seems like things will still be able to go as planned. I'm moving forward with everything, but I can't figure out what to do for flowers or the cake. I had wanted something really special for the cake, but right now I just want a cake. Those two things are the last major items that need to be taken care of."

"When did you say the wedding was?" Victor asked.

"It's a week from this coming Saturday. It's difficult to believe that is only eleven more days." I kind of made a grimace with my mouth like I wasn't sure I could pull it all off by then, but I was going to give it a good old college try.

"Paige and I will still be here then. We'd love to do your flowers and your cake, wouldn't we, darling?" Victor turned and looked at Paige who would have done anything he asked.

"Of course we would. Let us do your flowers. And I guarantee that you will be amazed at the cake we can produce. We'd really love to do this. Please say yes." Paige was all of a sudden like my lost younger sister.

This was amazing. When I saw Paige and Victor this morning, before I even knew their names, I knew there was something special about them. I was feeling pulled to them, and yet I didn't know why. Once again I couldn't help but know in the deepest recesses of my heart that it was God performing just another one of his amazing miracles. He knows our needs even before we ask.

"Well, I haven't even decided what I want. I don't know what I want." I looked at them with this desperate look on my face.

Victor, who was apparently used to working with brides, had a very calming way about him, and his next words were, "Are you able to go somewhere now and grab some lunch. You could come with us, and we could talk about it together."

"Actually," I said. "I'm done here for the day. There is a lovely seafood house just down the road. If you haven't been to The Devine Deveined Shrimp House, you are in for a treat. Actually, let it be my treat."

They both agreed. We went inside, and I checked with Mr. Parker while they wandered around the gift shop. They followed me in their car over to the restaurant. Over lunch, I got to know more about them, and I shared a little of my life. I told them about Gabe and Gilliam and my precious grandchildren. They asked to see pictures, and, of course like every proud mother and grandmother, I produced small recent family pictures of both that I carry in my purse. After lunch, the discussion focused on flowers first. I really wasn't all that concerned about the cake.

They shared with me that they aren't florists but running a restaurant you are called to do many things, and flowers had become so important in the dining industry that both of them had attended commercial florist classes and did almost all of the flowers at their restaurant and for catered events. I was convinced, but I told them I didn't feel it was fair that they should work on their honeymoon.

Their response spoke to my heart. They told me that their first love was each other, and their second love was their work. Using that reasoning they rationalized that by my allowing them to assist on such an important occasion as my wedding, that they could have both of their passions on their honeymoon here on Jekyll Island. I laughed. What delightful people these two are. Thank you, God, for sending me back to work today!

We talked about flowers and finally arrived at what we felt would be elegant and yet informal for an outside wedding and not difficult for them to pull together. I offered my home for the flower preparation since I had a large laundry room with wash tubs and my second refrigerator, which now was empty, would be perfect to store the completed flower arrangements. Since we were marrying in Mel's home, mine would be very available for a preparation area. Paige and Victor were excited. So was I.

I told them I had to run everything past Mel, but I was sure he would have no problem. I invited them to come to my house on Friday evening, if they had no other plans, to meet Mel and have dinner. They agreed. I gave them my address and phone number, and I headed home leaving them sipping wine at the restaurant.

It seemed like every single night over dinner either Mel or I or both of us had some significant thing to share with each other that had occurred during our day. I was beginning to wonder if either of us would have a meal together where we didn't discuss some unusual happening that occurred in our life. And I wondered when life became routine and average, if we would become bored with each other. I shared that thought with Mel, and his immediate answer was perfect, he just laughed in the most amused way and then followed that up with, "No, Helena, we will never be bored."

When I told him about Victor and Paige, Mel was extremely amused. "Only you, my dear Helena, would find someone to do their wedding flowers and their wedding cake on a historical tram tour. I'm looking forward to meeting them Friday night." He sat there and shook his head, smiling while he put another bite of sweet Italian sausage in his mouth.

"If you don't mind, I thought I'd invite Hank and Autumn to join us. It seems like our four lives are doomed to be meshed together." I laughed, and Mel joined me as he tipped his head slightly and raised his eyebrows.

"Did you tell this Paige and Victor about Hank and Autumn?" Mel asked.

"No, I think I'll just let it be a surprise. What's the worst thing that could happen? They won't do our flowers and our cake." I smiled.

"You're right, babe, bring it on." Mel slid his chair out and stretched out those long muscularly taut legs as his arms opened wide inviting me over. I jumped into his lap, throwing my arms around him; and we hugged each other as our lips met. Neither one of us cared what anyone thought about our crazy relationships. They worked for us.

Friday night arrived and so did the four invited guests. I introduced everyone and hurried off to get some drinks with Autumn's help. I heard Hank telling Paige and Victor that he was the contractor rebuilding Mel's house. After a few comments, I heard him tell them that he was my ex-husband. Autumn and I stood very still and apparently so did those in the living room for there wasn't a sound. Then Mel, God bless him, said, "Well I got Autumn pregnant, and my friend Hank said he'd step in and marry her; and since that left Helena all alone, I decided I'd better hitch her up or what would we do with her."

Again, dead silence, and then Hank and Mel started laughing uproariously. Paige and Victor had no idea what was going on, so Autumn and I decided we had better rescue our new friends and tell them at least a modified version of the truth. When we were done, our two new acquaintances from Louisiana were a bit confused, but I think they were also pleased to know people who were able to forgive and move on.

It was obvious from their comments that they understood a love that transcends all boundaries and allows even the unthinkable to come into existence. I could tell by their glances toward each other, and something perhaps in their eyes or in their demeanor, that they also had a story to tell. I hoped that someday we all would grow close enough together that they would want to share it with us.

Dinner was great. The conversation was excellent. The six of us got along wonderfully, and then the conversation moved to the flowers. Victor asked, "Mel, did Helena tell you that we offered to do the flowers for your wedding? Oh, and we offered to make the cake too!"

"Yes, Victor, she did. Isn't working on your honeymoon a bit strange?"

Paige answered, "We love to work with flowers together. We love to cook together. We love to bake together. Decorating cakes is our forte. Actually, we haven't found anything we don't like doing together, so it's not what we're doing but that we're together—that really matters. We talked in the room this afternoon at your wonderful inn, and we are just so happy to have made new friends over here on the Atlantic coast."

Victor interrupted. "Excuse me just a minute, darling. Everything Paige said is absolutely true, but in answer to your question, Mel, as to our working on our honeymoon being a bit strange. Isn't that like the pot calling the kettle black? I don't think that there could be many things stranger than what we heard here tonight about you four. So Helena picking up a honeymooning florist and baker on a tram tour she's guiding just seems to me like the most perfect fit."

When Victor finished, all four of us who had been leaning forward as we talked, sank back into our seats in peals of laughter. It felt good to laugh.

Autumn who is usually quiet until you really get to know her, decided it was time for her to add her thoughts. "I think I can say for Hank and I, actually all four of us, that you two are just the most pleasant delight we could imagine. I can't wait to take a trip to Louisiana now and spend some time with you on your home turf." She patted her burgeoning belly. "I hope you don't mind babies."

Victor spoke up quickly. "Not only don't we mind babies, we're having one."

With that announcement, it was like the music had stopped playing. Everything got very quiet for just an instant, and then people were jumping up out of their seats and rushing toward Paige and Victor and hugging, kissing, and pounding on backs.

"I knew from that moment I spotted you two on the bench today outside the museum that you had a secret to share. Have you ever felt so happy that you just can't stop smiling? Well, right now that's how I feel. I have completely fallen in love with you two." I stopped talking, but I couldn't stop smiling.

Paige, who was beaming, said very quietly as tears streamed down her face, "I love you too, Helena."

Victor gave his wife a big hug and said, "Getting back to the pre-baby announcement, we would love to have you guys over to Baton Rouge anytime. We have a big place with room for guests. We'll put you guys up whenever and for however long you decide to visit the west side of the Mississippi, and we'll even take you to our restaurant and teach you how to cook real Cajun. We kind of have free reign over the kitchen. You'll love our staff, and they'll love you, and I can't wait for my family and Paige's grandmother to meet you." It was obvious that Victor was a very genuine person, and that he meant the invitation.

Mel, who hadn't said much turned toward Helena. "Well this is just turning into one amazing evening, but I'm still wondering, since it was the original reason for our get-together, who is going to tell me about the flowers?"

I wondered, knowing that Mel was never able to have children and that his one unfulfilled dream was to have a son, if this was just getting to be a little too much for him. There were a lot of hormones flying around, and we were the only couple in the room not pregnant. Of course, we were also the only couple not yet married.

I was getting ready to encourage Paige and Victor to fill all of us in on the flower plans when my hesitation allowed Autumn to interject, "Yeah, Hank and I want to know too!"

As she said the words, our eyes connected, and I think she was having the same thoughts about Mel that I was having. She truly did have a sweet and caring heart and was very in tune with what others might be thinking and feeling.

Paige, Victor, and Helena all looked at each other, and the two women nodded toward Victor, deferring the floor to him.

"Okay. It looks like I'm the chosen one. With the two ladies' help, this is what we decided on…"

From the Roadside

> Don't walk in front of me, I may not follow
> Don't walk behind me, I may not lead
> Just walk beside me and be my friend.
>
> —Albert Carnus

I moved in to Mel's house last week, as soon as the contractor finished and moved out. Mel is staying at the clinic, and I am sleeping in an upstairs guest room with our soon-to-be-shared room downstairs currently deemed off limits to both of us.

As soon as Hank's five crews finished Mel's home, two of the crews moved to the house I had just vacated. The guys were quick to begin the renovations that Autumn and Hank had specified so that the soon-to-be parents could transition to their new address. The whole process was taking on the persona of musical chairs.

They even began the renovations with the laundry and kitchen areas, so they would be completed and out of the way when Victor and Paige began preparing the flowers and cake for our wedding.

While Mel and I were on our honeymoon, Hank would assign one crew to work on Mel's clinic updates and have everything completed by the time we returned. He planned that with Mel's blessing. It was a coordinated scheduling feat by Rivers Construction that truly amazed me as materials were delivered, and crews were moved from one worksite to another.

It is Autumn's goal to move in ten days, which is about three weeks before the baby is due. Most women who are pregnant can't wait for that final month to be over and to hold the baby in her arms instead of their burgeoning belly. Because of our wedding and the move, Autumn was hoping that Devon would opt for a late rather than the anticipated early delivery.

I figured with the way things were going for us, Autumn would go in to labor right about the time that Mel and I were ready to say "I do," and probably we'd have to stop the ceremony while Mel did the delivery on the spot. Truly, with the way the past months had been going, that wouldn't have surprised any of us.

Right now I'm standing on the second floor balcony off the guest room where I've spent the past week. Mel is two rooms away in the old master bedroom, standing also on the balcony. Both of us are looking down on the gardens, and we both know that very soon we will be facing each other and saying vows that we will keep for the remainder of our lives.

Downstairs is our new bedroom suite that we will share tonight for the first time. I'm anxious, and I'm scared. I think I'm more nervous about tonight than I was when Hank and I got married. I feel like a virginal blushing bride.

Autumn, very pregnant and preparing for a major move in just a few days, somehow gathered an entire group of local women who together decorated our new bedroom as their combined wedding gift to Mel and me.

Autumn and Hank had begun coming to church, and many of my friends, the women working with her on this project, have gotten to know Autumn better during this process. Following my lead, they are freely accepting her into this precious circle of friends. There is a lot of healing going on everywhere on this little island. God is surely present, and he is good, all the time.

Neither Mel nor I have seen our room yet, and we're not allowed to see it until Mel and I enter it as husband and wife. I'm a little nervous about whether or not we'll like the style and colors that someone else chose for us. But there was no way that either one of us could have turned down this love gift from Autumn.

As I look down at the place where we will stand in just a few minutes, I am awed by the fairy tale altar that Paige and Victor have created. Somehow they have crafted an arbor that has been covered with an off-white chiffon and held back to the sides with immense bows. Affixed to the bows are huge bouquets of the greenery that they have cut from alongside the roadways interspersed with the native Indigo Woodland Sage wildflowers that we decided would be not just fit for our wedding but would be both sophisticated and chic.

God provided the flowers for my wedding, all of them free for the picking. Paige and Victor called them roadsidea and woodwardia since all the flowers were cut from the meadows, roadsides, and in the woods of this precious island that I call home.

When they first brought the Indigo flowers to me as their suggestion for the wedding, I was mesmerized by the beauty of the blossoms. I had seen the flower before, since it grows wild on our island, but I had never actually seen it up close or studied it. It was, in both shape and coloring, like a soft delicate iris.

Victor explained to me that it's a tougher and more resilient flower than the Iris, and that he was delighted to find that it grew wild on the island. He said that after meeting Mel and I and knowing a little of our history that he felt this flower, that could endure difficult times, was very appropriate to be used as a focal point in our wedding. I loved that analogy.

The flower had a hint of a pinkish gray mixed in with the violet-blue as the white spotted streaks that run through the middle of each petal fade out into the deeper color of the outside edges. The little white spots make it look like it has a small amount of leopard in it. That also seemed appropriate since it brought into mind a piece of the animal kingdom.

Mel liked the flower too. He said it was amazing how it matched the violet-blue of my eyes. Victor winked at Mel and told him that was exactly what he and Paige hoped he would see.

Still standing on the balcony, Mel looks down the side of house to his right while I look to my left, and we smile at each other. The sun is beginning its slow descent down into the marshes that we can just barely see far off in the distance. It's now almost half past three, and the wedding is scheduled to commence at four. Guests are beginning to arrive and are being seated.

Mel and I glance again at each other and move back into our respective rooms. I glance once more behind me, hating to leave the breath taking sight of the sun shining over the place where our lives will very shortly be joined together. One consolation is that Mel and I will be enjoying the sunsets from this house for years to come.

It's difficult to believe that it has been only two years since my heart was crushed, and now it is full and happy and about to burst with the love that I feel for Mel.

This very afternoon I will walk down a flower strewn walk behind my precious daughter. I will be looking at my handsome son who will be standing beside the man to whom I will pledge the remainder of my life. Those who matter most to both of us, old friends, new friends, and our wonderful family, will witness this union, and God will put his seal upon it.

The door opens, and Gilliam comes back in. She has been with me most of the afternoon, helping me with my hair and putting on my dress. It's not a wedding gown as people think of wedding gowns, but I feel beautiful in this sleeveless linen sheath. I will wear the matching long-sleeved full-length coat for the wedding and then take it off for the reception. The bouquet I will carry and the one Gilliam will carry are greens with the Indigo woodland sage. Victor and Paige wrapped the long stems of both bouquets in wired silk lavender ribbon. As the bride, my bouquet is about twice the size as Gilliam's with long streamers that hang from the front, wired with more of the beautiful iris-like blossoms. Both creations are stunning. I will wear a small veil that sits very nicely amid my blonde hair that today I have left down so that it rides curly, bouncy, and shiny just below my shoulders.

The door opens again, and this time it's Amy, my very beautiful daughter-in-law. "Mom, it's time to come downstairs. Dad and Gabe have already begun their walk to the front with the minister."

I pause for a moment when I hear her say dad, but I know she is talking about Mel. I'm so grateful that my children love Mel and are accepting him not just as my husband but into a very key position in our family. I smile at her, and she comes over and gives me an air kiss on my cheek not wanting to leave a lipstick mark.

"Okay, sweetheart." I can feel the tears starting to form. I cannot believe that at the age of fifty-eight, I am starting life all over again. As I think of what I am going to do in just a few minutes, I can feel the panic rising in my chest, and I put my hand to my heart trying to get air.

Gilliam runs toward me recognizing better than I do what is happening. "Mom, Mom, it's going to be okay. I know what you're feeling. I felt that same thing just minutes before Mike and I got married. Usually it happens when you hear the first chord of the bridal song." She laughed. "It's normal, Mom. Just breathe. Come on, Mom. Breathe. You love Mel, and he is so in love with you. You are going to have an amazing life together, and we are, all of us, so happy for both of you. Even Dad and Autumn are thrilled about today. Everyone wants you to be happy. Can you believe all the healing and forgiveness that this family has learned and experienced in the past two years?" Gilliam knew she was rambling, but she was trying her best to divert my attention and calm my nerves.

It worked.

I took in a deep breath, and although I was still trembling, I was ready to walk down those stairs and straight into the arms of the man I loved. I wasn't scared; I was terrified.

Amy led the way walking down the stairs in front of me. Gilliam walked behind. I think they had me sandwiched in for a reason. They were not about to let me run. When we got to the bottom, Amy turned and kissing me on the cheek, she said, "I love you, Mom. Enjoy today. It's going to be the first day of the best part of your life." She moved away to find her seat before the procession began.

Gilliam moved up beside me and put her arm around my waist. I looked up at her. "Did you ever, in all your life, think that you would be your mother's maid of honor and be calming my nerves before I walked down that isle toward the second man I have ever loved in my entire life?"

"No, Mom, never in my wildest dreams could I have imagined this. But, Mom, I couldn't be prouder of you or happier for you or happier that Mel is going to be my stepfather. I know you are going to be so happy together. Even Dad thinks of Mel as the brother he never had. He told us this morning that you and Mel have agreed to be godparents and guardians to little Devon. What a family I live in." She pulled back, and we both laughed as we heard the first chords of the music.

We walked, hand in hand, over to the patio door that we would pass through before taking that walk down the flower lined path to the altar. Paige was waiting for us with our two bouquets and ready to make any last minute adjustments to our apparel or flowers. She was one terrific wedding planner, at least when it came to flowers and last minute details. How had she and Victor ever ended up on my tram tour that day? And we think we're in control. Never.

When Gilliam had walked about eight feet down the aisle, Paige gave me the sign to begin. This was the last walk I would make as Helena Rivers. Returning, I would be Mrs. Melvin Anthony Daniels. I kept my eyes focused on Mel, and I knew with every step, I was moving closer and closer to the life I wanted. Mel's face had the broadest grin I had ever seen him wear, and his eyes were positively shining with love. All I could think while I walked those rhythmic steps to the music was a saying my momma always used when I was growing up. "When God closes a door, he opens a window."

We had decided on a very traditional service even using the words, *love, honor* and *obey*, which few young brides want to say today. God asks us to become one flesh, and in doing so, it will be impossible not to obey. Mel and I also decided to be just a little modern, and so we wrote vows to each other that we would say just before being pronounced man and wife.

That part of the ceremony had been reached, and the pastor announced that we would now share vows with each other. Mel started. He did not use any notes, he just spoke looking directly into my eyes as he said,

"Helena, if you remember the first time I proposed to you and you put me on hold." At his words, almost everyone in the gathered crowd gasped slightly, and Mel paused long enough for the shock to pass. "That night I told you that marrying you was very important to me. I told you it wasn't a spur of the moment decision or one I took lightly. I told you that I thought our marriage would be the most expensive investment I have ever made in my life, and I knew that it would require a lot of time, effort, and devotion. I told you that I was prepared to do whatever it took, and that I planned this commitment to be forever. I also admitted to you then, and I admit to you now, that making this commitment to you is scary, but it's worth it. I promise to always be there for you, Helena. We've already been through some bad times together, and I know that together we can get through whatever life throws at us. We also have wonderful friends and a beautiful family that we love and that love us. I told you then, Helena, and I ask you now, to help me to make this marriage the center of our beings and the core of our lives. I love you."

I stood there looking at this wonderful man, and I wasn't sure I could say the few words I had planned. I looked over at Gabe who was beaming, and I turned and looked at Gilliam who was smiling with tears running down her cheeks. I looked out at my family and friends, and I spotted Hank and Autumn who were displaying almost the same reaction as my children. I took a deep breath and squeezed Mel's hands.

"Mel, thank you for those words. As you have just vowed to me, I vow back to you that I will make our marriage the very epicenter of my life, of our lives. I will work with you to be all that we can be together. I will try not to make the mistakes that I have made in the past. I will try to never take you for granted and to always put you first, just slightly behind God. I thank you so much for your love, for wanting me, for accepting my family as your own. You are such a good man. I love you so much.

What I prepared as my vow are not my own words. These words are borrowed from the poet, Roy Croft. It is his poem called *Love*. I wish that I had written these words for you, Mel. They are said to you today as if they come from my own heart. This poet must have been able to look ahead into the future to see into my heart and know every feeling that I have for you today. Every word flows from my heart to your heart."

I looked at him with all the love that I felt in my heart, squeezed his hands as we held onto each other and recited the poem that is written into my memory.

I love you,
Not only for what you are,
But for what I am
When I am with you.

I love you,
Not only for what
You have made of yourself,
But for what
You are making of me.
I love you
For the part of me
That you bring out;

I love you
For putting your hand
Into my heaped-up heart
And passing over
All the foolish, weak things
That you can't help
Dimly seeing there,
And for drawing out
Into the light
All the beautiful belongings
That no one else had looked
Quite far enough to find.

I love you because you
Are helping me to make
Of the lumber of my life
Not a tavern
But a temple;
Out of the works
Of my every day
Not a reproach
But a song.

> I love you
> Because you have done
> More than any creed
> Could have done
> To make me good,
> And more than any fate
> Could have done
> To make me happy.

When the last word left my mouth and I continued to look into Mel's eyes, he dropped my hands, took one step forward, and embraced me. My arms came up around him, and we stood there for just a moment held in each other's arms. It was a place of comfort and a place of safety and rest.

The pastor didn't wait for us to separate, he simply cleared his throat and said, "I now pronounce you husband and wife." As he looked up at the gathered crowd, he continued, "May I now present to you, Dr. and Mrs. Melvin Daniels. You may, as soon as you can part just a little, kiss the bride."

Dr. Melvin Daniels, Blue and Grey's doctor, planted a kiss on me that I was not expecting. It took my breath away.

Everyone was standing, laughing, and clapping, and I even heard a few whistles and hoots.

Gilliam handed me my flowers, and Mel and I walked down the center isle toward the covered porch.

It was a beautiful service, and one that everyone there would remember for many years. I'm sure Hank understood my comments about not repeating past mistakes. I hope he understood it was my way of apologizing to him for not being all that he needed me to be. I'm also sure that Mel knew that nothing or no one would ever mean as much to me as he does. My men. My husbands. One behind me and one in front of me. God is good, all the time.

After the service, it only took moments before the reception began. The champagne corks started popping, trays of food began appearing, and Mel and I began moving from table to table. The band was playing, and they were great. I took off the long coat since it was a warm day, and I was delighted when one of the first couples we greeted was one of Hank's clients who had delayed their building for us. We thanked them again, profusely, and they told us what an honor it was that they were able to make that very small concession for us. We assured them it was far from small, and we were so glad that they also had decided to join us. We suggested that they might like to roam inside the house sometime before they left and take a look at all that Hank and his crews were able to accomplish for us thanks to the sacrifice that they made.

I don't think that things could have gone any better that day. Except for that one moment of panic before walking down those stairs, I was relaxed and happy, and I was so glad to be an old married woman once again.

That time, those several years between my separation from Hank and my marriage to Mel, had allowed me to realize who I was. I could do whatever I made up my mind to do with or without a husband, but I knew that first and foremost what I really wanted to be was a good wife to a good man. I had been married to two good men. How many women ever get to say something like that in one short lifetime?

It was a great party. The interesting thing was I hadn't seen a wedding cake. I was sure that Paige and Victor had planned a cake, and so when the announcer said it was now time to cut the cake I was confused. What cake?

Mel and I were on opposite sides of the room, but with the announcement we looked around, and spotting each other, we headed to one another's side. On a large rolling cart, coming out through the French doors from the kitchen, was the most amazing cake I had ever seen. It was a horse and in the saddle were a bride in front and a groom behind, holding on to her with one hand and the reigns with the other. The horse part of the cake was done in a medium cream colored frosting, the bride was in pink, and the groom in black, and it was amazing. The horse stood about three feet high and was also about three feet from nose to tail. The bride and groom added about another foot in height to the middle of the cake.

Everyone gasped, and Paige and Victor beamed. They continued to carefully push the cake to the center of the gathering, attempting to not jostle it any more than necessary. Paige handed Mel a beautiful silver cake knife with lavender streamers tied around the handle.

With both of our hands together on the knife but before making the actual cut, I looked up and said, "This is truly amazing. Everyone, please, let me introduce our new friends from Baton Rouge, Louisiana who made this spectacular cake and who did all of the beautiful flowers and acted as our wedding planners. They are here on our beautiful island on their honeymoon, and I met them a week ago on one of my tram tours."

Once again, the group erupted with cheers, gasps, laughs, whistles, and shouts.

The cake was cut and consumed, the garter and flowers were thrown, we danced our wedding dance, all the necessary things were done, and the crowd began to leave just about the time that the sun began its dissent into the west, which was pretty much what we had planned. With the guests gone, the cleanup crew using the final shards of daylight took about a half hour to finish putting away food and clearing dishes. Tables and chairs could be done in the morning.

We waved good-bye to the last truck out of the driveway, and then turning, we walked back into our house, our home, and into each other's arms. This was our first embrace as husband and wife without a hundred witnesses, and it felt so good. We whispered words of love into each other's ears and then slowly began the walk to our new bedroom.

When we opened the door, we could not have been more shocked. This was the most gorgeous room I had ever seen. Not only was I thrilled, but it was beyond anything I could have imagined. Mel just stood there stunned. We both looked at each other and in unison the word "wow" emanated from both of our mouths.

In the middle of the room was our large four poster bed. The bed skirt was blue and beige stripes running vertically. On top of the bed was a down comforter in ocean blue with small tan and gold wavy stripes, almost like the wild rice of the marshes bending in a gentle breeze. There were numerous pillows in blue and beige and gold stacked at the head of the bed and a light brown coverlet across the foot.

The drapes matched the bed covering. It was the beach, the ocean, the marshes, the meadows—everything we loved reflected in this precious room where we would start our life.

In the bathroom, the colors were matched in towels and sink top accessories. It was remarkable and stunning.

The crowning touch was a painting that was obviously carefully chosen for Mel and me and that now hung over the top of our bed. It was horses, like the wild horses that ran the islands of the outer banks. They were chasing across a meadow with water and marshes in the background and a sky the color of the sky I saw just a few days ago and couldn't believe was real. The painting was in an amazing gold filigreed frame. It was a painting that we would share and love together for many years.

How would we ever be able to thank Autumn or the other women who had put this all together just for us. I have never before felt so loved or valued. I knew I also had a husband who cherished me, and I adored him.

I turned my back toward Mel and asked him if he would mind lowering the back zipper on my dress. He put his hands on my shoulders, and leaning down, he kissed me on the back of my neck, which sent a shiver down the full length of my spine. I think he knew that I would make a little shutter as the feeling drove the full length of me. I heard his deep satisfied laugh as his hands began slowly lowering the zipper.

It was indeed a wedding night to remember, and it is completely amazing how two people who were as tired as we were when we waved good-bye to the last wedding guest somehow rallied so astonishingly in such a short few minutes.

The next morning, we spent some leisure time just snuggling together in bed. Mel was kissing my eye lids, and things were beginning to once again heat up when the phone rang.

"Don't answer it," I whispered in his ear as I nibbled on the lobe.

"Ohhhhh, Helena, I have to," I knew he didn't want to, but he rolled over and picked up the phone that was on his side of the bed.

He listened for a moment. I couldn't hear the words, but I knew it was a man's voice.

"No kidding," Mel pulled the covers up and snuggled the phone next to his ear as he laid on his side looking at me. "Really. When?" He listened. "How big?" More waiting. Then laughter. "How long?" Another pause. "No, that's hard to believe."

I was getting curious now and impatient. I mouthed to him, "Who is it? What's going on?" Mel smiled at me and just kept listening. I wasn't happy being ignored.

"Well, Hank, congratulations to both you and Autumn and Devon and Dodge. Twins. That's hard to believe, and they didn't show up on the ultrasound." Another pause while the voice I now knew was Hank's said a few more words of explanation. "And the doctor thinks one was hiding behind the other. That is amazing. Well, buddy, I am sure glad that everyone is okay. Helena and I will come by the hospital a little later today. You give a kiss to Autumn for us. We love you guys, all four of you." Again the disembodied voice on the phone spoke. "Oh, sure, what's one more godson. Bye."

He hung up and started laughing as he hugged me close and gave me a big kiss. "Did I tell you before how very happy I was that it was Hank and Autumn who were having a baby at Hank's age and not us? Well, baby, that goes double now. They just had twin boys. I don't know whether to laugh or cry. Hank sounds like he's in shock." He started laughing and kissing me, and then he was doing more than kissing me, and we made the sweetest love in celebration of two new boys who weren't ours. I guess that Mel was over wanting his only unfulfilled dream, at least in the traditional way.

It was about two o'clock before we piled into the car and headed toward the hospital. When we arrived the two boys were in the room with Autumn, and Hank was there too. They were the most adorable boys. Autumn looked happy but tired. Hank looked like he won the prize for man of the year. The shock had worn off for now, but I was thinking he's going to have to start a second trust fund. It's a good thing they have the big house for raising the boys in. They are going to need it.

I reassured Autumn that Mel and I were absolutely delighted with the bedroom, and that we would now begin work helping Hank get their new place in shape for her to bring the boys home. I really felt that we could get enough things done that she could go right from the hospital to the big house. I knew Hank's crew planned on finishing up all the changes today. Tonight, Mel and Hank and I could start moving things with some help from friends, and tomorrow I could get everything set up and ready for her to come home the next day.

I was beginning to think that we were all truly amazing super powers, but it wasn't us individually that have been able to do so much—it has been us together with help from everyone willing to pitch in. As a team, we have been able to achieve remarkable things in very short periods of time.

Remodeling, rebuilding, decorating, planning weddings, putting together the flowers, catering, healing, moving—all the things of life and alone they seem to be mountainous tasks, but with help, there is nothing insurmountable about them individually.

I had called Paige and Victor about the babies, and their smiling and beaming faces appeared in the doorway with congratulatory balloons.

Paige ran over to Autumn and gave her a big kiss while turning to the babies she began to *ohhh* and *ahhhh*. In the meantime, Victor shook hands with Hank, and they both asked when they knew they were having twins. Hank laughed and answered. "Right about the time the second one's head appeared, then we knew."

Everyone laughed, and Autumn reached out for Hank's hand and gave it a big squeeze. What a family we are. Family, oh my goodness. "Hank," I asked, "Has anyone called Gabe and Gilliam and told them about their new brothers?"

Hank looked at me and shook his head that he had not called them yet. "Do you want me to call them?"

"No, Helena, thanks. I'll give them a call in just a couple minutes. I think the call should come from me."

I answered. "I'm glad. The kids are going to be so excited; it will be good for you to tell them and hear their reaction."

The kids were going to be amazed to find out the family had doubled from two children to four children. Actually, I think we were all amazed, but I wondered how Autumn was really doing. I moved over to her, and putting my hand up to her forehead, I gently pushed the hair back that was hanging into her eyes. "Autumn, I'll be here for you. I just want you to know that. I know you don't have a mother to help you out, so perhaps for a couple weeks when you get home, I can come by and help with the little ones. If you'd like me to."

I could see the look of gratitude in her eyes, and Hank who had heard my offer came over beside Autumn and looking at me mouthed the words, without any sound, "thank you."

"I think that Mel and I had better get going." Turning to Paige and Victor, I said, "How much longer are you two going to be around? By the way, and this is not an afterthought, the flowers were spectacular. And that cake. Not only was it the most beautiful thing that I have ever seen, it was also the tastiest. If you guys ever get tired of being restaurateurs perhaps you'll want to open a bakery or a flower shop or oh why not all three. And I haven't forgotten, I know we need to settle up on what we owe you before you head out of town."

Paige answered. Apparently, she and Victor had been conferring. "You don't owe us anything. The flowers were free, and what little we did spend on the few things we needed, you can consider a wedding gift from us. We had so much fun doing it, and we have loved making four, now six, new friends to boot. What a marvelous honeymoon you guys have made for us. We were going to go home tomorrow, but we'd love to stay and help you get things ready for Autumn and Hank and the boys if we can do anything."

I jumped in. "Do anything? Oh, if you really mean your offer, we can use the extra hands. Thank you guys so much. I'm thinking you need to be planning yearly vacations to Jekyll from now on. Both of us couples have lots of room for guests."

Victor answered. "Well, that's settled then. When do we start?"

"How about if everyone comes over to our house for supper tonight. Anyone, that means you Hank, who wants to come is welcome as long as you understand that you'll be eating leftover reception food, including champagne. We can start doing whatever right after we eat." When I finished talking, I looked over at Mel and got a nod of confirmation. Of course, what choice had I given him?

Hank spoke up looking at Mel and me. "Aren't you two supposed to be on your honeymoon? Four people who are on their honeymoon, and they're working to get Devon, Dodge and their parents into their home. I'm not sure I understand this modern world. In my day, honeymoons were for other things."

Victor laughed. "Yeah, and they still are." He smiled at Paige and put her hand in the crook of his arm. I slipped my hand into Mel's, and Hank bent and kissed Autumn.

"Actually," Mel said, "We don't leave for Aruba until Wednesday, and it isn't you and Autumn we're planning to work so hard for— it's Devon and Dodge! After all, I am their godfather and a very proud one!" The babies started crying. All, at that moment in time, was well with the world.

Fatherhood

> Blessed be the hand that prepares a pleasure for a child,
> for there is no saying when and where it may bloom forth.
> —Douglas Jerrold

We had a good time that evening, the five of us, eating, laughing, and planning what we would do the next two days to make things perfect for the arrival of the babies. As soon as we had thrown away the paper plates and napkins we had used, we all headed over to Hank and Autumn's place.

As I walked in, I was pleased with the changes they had made. Hank's crew had replaced the kitchen appliances with the new dull fingerprint proof stainless and installed beautiful navy and white flecked granite countertops. The kitchen cupboards were no longer the golden oak I loved but were now a shiny white trimmed in navy blue, and an angled bar with eight bar stools now circled the room, providing a natural boundary between it and the family room. It really opened the place up and brought it into the twenty-first century. In the family room, they had updated the old red brick fireplace wall by painting the brick white and adding a beautiful white built in entertainment center on one side and wet bar on the other. It was delightful. The floors had been sanded and urethane applied, and they were shiny with the new patina.

The dining room had a new chandelier that was made of capiz shell and silver, and that hung over a glass and chrome round table and chrome and white leather chairs. Again, the room was light and bright and a reflection of much more modern taste with a strong note of elegance. It was far more versatile for family dinners or entertaining guests. I was impressed, and although my pleasure wasn't important, I was pleased with what I saw.

I whirled around taking in all the updates and changes, and I was thrilled for Hank and Autumn.

"Hank, this is positively stunning. Did you come up with all these ideas?"

"Not a single one of these ideas are mine. They are all Autumn's. She has kept the rooms that she and I and the kids will use most rather family oriented and kid friendly, but in rooms we'll use strictly with adults, like the dining room, she has dared to introduce glass and shell and things that she says speak to her of the island. I am amazed at her creativity. I'm glad you like it, Helena. I'm sure it's difficult to walk into the house you had decorated so wonderfully and see the changes."

"Actually, Hank, I couldn't be more delighted. I'm glad that you two have made it your house now. I think Gabe and Gilliam are going to also love it. It's much more in keeping with their younger taste and not quite so old fashion. It was time for this old place to get a face lift. I can see those boys running around in here with Autumn and you chasing after them. It will be a home that will bring you all many years of happiness."

Mel came over, and putting his arm around me, he gave me a squeeze and kissed my cheek. "Okay, okay," he said, "let's not get too emotional, we have work to do. Where do we start to get things ready to bring my boys home?"

"Your boys?" Hank slapped Mel on the back. "Seems like I'm rapidly being moved out of the picture. Well don't forget old buddy who their daddy is?"

Mel laughed and gave Hank a little elbow in the ribs as he came back with, "And don't you forget who their god daddy is?"

Victor just stood there shaking his head while Paige had an amused little smirk of a smile on her lips. I think the two of them just continued to be both puzzled and amazed at the relationship the four of us had developed.

Hank led us to the room adjacent to their bedroom that would be the boy's room, at least for the first year or two. The room had an adjoining door for both convenience and privacy. It was a good design feature and obviously one that had been accomplished within the past month. The room was already decorated for a boy, and there were boxes containing two cribs, two dressers, a dressing table, and several other items that had been delivered but not put together.

"Here is our nights' work. If you guys want to work as couples, I'll go grab us some tools, and we can start the assembly process." As Hank turned to leave in pursuit of tools, both remaining men reached into their pockets and pulled out their Swiss Army knives. Why is it that all men feel the need to carry that knife-sized toolbox? Both of them, almost in unison, popped out the knife blades and started opening the boxes, each one choosing to begin with one of the cribs. Paige and I just looked at each other, shrugging our shoulders and smiling.

When Hank got back, the guys were ready for the pliers, full size screw drivers, wrenches, and even the hammer that Hank brought with him. He came in the room carrying three pails and set one down between each couple and carried one to where he would be working. He also turned on a portable radio that he had stuck under his arm and soon the sound of soft jazz was filling the room.

While we worked, we talked, sang, whistled, and did a few hand beats on the cardboard in time with the music. At one point, almost in unison, Mel and Victor grabbed their wives and began dancing us around the room while Hank looked on smiling. Finally, he put up his hand and said, "Enough. Enough. Back to work, everyone. Your break is over. Honeymoon on your own time." The guys retorted back something about Hank being a slave driver, and each of us returned to our respective jobs. It was a very companionable group, and we were all working hard and having fun doing it.

Every once in a while, someone would ask for another pair of hands or call on Hank to explain something in the directions. At one point, I asked Hank if there was anything cold to drink in his frig, and he told me I knew where it was, to help myself. I felt a little strange prowling in a house that was no longer mine, but yet it also felt comfortable that Hank didn't mind that I would make myself at home. I came back up with a six pack of cold Bud, some cheese and crackers, and a couple of apples cut into slices.

Everyone stopped, and we sat on the floor in a circle munching, slurping, and gulping, and then it was back to work. It took us about three hours to finish putting together the last of the furniture items. We all marched to Hank's truck with our arms filled with empty boxes, paper, and tools.

Returning to the house, I grabbed the vacuum and ran it over the medium blue short nub carpet that was perfect for a boy's room.

When the floor was clear of all debris left from the assembly process we placed the cribs, the dressing tables, the dressers, the bouncy chairs, and the two platform rockers with the matching ottomans on both sides of the room.

Standing back and observing the final outcome, it was like a room with a mirror image. Each side was set up to replicate the pieces on the other side of the room. In the middle was the door that led to the master bedroom, so when Hank or Autumn, or both of them, came through the door, they either went to their left toward one son or to their right toward the other. I liked it. It was simple and practical and would make it easy for the caregivers.

Looking at the room now, seeing it with eyes that know twins are going to reside in here, I had an eerie feeling that it was originally designed for not one but two babies. I know it wasn't possible, but as I looked at the two sides, I began to notice that there also was a closet on both sides of the room, a bathroom that butted up to Hank and Autumn's, and a day bed on the far empty wall that rested nicely with about four feet on each side, between the two cribs.

My curiosity got the better of me, and as I cleared my throat, I said, "Hank, when was it again that you and Autumn knew you were having twins?"

"I already told you guys. We knew it when Dodge started out head first right after Devon." He didn't seem to really pay much attention to the question, so I decided to try again.

Once again, I cleared my throat. "And, Hank, who designed this room, was it you or Autumn?"

This time he looked up at me. "What are you getting at, Helena?"

"Well, Hank, look around. Two closets, a bathroom, a day bed, and room for two duplicate sets of everything. Does this look like a room designed for one little baby boy?"

"My, my, Helena, aren't you the suspicious one. Obviously the gig is up. It wasn't designed for one baby boy. When Autumn and I designed the room, we thought it might be smart to think out a little further than two years, so we designed it to be a room that would accommodate twin beds, two dressers, two closets, and a bathroom for Devon as he grew older and might have little boy guests or even later for just a guest room. After all, Helena, as you might recall, children have a tendency to grow up. Now it's your turn to grow up."

The air in the room stopped, and everyone looked at us very strangely. I had carried the interrogation a little too far, and it really was none of my business.

"Hey, Hank, I'm sorry. My questions were definitely out of line, and with all the other great ideas that you and Autumn have had for this house, I don't know why I didn't think about later. I guess I'm just a short-term thinker. Forgive me?" I smiled.

Hank got up and walked over to Mel. "Mel, I know you've only been married one night, but you have your hands full, my friend. She's a great woman, and you've got to love her, but she's tenacious as all get out. She's like a bull dog."

Then he walked over to me and gave me a big hug and a kiss on the cheek. "You're forgiven."

The moment passed, and you could feel the air noticeably lighten in the room.

Paige had hesitated in her job of opening the linens, and now she continued. Together we began making up each crib with the matching sheet and comforter in the blue and red pattern. It was interesting that one red and blue set had hammers and saws and all sorts of tools all over it, and the other was decorated in old fences, meadows, barns, and horses. I wonder if she was planning on one joining Hank and the other joining Mel. It seemed like she was patterning their future before they even had come home from the hospital. Mel noticed it too.

"So is Autumn planning on one boy following in their dad's footsteps and the other in his godfather's?" Mel said.

Hank looked smiling, "I'm glad you noticed, but I think you're forgetting something. Autumn didn't know she was having two boys. I purchased the second set of all this furniture, just duplicating what Autumn had purchased for the first boy. She planned on our son following in my footsteps. She bought the coverlet and accessories with the tools to honor me. But now that we have two boys, I thought it wouldn't hurt to give one of them a little push toward their godfather and see what develops in a few years."

I could see that Mel was truly touched. What a kind and loving gesture. Hank knew that Mel had always wanted a son, and his willingness to share his was not just kind it was a truly generous and loving gesture.

"So," Hank said before it got too thick with emotion in that small room, "Anyone want a tour of the rest of this floor?"

Everyone nodded, and he led us through the connecting door into the room that he and Autumn shared. It too had been remodeled and redecorated, and it was stunning. A very large round king size bed sat in the middle of the room. Actually, there were no corners in the room. Hank's crew had created a round room so that it felt like one was entering a tower. The furniture was spaced around the outside edges of the turret. Nothing was wide. All the furniture including the dressing table, chairs, and dressers were all narrow and tall, and each piece appeared to be slightly curved so that it all flowed smoothly around the outside diameter of the amazing room. The color of the room was a beautiful dove Grey from about four foot down to the floor and had been faux painted to look like concrete blocks with ivy climbing up the walls. From the top of the blocks to the ceiling the room was alive with shades of mauve, orange, and yellow reflecting what might appear to be the colors of the setting or rising sun.

There were narrow, floor to ceiling, doors that led out to a balcony that was edged with a black iron railing with vertical bars spaced only two to three inches apart. The balcony had been roofed, and the furniture consisted of heavily padded large chairs and tables that looked to the west affording a beautiful view as dusk raced to meet the horizon.

I wasn't sure if I had entered a bedroom or a Disney film. We were all struck dumb as we just kept twirling around in the room taking in the effect that had been amazingly created.

Paige, God bless her, was the first to speak. "Hank, this is the most amazing room I have ever been in. You must feel like the prince who just rescued Sleeping Beauty or Rapunzel every time you come in here."

"Actually, Paige, I haven't gotten used to it yet, but it was what Autumn wanted, and so I told her we'd give it a try. I personally think she went a little overboard with it, but it certainly has given my crew something to stretch their imaginations and talent. Sometimes they need something that's a little out of the ordinary and this certainly is. The one thing that everyone who worked on this room told me, and I don't think it's because I'm the boss, is that Autumn is wonderful to work with. The guys told me that not only does she have ideas, but she has ideas about how they can accomplish her ideas." He stopped realizing he was going on maybe more than he needed to.

Paige encouraged him. "Well what is Autumn's background?"

"Her father was an architect, and she has a degree in art. That more than says it all."

Hank then led us into the hallway and showed us the other rooms on the second floor. Each was beautifully furnished and decorated, but none of them were like the room that she and Hank shared. I wondered personally, how long they would keep that motif. I think that it wouldn't take long to get a little tired of it and want a change, but it also wouldn't be difficult to repaint. I did think the round bed in the middle of the room was a little over the top, but one thing for sure, neither one of them would ever have to worry about getting up on the wrong side of the bed.

After the tour, the guys headed downstairs to put together high chairs, unpack car seats, set up the two-seater stroller, and the side-by-side buggy.

Paige and I stayed in the nursery and unpacked and put away all the boxes of shower gifts and other purchases that she and Hank had been making for months. We put out the Pampers, the jars of petroleum jelly, baby oil, and lotion. We opened drawers and folded and put away the onesies and little snap pajamas, the tiny little blue jeans and shirts. We folded little socks and booties and sat up the tiny shoes. We had stacks of receiving blankets and soft little towels with hoods, tiny wash cloths, and all the things a little one would need.

We sorted everything into piles by color. It is amazing that it isn't just blue for boys anymore. We had piles of red, blue, green, yellow, and white so that Autumn would just have to choose what she wanted and go to that pile.

When we were done, the room looked like it was ready for the arrival of the babies. Burp cloths were laid over the backs of the rockers along with little lap blankets. We even had two little baskets where we divided up the rattles, pacifiers, teething rings, and teddy bears. In one basket, we put everything that was blue and in the other everything that was green.

We found two mobiles and attached them to the top of each crib so that Autumn could wind them up and allow them to move and play their little tunes encouraging Devon and Dodge to grow heavy eye lids that would herald sleep.

Paige looked over at me while we were working and confessed, "I can't wait until the time when Victor and I have our little one. We had decided to wait for a little while since we both work together, but God had other plans. We took a mini-honeymoon in Florida after we had been married a few months. It was an amazing time. Someday I'd like to share with you the amazing thing that happened on that trip. Victor helped me to get past some things from my childhood that I had been hung up on for years."

She paused, and I could see her thoughts moving backward. I didn't say anything; I just waited until she rejoined me in the present. "I'm younger than Victor, so we could have waited for a while; but sometimes when you put things off too long, you get stuck in your little ruts and decide not to change the pattern. I'm glad God took that out of our hands. My pregnancy was a surprise for both of us, but we are both positively delighted. My sister-in-law who also works with us at the restaurant is pregnant with her second baby, and they'll be due fairly close to the same time." She looked up and smiled. "I'm just so happy, and I'm so glad that you and I have become friends. I love you, Helena."

I gave her a hug. Paige was younger than Gilliam, so I knew I could offer some motherly advice to this motherless girl. "I'm so glad you both are happy about the baby. Being a mother is the best thing in the world. You'll make a wonderful mom. Just don't do what I did in my marriage to Hank. Don't forget about his needs. Men are babies too! They need a lot of encouragement and support."

"Thank you, Helena. Victor and I are grateful that we had the opportunity to meet your children and grandchildren while we were here. Your wedding was so special, and I fell in love with all your family and the people from this amazing island. Everyone we met is wonderful, just like you." She smiled and continued lovingly touching the baby things as she folded and put them away.

"My kids are wonderful. I am also glad that you got to meet them. I don't think when you leave that this will be the last time you see us or our children. I think you're going to, over the years, get to know all of us very well. I have a feeling you're going to be coming this way often, and we'll be coming to Louisiana. You have friends here, now, and we have friends there. Friendships are very important. We'll stay in touch. Often."

"I know we will," Paige replied and looked up to me with a huge grin on her face. This young lady who came here on her honeymoon arrived a member of a very small family, on her side—just her grandmother and on Victor's side a few more members; but she was leaving with at least eleven more members added to her family, and two of them were tiny little newborn twin boys.

A New Routine

A child is an angel dependent on man.

—Count de Maistre

Paige and Victor left the next day needing to get back to their restaurant and relieve their new friends who had taken over as acting chefs while they were away. They explained how various restaurants in Baton Rouge with husband and wife chefs had been helping each other when important occasions occur. They talked about weddings and honeymoons, events with children, funerals, and vacations. I told them that Mel had that kind of relationship with the other veterinarians in our area. It was good to have friends.

It was a tearful good-bye. We packed up a box of snacks and drinks for them to use as they drove and made them promises to stay in touch. We had already exchanged addresses, phone numbers, and e-mail addresses, and were all, by now, Facebook friends.

Mel, Hank, and I had met them at the diner for breakfast. When we parted, watching them heading back to Baton Rouge with their car full, Hank was headed for the hospital to be with Autumn and his boys while Mel was headed to the clinic, and I was headed to the club to see who was waiting for a tram tour. Tonight Mel and I would pack for our honeymoon.

Today was the first normal day we'd had in a while. It had been a considerably long time since I had a day where nothing significant or unusual happened. That night as Mel and I ate, we shared our day, which was rather dull and drab compared to what had recently been occurring in our lives. I talked about packing for our trip to Aruba and Mel said, "Helena, would you mind if we postpone our honeymoon for a short while?"

"Of course I wouldn't mind. Is there something going on you haven't shared with me?" I asked.

He looked at me with eyes filled with love and said, "No. I just keep thinking about Autumn, and I think she's going to need us here with her the next several weeks. I can't imagine how she is going to manage those two boys all by herself."

I had already thought of that, but remembering that my mother always told me to put my husband first, I didn't want to suggest delaying our honeymoon. I shook my head very slightly from left to right as I looked with wonder at this very special man who was my husband. "You know, Dr. Daniels, you constantly amaze me with your perceptions and insights. No wonder I love you with all my heart and soul."

Mel smiled and feigned a shy embarrassment. That night, he called all the required numbers and cancelled, for the time being, our Aruba experience. We both felt happy about that decision. He told me that when he explained the reason for our cancellation and that we would be re-booking the same vacation within several months, everyone forgave the cancellation charges. With or without charges, we were doing the right thing.

After all that Hank and Autumn had done for us recently, it would have been a terrible injustice for us to walk happily away when they had a need we could help with. We went to bed early that night and spent the night cuddling after sweetly making love.

In the morning, we had breakfast together, and Mel took off to assume his day's duties while I drove over to the stables to ride my girls. Old Bill waved, and I saluted. Celeste yelled a greeting, and I yelled back. The girls happily accepted the carrots that I had in my pocket, and I rode first Blue and then Grey, both encounters without incident.

Before I left the stables, Victoria, Celeste, and Old Bill told me how much they loved the wedding. They thanked me again for inviting them. "Are you kidding," I said, "we're family."

I ran over to Autumn's to check on how she was doing with the boys. Here is where the routine part ended. Autumn answered the door with a squalling baby in both arms, and she quickly handed me one.

"What's up, Autumn?" I asked.

"What's up? What's up? Me. I've been up all night with these two boys. I get one to sleep, and then I work on getting the other to sleep, and just about the time I lay the second one down, the first one wakes up. I can't do this, Helena. I never bargained for twins. How does anyone handle twins?" She spoke like she was about to have a nervous breakdown.

"Sweetie," I cooed, "Everything will be okay. It's just going to take some getting used to and setting up some method to take care of both of them. And right now you're still healing, and you're tired. This too shall pass. Is Hank helping?"

"No. Hank is not helping. He comes home and expects me to have his dinner ready. Honestly, how am I supposed to fix his dinner when my hands are full of these boys all day and all night?"

"Okay. Well I'm here now. I've never had twins, but I did have two in diapers at the same time; and I still remember what that was like, so I do have somewhat of an understanding. Come on over here on the couch."

I went over to the playpen that was sitting in one corner of the room and laid down the boy I was holding. He cried, and I let him cry. Then I went to Autumn and took the other boy from her arms and put him next to his brother in the playpen. Now they both cried. I let them.

With the boys in the playpen, I went over to the sofa where Autumn was sitting, and I sat down beside her. I put my arms around her, and when I did, she turned burying her head in my shoulder, and the tears started along with an immense round of shaking and sobbing. I patted her back and comforted her. "It will be all right, Autumn. I will start coming over here every morning for however long that I can, and I'll help. I promise."

Between hiccups, Autumn got out, "Thank you, Helena. I really...need...help. I'm so scared and so sad and mad and stressed. Do you think I have postpartum depression?"

"I hugged her and patted her on the back. Well you might, but it sounds more to me like you are just overwhelmed and tired."

I sat for a short while letting her cry and then I said, "Okay. The first thing I want you to do is go upstairs. Take a nice hot shower. Put on something clean and comfortable and then lay down on your big round bed and take a nice nap. I'm going to look after the boys while you do that, and I'll come wake you up in just a little while."

"But"—Autumn looked up at me with huge tear soaked, red-rimmed eyes—"the boys are crying, and they probably need changed, and they need fed, and the house is a mess. I don't have time to lie down."

"Yes, you do," I reassured her, "Now go and trust me. I'll be right here. I'll change the boys and feed them, and I'll pick up the house a little. Please, Autumn, go rest. You won't be any good to these precious boys if you fall over from exhaustion."

She looked at me and even in the middle of her rattled condition she remembered that I was scheduled to leave on my honeymoon today. She asked me about it, and I told her that at Mel's suggestion, and with my agreement, we had postponed the Aruba trip for a short while. We both believed we were needed here.

"You cancelled your honeymoon for us?" She asked.

"For you and for us. These are our godsons, and you are our good friends. Mel and I love you, and we want to be here for you like you and Hank have been there for us. That's what friends do." I smiled at her, and standing up, I indicated it was time for her to pay herself some much needed attention.

Finally, she went upstairs. As soon as I heard the water running in the shower, I picked up the phone, and I made two phone calls. Thirty minutes had not passed before two of my friends arrived. Each friend took a boy. They changed him, fed him, rocked him; and finally with both babies asleep, the women took their leave.

While they were tending to the boys, I picked up the house, loaded and ran the dishwasher, made formula, and refilled all the available bottles storing them in the frig. I did a load of laundry and then defrosted some hamburger and made a huge pot of pasta sauce. I cut up a big bowl of salad and a huge bowl of fruit. I sat the table for two with candles in the middle. I went to the stereo, and finding several CDs of soft jazz music, I began the music playing. I lit jar candles around the house.

The boys were still sleeping, and I hadn't heard a peep from upstairs. I unloaded the dishwasher quietly and put all the dishes away. I found the remote for the gas fireplace and began the fire burning. Looking around me, it appeared that right now everything in the house was perfect.

I sat down on the couch and dialed Mel. I told him about the situation and asked him what he thought I should do. "I think you've done what you should do, hon. Now it's my turn. I have just finished with my last patient, and I can leave, so I'm going right over to Hank's office and have a long talk with him. He wanted to be the world's greatest husband and father, so I'm going to challenge him to step up to the plate. He either needs to help this poor girl or get her help."

"I told her I'd come over every day and help her, Mel." I said.

"Yes, I knew that you would, and I think you should, but you can't be there all day every day; and until Autumn gets more comfortable with motherhood and learns how to handle the two-for-one package she's been handed, she needs some around the clock help. A live-in nanny is what she needs for now. Perhaps that's why there is a day bed in the boy's room. And if that isn't why it was put there originally, it's going to come in very handy if a live-in nanny is required.

Hank can afford it, and I think one of those women you called today would probably be willing to fill that bill for the next six months. Maybe both of them, taking turns, will want to be part of the Rivers family life for a little while." Mel stopped. "Don't forget you're a new bride, and you have a groom to keep happy."

"Really, Mel?" I'm sure I had a little edge in my voice as I continued, "Do you think that my helping Autumn would short change you?" I was flabbergasted at his remark.

Mel started to laugh. "Hank was right, you are a handful, and it's so easy to trip your trigger. Of course I don't think you'd short change me. In fact, that's the last thing I'm worried about, or I wouldn't have kidded you about it. Ease up, baby, I'm all for doing what we need to do to help our friends."

"You're so right, hon. Thank you for helping out here. I'm sorry I'm so sensitive. I just don't want to make mistakes. I love you, and I want to be everything you need me to be. Autumn really is at her wit's end with these boys, and I can see why. I couldn't handle these two at the same time, and I am a semi-experienced mother. Doing this for the first time without any previous practice would be impossible." I paused for a moment, and Mel waited for me to continue.

"I'm going to go up in a few minutes and wake her up. She's been sleeping for four straight hours. I think that will help, and the boys were exhausted too. I think they are feeling her stress, and that's what's keeping them agitated all the time. I'll have a little talk with her before I leave, and then I'm going to get out of here before Hank shows up. Have fun talking with him. Maybe you should call first before you go, so he waits for you in case he heads home early."

"I got it. Good idea. Let's hang up now, and I'll call Hank. Good-bye, my sweetheart. I love you."

"I love you back, my prince." We hung up.

I sat there for a few minutes. The music was soft and sweet. I could hear the soft breathing of the boys. The candles and the fireplace were flickering, and the sun was just coming across the roof line as it lowered itself into the west.

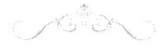

***

Here I was, experiencing yet another day of things that were not routine. That every day would be unpredictable is becoming the pattern of my life. An unpredictable life can be a profound reason to get up each morning. Many evenings, looking back on my daylight hours, I comment, "Who would have ever suspected that that was going to happen today?"

Both Mel and I have life experiences that are anything but dull. We could play a game over dinner of "who had the most unusual thing happen to them today?" Maybe I should take notes, and one day we can write a book.

Speaking of writing a book, I am almost done with my Jekyll Island book. I need to take the final pages in to Mr. Parker and get his comments. He had already found a company that said they might be interested in publishing. Once that was behind me, maybe I could start another book. I sat there for a minute trying to think of a catchy book title. *Channeling Change* came to mind since I was gaining significant experience from the myriad of transitions confronting my life in the past several years. A book on change would have everything to do with starting over, and I have more than a little experience in that. I've always heard that you should write about things in which you are familiar. Well, starting over is one of my fortes.

It would be a challenge to write a book about how people put the pieces of their lives back together and give it another try? I loved the idea. I would have to ponder on that for a while and maybe make an outline and some content notes. Would it be a self-help book? Would I want to develop something to help people through rebuilding their own lives when something difficult happens? Would I rather it just be an inspirational book of stories about people and how starting over has given them a new perspective and a new zest for living? Would it be about people who suffered medical conditions like a stroke or cancer. Would it be only people who experienced the loss of a spouse through death or divorce. Would I want to include people who have lost children in war, accidents, or suicide? There were a lot of questions, and I would need to answer them all before I could decide how and where to begin.

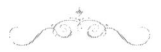

I heard a creak on the stairs pulling me out of my deliberations, and looking up, I saw a fresh and bright Autumn coming down the stairs. She was dressed in black leggings and a hip length, red, long sleeve tee shirt top with a black belt slung across her narrow middle. I could not believe she had just given birth to twins. She had on black flats, and her long auburn hair had been brushed till it shone and was hanging on her shoulders. She had applied make up, and she looked beautiful.

"Wow. Is this the same woman who opened that door about five hours ago?" I said looking over at her as she approached me.

"Has it been that long? I really needed that rest. I actually feel like the world is going to be okay. I can't thank you enough." She looked around and then back at me. "You have picked up the entire house."

"Only the downstairs." I laughed.

"I also smell something yummy besides the candles, which I love that you lit and the fireplace. The music is wonderful. Thank you." Autumn sat down beside me and put her hand on top of mine.

"I made some pasta sauce and cooked up some macaroni. It's an old recipe from my Mom. She called it goulash. It's all mixed up in a casserole dish in the microwave, and you can just reheat it and serve it with some Italian bread and butter, some parmesan cheese grated on top, a fresh salad, which I also cut up and have Hank uncork some red wine. I cut up some fruit for dessert."

"You are amazing, Helena. How long have the boys been sleeping?"

"Autumn, I think the boys were as exhausted as you were. They are probably picking up on your stress, which is also what is making them so edgy and fussy. Now don't get worried. As soon as you get the knack of all this, you'll relax and so will they. It's just part of learning to be a new mother, so don't be hard on yourself." I pulled my hand out from under hers, and placing mine on top, I patted her hand this time.

"I'm hoping you won't get upset about what I'm going to tell you next, but I called Mel and told him I'd be coming over here a part of every day for the next few weeks. I told him why. He is with Hank right now, and he's going to tell Hank that he thinks it might be a good idea for you to have a nanny for a few months. I agree, it is what you need."

Autumn let out a long sigh. "I know I need help, but I wasn't sure how to approach Hank about it. I think coming from Mel might be the best thing. He really respects Mel, and they are both independent, business-owning men. That makes them part of a club sort of thing. I'd better go do the dishes before the boys wake up."

Smiling, I said, "The dishes are done. I even threw in a load of laundry, which is all dried and folded in the basket in the laundry room. I hope you don't mind." I paused for a moment as Autumn gave me a brief hug.

Continuing, I told her, "I called Maggie and Linda, my two good friends from church who are sisters, they came over and took care of the boys while I did the house things. Once they got the boys changed, fed, and sleeping, they left. They were here about an hour, and they loved every minute of it. Those two might be worth talking to if you decide to get a nanny. They might want to think about a job share arrangement between them, if you wanted them to. I'm not trying to interfere in your life, but you really do need someone in addition to me. Autumn, no woman could do this alone, not even Super Woman. I'll come over every day for a few hours for as long as you need me. You need to get your rest, and the boys need theirs. Am I sounding pushy?"

"If you're being pushy, Helena, it's probably because I need you to be right at this moment. What would I have done today if you hadn't stopped by?"

As Autumn finished her sentence, my phone rang. My ringtone for Mel calling me was "Happy Trails to You," the old Roy Rogers song, which I have always loved. I picked up. "Hi, Mel. He is? Okay, I'm out of here; I'll meet you at home in ten minutes. Love you too." I flipped my phone closed.

"Hank is on his way home. Mel just left him. He says Hank loved the idea of a nanny and wishes he had thought of it first. He knows I've been here helping this afternoon, so now the ball is in your court. I think you need to let those little ones sleep for a while longer, and maybe it will give you and Hank some quiet time to talk things over. I love you, Autumn."

"I love you back, Helena." We both stopped and looked at each other. We had never said those words to each other before, and this time they came out so easily and naturally, like two good friends or sisters.

After quietly shutting the door behind me, I hurried down the front path and slid behind my steering wheel. Driving home, I felt good. I couldn't wait to spend the evening with Mel. I wanted to hear about his day and about how it had ended. Hearing about his discussion with Hank would be interesting.

Hank wasn't a bad man, but he wanted so badly to be a better husband and father, and the way he was starting this off wasn't much different than it had been when we were raising Gabe and Gilliam. He still went to work and left everything to his wife to handle. He slept through the night and felt it was Autumn's job to get up with the babies, just like he had done with me. Getting a nanny for Autumn was a good thing, but he needed to also learn how to share those child rearing duties with his wife and to become a part of bringing up his boys. I wonder if it's possible to teach an old dog new tricks. I'm pretty sure it can happen if he wants to learn. Hank had a good heart, but like Autumn, he really had no idea how to do the new baby things that needed to be done. Then I had an idea. I did know who was very proficient at raising children having two of his own that he is helping raise. Gabe.

What if we called Gabe? He might be the perfect person to help his dad learn how to be a dad to his two new sons. Imagine a son teaching his dad how to be a dad. What a splendid idea. It would be something that could really work to bond Hank and Gabe together and also to bond Gabe with his two new half-brothers. I loved the idea, but I didn't know if Gabe or Hank would.

I would surely talk with Mel about it tonight and get his male assessment on my thoughts. I know that Amy had told me that Gabe was a wonderful father, and that he had helped her with everything from the stuff required to get her through the birthing process and all the essential things required to help with the baby. Gilliam had told me almost the exact same thing about Mike. It seems that fatherhood to men today is much different than it used to be. Men want to be a part of raising their children. They can handle being the breadwinner, but they also want a bond with their children. Maybe it was time for Gabe and Gilliam to come home with their spouses and children and help their dad and stepmother, it could be a real family experience. I was getting truly excited about the prospect.

By the time I pulled into our driveway, I was pumping on all cylinders. Mel was already there, and the porch light was lit even though outside it was just turning that lovely mauve grey of dusk.

I closed the car door and almost skipped up the driveway. As I approached the door, it swung open, and Hank handed me a glass of wine. "Oh, are you just the most marvelous man in the entire world or what? Thank you, hon. I need this."

"I had a feeling that you would. I know you already cooked one dinner tonight, so I stopped and brought home some fried chicken, mashed potatoes, and those wonderfully soggy green beans cooked in ham fat that we both know is horrible for us but that taste so good." He smiled.

"So you stopped at the diner. How is Rose tonight?"

"She's great. She sends her greetings and said to tell you that she hopes you enjoy your dinner."

I looked up at Mel and gave him a generous kiss. Pulling back, I took a sip of wine and said, "Oh, baby, I can smell the food. Quick let's eat it while it's hot. I'm starved. Oh, shoot that is not a ladylike thing to say." I laughed and so did Mel as I started over in my most formal lady voice.

"Would it be okay with you, my dear, if we begin our repast now rather than later? I didn't have any mid-day meal today, and my tummy is talking to me just a tiny bit?"

He took the wine glass from my hand, and sitting it on the counter, he lifted me up off my feet and twirled me around. "Please, Helena, don't ever turn into that woman you just mimicked. I love the old famished and ravenous you and every single thing about you."

He sat me down and handed me back my wine glass. Taking me by the hand, he led me to the kitchen table that he already had set, and the dinner was there waiting for us. He pulled out the chair while I sat down and then gently pushed it back into the table. "Will there be anything else, my princess?"

"Just you, dear. It feels so good to be home. I now know why you have been saying all along that you were glad that it's Hank and Autumn having the children and not us. We are definitely too old for that job right now. Being a grandparent or a godparent is one thing. Taking care of them and then leaving to come to the quiet comfort of our home is really quite nice. Poor Autumn was near to a nervous breakdown when I arrived today. I called for reinforcements, and while she rested, the three of us took care of the boys and the house. She just cannot do that without help."

"I agree. So does Hank. I don't think he had any idea how bad it was for Autumn, but after I explained what you had told me and we talked about it man to man, he was going to go home and do what he could tonight to help her. He's going to cut his hours, and he even said he thought he'd invite his other two kids to come over for a few days. He mentioned that both his son, Gabe and his son-in-law Mike were of great help to their wives, and maybe they could teach him. He was thinking that while the guys got him up to speed, the girls would be able to help Autumn and give her some tips."

I laughed. "Great minds do run in the same channel. I had the same thoughts on the way home, and I was going to talk those thoughts over with you before I called the kids. Is Hank going to call them?"

"Not until he's talked it over with Autumn." Mel's look was thoughtful. "You know, Helena, Hank may be oblivious to a lot of things; but he does have a good heart, and he doesn't want to do anything to create problems with Autumn. He told me today that he had blown being a good husband and father once, and he didn't want to make the same mistakes twice. I suggested to him that he might be doing just that, and I think it really shook him up." Mel took a sip of his wine and continued. "I didn't want to hurt Hank, but sometimes you need to shake people up in order to get their attention."

"You are so kind when you shake things up, Mel. I'm sure Hank appreciated that you cared enough about him and Autumn to come talk with him today."

"That is exactly what he said when we left together. I told him I was stopping by the diner to get dinner since you'd had your hands full all day with your godsons." When I said that, Hank stopped, looked at me, and asked, "How do you know to do those things, Mel?" I told him to just start thinking about someone other than himself, and it will come more naturally every day."

I smiled at this man I loved more than life itself. God, I said under my breath, thank you for bringing us together and allowing both of us another chance at life.

Melding and Dividing

> Seek not proud wealth; but such as thou mayest get justly, use soberly, distribute cheerfully, and leave contentedly.
>
> —Bacon

Hank called Gabe and Gilliam and told them what he was thinking; they both arranged to arrive that next weekend to spend the entire week. They were ready to pitch in and help in any way they could. Hank was bowled over by the excitement, enthusiasm, and love that he heard in their voices.

Both Gabe and Gilliam were still reeling with the thought that they now had two little brothers, and they were both anxious to meet the boys and help their father and Autumn. Their being here just a few weeks ago for the wedding had made such a difference. When our children saw how Hank and Autumn had put so much energy and kindness into helping Mel and me begin our new life together, all the previous anger and letdown disappeared. The grandkids couldn't wait to come back. They wanted to be introduced to their new uncles.

I went to help with the boys every morning. Some days it was only for an hour or two, but it gave Autumn a chance to take a quiet walk or sit outside in the sunshine while I tended to the boys needs and did a few chores for her around the house.

I helped her prepare the guest rooms for the kids. When I asked Autumn if she thought their coming would be intrusive, she responded that it would be wonderful to have a family. This woman is lonely. We are her family now, and I was glad to share my children with her as she was sharing her children with Mel and me. She was looking forward to getting to know Gabe and Gilliam better.

Each day at home while cooking for Mel and me, I prepared some of the kids' favorite dishes and put them in the freezer. Either Gilliam or Amy could heat them up in the oven or microwave without spending a lot of time in the kitchen during their stay.

That weekend, everyone would be together. Both families were planning to leave their homes on Saturday morning, which would put them at their father's by late afternoon. Gilliam and Amy had gotten their heads together and were bringing dinner for that first night. They told Autumn that they would shop on Sunday, so she wasn't to worry about what the kids might like.

I was so proud of those two. The boys had already begun preparing a "How To Do It" book for their father. It was meant to be funny and yet practical, and I really thought Hank would love it. Each boy was typing out "how to" things, and they were sending them back and forth to each other via computer. Gabe had sent me the "how to change a diaper" page that Mike had written, and that night, I thought that Mel and I would die laughing reading it. It was a great guide, and he was so humorous in how he wrote it.

How to Change a Diaper

One— start with a kid, preferably one who is still wearing diapers and weighs less than forty pounds.

Two— remember little boys have their own built in squirt gun, and they love to play "got ya."

Three— protect yourself by placing a large plastic bag over your head, preferably with a hole through which your head might stick out or wear a wet suit.

Four— before you remove the old diaper, spread out the new one keeping it handy to grab

Five— check to make sure the baby is only wet. No one likes lumpy pee pee or smelly surprises!

Six— make sure the following goodies are close by and can be accessed with one hand: wet wipes, a plastic bag, baby powder, baby lotion, petroleum jelly, rubber gloves, a clothes pin, goggles, Lysol disinfectant spray, a cinnamon scented candle, a rubber sponge, a pail of clean soapy water, four gallons of bleach, fresh onesies, clean pajamas, (perhaps more than one pair), unsoiled rubber pants, two extra hands, and a partridge in a pear tree.

Okay. With all that assembled, you are now ready for step seven, which actually takes you back to step one, which was significantly out of order; but without number one, you really didn't need the other steps.

Seven— you are now ready to pick up the baby.

Caution! Be sure and hold his head with one hand while you hold his little tiny rear end with the other.

Note: The little tiny rear end could hold a surprise! Your nose will probably have already told you that. If it did, apply the clothes pin to your nose and light the cinnamon candle, which you should have previously gathered (see above) and proceed.

By the time, Mel and I had gotten to that point we were both grabbing our stomachs and trying to catch our breath from laughing so hard. Mike was amazing. What a sense of humor he had. I could not wait for Hank to get the fellows "How To" book. I think the fact that they were handling the entire situation in such a laid back manner was going to be terrific for all of them. They were rather like the Dave Barry of baby care. Perhaps they should collaborate and put out a book for new dads. The way this is written, it would be an instant best seller.

I had been hoping, actually praying, that the seven of them coming at the same time wouldn't overwhelm Autumn. Every time I had talked with her about it, she seemed to be truly excited that the family was coming. With the extra hired help, me for short periods, and Hank trying to do more things around the house with the babies, Autumn seemed to be much calmer than she had been that first week home from the hospital. As a consequence, much like I had suspected, little Devon and Dodge also seemed to be more content and a lot less fussy. It was a cycle. Less stressed mommy equaled less stressed babies.

Hank and Autumn invited us to join them Saturday night for dinner, but we graciously declined and suggested that they let us bring Sunday dinner over to their house to feed the gang. I planned to take my wonderful barrier island barbeque, red skin potato salad, slaw and baked beans with rolls for anyone who wanted a sandwich. Hank said he'd get a case of beer for the adults and soda for the kids. Sounded perfect to me and when I shared my plan with Autumn, she squealed "picnic." She said she'd make sure the outside patio, tables, and chairs were clean and ready, and the kids could romp in the yard while we grownups talked.

We planned to come over for a mid-afternoon lunch about two, which would give us time to go to early church, change our clothes, get the lunch heated, packed and delivered. I told Hank I'd throw in paper plates, napkins, plastic cups, and plastic flatware, so there would be no dishes.

Autumn called me Saturday night after all the kids arrived to let me know they were there. "I figured you'd worry until you knew everyone was safe."

"Thanks, Autumn, are you okay?" I asked.

"I'm better than okay, Helena. I have a family, your family, our family, and I'm loving it. I just wish you and Mel were here." She paused.

"We'll be there tomorrow afternoon. Enjoy the night just you guys. I'm so glad the kids are there for you and Hank. It's important to all of you, and I'm right here if anyone needs me.

You have a great evening, and thanks for calling. Oh, before I hang up, are my two godsons doing okay?"

"They are actually perfect. They are so much less fussy now. I don't really understand what happened. Do you think it was me?"

"Yes," I answered, "I think now that you have settled down a little and are more confident around them that they sense that new peacefulness about you. Babies really do take their clues from those around them."

Autumn let out a little "Hmmmmmm," and finished with "I guess they do. See you tomorrow. Bye."

I enjoyed my quiet evening with Mel. It was nice to have a little time with my new husband all to myself. I was very happy that my children were just down the road, and that we'd see them tomorrow. Tomorrow being the operative word. Tonight was for Mel and me, and we were both ready.

We had a quiet dinner with candles, soft music, and good wine. We talked about our week. It was another week of taking care of problems as they presented themselves. We used our time for finding solutions, providing help, giving encouragement, and supporting people we care about. Neither Mel nor I knew what a routine day looked like. I laughed as I told him that the first fifty some years of my life were all about routine, and now my days didn't even recognize the word.

I told Mel that I was happy that tonight he wasn't spending it at the clinic tending to a sick friend, and that we could share this quiet boring night alone, together in our beautiful home.

"Helena," Mel started, "I am so very content. I'm glad the house is done and the clinic is done with all the renovations, which turned out to be more than I could have asked, and I'm most of all glad that we are finally husband and wife. I could not be happier, and I love you so very much."

I looked up at Mel, my head was slightly bent downward, and my eyes were looking up at him as he sat so handsomely across the table from me. The evening had been light and fun, and then he had changed the aura with his serious and loving remark. I had been waiting for the right moment to say something I had been feeling, and the door was open so I walked through. "This may sound a little silly to you, Mel, but it is so nice for me to be married to my best friend. I feel so comfortable with you as your wife. It's like God made us to fit together and has just been waiting for us to finally find each other and slip into one another's arms. Do you know what I mean?"

Never taking his eyes from mine, he stood up; and walking to my end of the table, he helped me up and gave me a gentle and sweet kiss. "I know exactly what you mean, Helena. I feel the same way. So, my dearest and best friend, let's go for a walk, just like we did that night, the first time I proposed. I think a little hand-in-hand stroll is just what the doctor ordered for both of us. I can see the huge harvest moon lighting up the outside like a stage, and it looks almost as beautiful outside as you do here beside me. Let's pretend there's a rainbow since we've both already found our pot of gold."

I was continually blown away by the poetic heart that beat inside this wonderful man. He was a true romantic. How did I get so lucky to have him as my husband. Oops, forgive me God. I forget sometimes that in this world where you have placed us that there is no such thing as luck, it is by your great design that these amazing things occur. Thank you, God, for putting Mel and me together.

Sunday was wonderful. I felt blessed and comforted by our pastor's message. I was ready for a week of whatever came my way. Mel and I drove home with the windows down. It was a beautiful day. Not hot. The air was blowing in off the Atlantic, and it was fresh and sweet and made your skin feel alive. Once home, I took off my heels, skirt, and little waist length jacket and slid into my comfortable jeans, a red tee shirt, and my riding boots, the most comfortable shoes I owned.

I had slid the pans of barbeque and beans into the oven when I got home and turned the oven to a slow heat. When I emerged from our beautiful first floor master suite, I could smell the luscious aroma beginning its slow drift through the house. There wasn't much to do except grab a glass of sweet tea for Mel and me, put the Sunday paper under my arm, and go out on the patio where Mel was already enjoying the beautiful afternoon. I sat the tea down beside him and laid the paper out on the table between us.

We both sat there quietly sipping and reading until it was time to put the food in boxes, load them in the car, and take off for lunch with the family. It was a great day. It was so good to see the kids. The new babies could not have been more perfect. They were hardly making a peep anymore. When I looked into their little bassinettes, they were cooing and playing with their toes. Babies are just so darn adorable.

I noticed that a couple times, Hank went over; and reaching his hand toward his boys, he rubbed their little arms or legs and talked gently to them. He was trying very hard to become more comfortable around them, and it looked like he actually was enjoying paying attention to Devon and Dodge.

Babies can be addictive if you let your guard down long enough for them to penetrate your heart. Hank was getting there. I could see the love in his eyes that he finally dared to show. That impenetrable manly exterior that his father had taught him to cloak himself with, was beginning to crack. The gentler side of Hank was showing through thanks to Autumn, Devon, and Dodge.

Before we left that night we made some tentative plans for the week. On Wednesday, when Maggie and Linda, who were serving as part time nannies, said they could be here for the entire afternoon to look after Devon and Dodge, it was decided that the guys would take the older kids to the sea shore while we four ladies had a girls afternoon out. We decided on a spa day. I called ahead to the Sea Spray Day Spa and arranged for each of us to have a thirty-minute massage, a facial, a manicure, and a pedicure.

It had been months since I had treated myself so decadently, and the other women were as excited about the pampering as I was. Sometimes women just need to be spoiled.

On Thursday, my cell phone rang when I was leaving to pick up Sean and Jeffrey to take them riding at the stables. The plan was that we would go riding first and then, at Mel's suggestion, we were going to the clinic. The boys had clamored during dinner last night that they wanted to see what Grandpa Mel did, and he agreed that a late afternoon visit today would be wonderful, unless some unforeseen emergency arose.

There was no hello when I answered my phone. What I heard was "Helena, I need to talk with you." It was Hank.

"Okay. Right now, I'm heading over to pick up our grandchildren to take them for the afternoon. When do you need to talk and about what?" I was curious but not alarmed.

"Gabe and I had a long talk yesterday while we were out together. Mike and Mel were having a great time romping with the boys while little Christie was sound asleep under a beach umbrella. Gabe asked me if he and I could stroll down the beach alone. Don't get excited; Mel came and sat with Christie while we were gone. When we got out of earshot of the rest of our gang, Gabe hit me with wanting to know about my end of life plans. You know, Helena, he wanted to talk with me about my will. He wanted to make some suggestions about my business. That's what I'd like to talk with you about." He sounded confused.

"Okay, but why talk with me. Why not Autumn?" I asked.

"I will talk with Autumn, but I'd like to run by you what Gabe suggested first, if you will let me." He didn't just sound confused; he actually sounded a little scared. Probably thinking about his demise was not a very comforting thing for Hank to ponder. He'd just become a father to two new baby boys, and I already knew Hank had thought about his age when they would be entering college. I couldn't figure out what Gabe was doing. He was usually smarter than that.

"Do we need to talk right away, or can we wait until after the kids leave in a couple days? I think they're planning to leave on Saturday morning." I was trying to sound business like and reassuring, but I'm not sure if I was accomplishing my goal.

"Helena, I'm sure that the discussion could wait, but I'm not sure that I can hold out that long. I doubt if I'll be able to get this out of my mind until I talk it over with you. Don't you have any time today at all?" He was truly flustered. What in the heck did Gabe say to him that had his dad in such an unnecessary frenzy?

"Well, the boys and I are going riding, and then I'm going to take them over to the clinic to visit with Mel, so they can observe him working with some of the animals. How about if I leave them with Mel and come have a cup of coffee with you. Let's say we meet at the diner around three. Would that be okay?"

"Thank you, Helena. That would be perfect. I'll see you then. Bye."

Well if that didn't beat all I don't know what did.

The kids and I had a wonderful ride. I had phoned Celeste and told her which horses I wanted for the afternoon. Jeffrey, the oldest, could handle Blue, I'd ride Grey, and Sean would be on the gentler roan, Clicker. When I arrived, Old Bill had Blue, Grey and Clicker saddled along with Rico, Celeste's horse. I began to question why the fourth horse when Celeste ambled into the paddock saying, "I thought I'd ride along with you and your grandchildren today, Helena, if no one objects. Rico really needs the exercise." She winked at me with a smile on her face.

"You are a true friend. Thank you so much, Celeste. I really appreciate this." Being the horse woman that she is, she would instinctively know that one experienced rider with two novices could have her hands full. One-on-one was so much safer.

"Helena, I thought I'd let you lead the way on the path, and I'll follow up in the rear. If something should happen while we are on the trail we'll be in position to respond quickly."

As it happened, we got everyone secured in their saddles, reins in hand; and with a few brief instructions, we took off. We spent an hour walking the horses along the path. We went down on the beach and did a short romp in the surf with both Celeste and I watching closely for anything in the water. Then back up to the path and back to the stables. The boys were excited and thrilled to have been allowed to ride alone, the first time that they hadn't ridden in front of me on the same horse.

On the way to Mel's, they couldn't quit talking about what a great time they had. Sean said, "You are such a cool grandma." In unison I heard, "Thank you for taking us." I smiled, pleased that they had a good time.

When we got to Mel's, they were given gowns to put on, and they filed back into the treatment room. Mel was busy examining a beautiful Black Lab. He told the boys that the dog had been hit by a car, and he was going to put a cast on his front leg. He invited the boys to sit in the chairs that he had placed on a nearby side table. I want you guys to sit up here and watch me. You can ask questions if you want, but you must not get down off the table. My assistant, Miss Marie, will be assisting me. From where you are sitting, you will be able to watch everything that Miss Marie and I will be doing. Is that okay?

They all thought it was very adult and very interesting. They told Mel it was just like they'd seen on television when people are operating, and you look up and there are other doctors watching their every move. It was a great plan to keep the children involved and yet removed. Mel would not have to worry about them touching anything around the patient and contaminating or causing an infection, which can easily occur. I could tell that our boys would be riveted to their seats watching Mel. They probably wouldn't even know that I was gone.

I whispered into Mel's ear that I was going to run quickly to the diner to meet Hank. He raised his eyebrows in question. "He called this morning with something urgent he needs to talk about," I whispered, "I'll fill you in on it tonight." We shared a look, and he nodded. The look said good luck, and I can't wait to hear about this one. I smiled and took off.

When I got to the diner, Hank was sitting at a back table, and I joined him. Again, I caught a few interested and quizzical looks as I walked back to join Hank. I smiled to myself. Let them talk. Everyone needs someone to talk about.

"Hi, Hank," I said as I slid into the bench of the booth.

"Hi, Helena," Hank responded, "Thanks for meeting me. Does Mel know you're here with me?"

"Of course," I replied.

"Good. What I'm going to lay out to you, which is what Gabe laid out for me, I'd like you to also run past Mel, and the two of you can let Autumn and I know what you think. I'll discuss it with Autumn after the kids leave on Saturday."

"Okay," I responded, "I'm not sure what Mel and I have to do with it, but you certainly have got my curiosity up."

"Gabe told me that he and Gilliam and their mates have discussed this and agreed that he should approach me about it. I don't think it's selfish on their part, I think they want the best for me and you and our new partners. Our children are concerned that if I don't let go of some of the things I'm currently doing, I won't be around to see Devon and Dodge graduate from college. Gabe says that he and Gilliam don't want me to wear out, which they both think I'll do staying on my current schedule."

He paused and I said, "Okay, I get it, they are concerned about you in your doting years."

"Helena, why do you always make me feel so old?"

I laughed. "Do I? Well remember we're the same age. I'm just trying to tease you a little to lighten the mood."

"Oh, okay. Well, Gabe says that the four of them think that I should make Jim a partner and let him start taking over more of what I'm doing, letting me have more time with Autumn and our baby boys."

"That's not a bad idea. Jim started with you when he was nineteen and has been with you what, twenty years now? That would make him just under forty. He's got the maturity and the experience. He'd make a perfect partner. Did Gabe suggest how he thought you might do that?"

"Yes. He suggested that I give him nine percent of the business for past service and loyalty and sell him twenty percent to be paid off over the next five years, some of it being in yearly bonuses and yearly raises applied to the purchase price and the rest in a no interest loan that Jim would pay off in monthly installments, like a house mortgage. At the end of five years, Jim would have the full twenty-nine percent partnership. Gabe says we need to go to a lawyer and get it all written up so that it works to the best interest of both of us."

"So Jim would own twenty-nine percent, and you would own seventy-one percent." I nodded while I was trying to figure out how Gabe came up with twenty-nine percent.

"Right, but there's more. Here's the rest of what Gabe said the four of them came up with. Gabe and Gilliam would each be left ten percent of the business in my will to receive it upon my death. That would be the total of their inheritance from me. They understand that Autumn is much younger, and that she will need to be taken care of if something happens to me."

"Well, ten percent of your business as their inheritance sounds pretty fair and certainly not greedy." I again mused that over in my thoughts as I sat there.

"I thought so too. There's more. My new boys, Devon and Dodge, they think I should leave fifteen percent of the business to each of them. I told Gabe that I had already set up a college fund for one of them, and now that there were two of them that I would be doing the same for the other. He was really glad to hear that. He told me how grateful he was for the education I had given to him and to Gilliam. Helena, I don't think that he'd ever said thank you to me before. It touched my heart that he realized that I did care about him and wanted him to have a good life." His eyes were so serious and somewhat sad.

I reached across the table and squeezed his hand. "You have been a good father, Hank. The kids know that and so do I. So is that it?"

"No, there is one more thing. Autumn. They think I should leave twenty-one percent of the business to Autumn. They have really thought this through. It wasn't until I got back and sat down and wrote the figures down that it began to make sense. If Autumn gets twenty-one percent and Devon and Dodge each get fifteen percent, the three of them will hold, together, the controlling interest in the Rivers Construction Company, fifty-one percent. That really is quite brilliant. Gabe suggested that I make a legal stipulation that if any of them want to sell their shares, it has to be to one of the other two unless all three of them sell to outsiders at the same time. He also said that if I should die before the boys reach legal age, that the fifty-one percent should be held in trust for them with Autumn as the executor of the trust." He looked over at me, and I actually thought that just talking it through out loud had given him a viewpoint on the entire thing that was allowing him to relax a little.

"Even if Gabe and Gilliam should sell their ten percent each to Jim, he still could never own more than forty-nine percent with his twenty-nine percent and their twenty percent combined. It's actually a rather brilliant and well thought out plan. What do you think?"

"I think your children love you. I think Gabe and Gilliam are giving your new marriage and your new wife and children their blessing. I think that our children are trying to tell you to back off working so hard, so you'll live long enough to dance at Devon and Dodge's weddings like you did theirs." There it was out on the table. I liked my children's idea.

"I kind of got that feeling too, Helena. I wanted to run it past you to see if you would see it the same way I did. And, you did." He cleared his throat and continued. "I did ask Gabe why he thought Devon and Dodge should get a larger share of the business than he and Gilliam? His answer blew me away. 'Dad,' he said, 'Devon and Dodge are our brothers, our much younger brothers. Gilliam and I have great partners; we're building wonderful lives. Thanks to all you and mom already have given to us. What we suggest is fair, and we're more than happy with it. You could leave us nothing, and we'd still feel that we have received more than we could ask.'" Hanks eyes were pooling with unshed tears.

He shook his head as if to clear it. "Helena, if not for you, I wouldn't have this business to divide up. You were always a good partner. Sometimes we forget to tell people how much they have done for us and to thank them. Thank you, Helena." This time, he reached across the table and squeezed my hand.

Would miracles never cease? This was the first time in our lives that I think Hank ever had said thank you to me. "You're welcome, Hank. We did do really well, didn't we? Together we made a successful business, had a wonderful home, and raised good kids. Now we're still friends, and we still love each other. Not a lot of people can look back at their lives and make such a statement. I'm glad we can, and I'm happy that we both are where we are with our lives. It is looking pretty good from my seat."

What About Mel?

Dreams are illustrations…from the book your soul is writing about you.
—Marsha Norman

At dinner that night, Sean and Jeffrey could not stop talking about their day. For Sean, his favorite part of the day was riding the horses on the trail and down on the beach. For Jeffrey, he was thrilled with what he had seen at Grandpa Mel's clinic. He announced at dinner that when he grew up, he was going to go to veterinarian school and be a doctor just like Grandpa Mel.

We all laughed and told him that was a great idea. Mel was rather quiet. He reached his arm around the boy and gave him a grandfatherly hug. It was interesting that tonight Jeffrey had moved around the table seeking out the seat beside Mel. It appeared to me that a true bond was being formed between Gabe and Amy's oldest boy, Jeffrey, and my sweet husband, Mel. Jeffrey would be turning eleven in a couple of months and would be starting into seventh grade next year. He was a very smart boy. He had already taken several languages and was extremely smart in math and biology, subjects that usually weren't taken until the freshman year, but he was in an accelerated learning class and was taking some subjects at the college level already. Gabe claimed he took after him, and he was nothing less than a little genius.

It was quite astonishing that Mel, who just a few months ago had dreamed of having a son, now was surrounded with sons. The words "I do" were as magical for Mel as "Abracadabra." In a mere instant, he had a son, Gabe; a son-in-law, Mike; two godsons, Devon and Dodge; and two grandsons, Jeffrey and Sean. I believe that his quietness tonight was the realization that his cup surely was running over.

I questioned in my mind as Mel sat there whether he wondered if Jeffrey would really continue on the path that he himself had taken when he followed in own his father's footsteps. I was sure that Mel was thinking that he was about Jeffrey's age when he made up his mind that he would one day take over his father's practice. Sitting there, I was getting more and more lost in my thoughts as I reflected that Jeffrey didn't even own a dog, a cat, a bird, or even a gold fish. Did he truly have an interest in animals? Lost in my meditations, I was quickly shaken from them when I heard Jeffrey speaking.

"Grandpa Mel. When I get out of school in June, could I come spend the summer with you and Grandma and help you at the clinic?"

"Jeffrey, I think that's something you'll need to talk over with your parents, and I'll need to talk over with your grandma. We have a few more months before we need to make that decision, but I'll certainly give it some serious consideration." He ruffled Jeffrey's hair while Jeffrey returned a look of genuine adoration.

It was time for me to break into this discussion and get on to something else. "This certainly has been an amazing week. One more day to go, and then we're all going to hate to see you guys pack up and head home. You need to do this more often. I know it's a rather long drive for a weekend, but when you have four-day weekends, which pop up a lot more frequently on calendars than they once did, you really must plan to come over to the island. We're doing a pretty good job melding together as one big family that appears to be getting bigger every day. Between Autumn and Hank, and Mel and me, we do have lots of empty rooms in our big houses, and they are calling out to be filled." I smiled and wiped my mouth with my napkin.

"Grandma," Christie began in her charming little girl talk, "If Jeffrey comes to stay with Grandpa Mel for the summer, can I come and stay with you?" Christie wasn't addressing that question to me; she was looking directly at Autumn. Everyone at the table glanced at Autumn and gave her a big smile. You could tell she was overcome with emotion. None of us, including Autumn, had previously allowed that reality to permeate. Not only had Autumn recently become a mother, but she was now also a grandmother.

"Yeah," piped up Sean, "How about me? Can't I come too?"

Everyone at the table laughed. Looking over at my son and daughter, they were looking at me. Did they think I wouldn't want to share the title of grandmother? They were wrong. I could not be happier.

"With your parent's permission, I think that Autumn and I would like nothing more than to have month long Gram Camp every summer for the rest of your lives. I'm betting that since Jeffrey wants to spend time in the clinic, and Christie loves her new baby brothers, and Sean likes the stables that we could find a lot of things to keep you guys happy and give your mothers and fathers a little time just for themselves. But we need to do a lot of talking between us adults before we give you any definite answer. Okay?"

With that, I heard three simultaneous "Okays" yelled from various seats at the table.

I'm not sure what I was letting myself in for, or committing my cohorts in crime to, but it actually would be great having them here for a month. I have missed my children and my grandchildren. I was so grateful that they wanted to spend time with us. I hoped that my children would consent, but first Mel and I needed to talk and so did Hank and Autumn.

The months before summer passed quickly, and soon the three grandchildren were preparing to arrive. Devon and Dodge were getting bigger and were now a significantly larger handful to manage then when they were only weeks old.

Gabe and Gilliam decided that they would leave their homes on a Friday night after work putting them in to our house about one o'clock in the morning. I told them I would have the bedrooms ready, and they could just carry their sleeping kids into the house, dump them in bed, and plop into their own beds. Having the entire second floor as their private guest quarters was going to work out really well.

I greeted them when they arrived. Helped them upstairs to the bedrooms I had set up for everyone, and when I was sure that there was nothing else they needed, I turned off all the downstairs and outside lights that I had left burning, locked the doors, and snuggled in beside Mel. He rolled over and whispered, "Did everyone get here okay? Are they all settled?"

"Yes and yes," I replied, "Go back to sleep; I'll see you in the morning."

The six adults sat around the table in the morning, the women in their pajamas, and the men dressed for the day. We were sipping coffee and talking. I was catching them up on what had been going on when Gabe said, "You know, Mel, Jeffrey has not stopped talking about you and that clinic since he got back to our house after the last visit. I don't know if you want to encourage him or not."

Mel looked up at Gabe. "Do you have a reason that I shouldn't encourage him?"

"No, not at all," he replied, "I just don't want him pestering you to death."

"He won't pester me. I was his age when I decided to become a veterinarian, and if you don't have any objections, I'm not going to discourage him in any way. I'm planning on showing him things and observing him. I'll know at the end of the month whether he should be encouraged further or not. If not, I promise you, I will try to persuade him that perhaps he might want to consider something different." He smiled. "I care about your young man. I care about all the kids. After all, I love their grandmother." Mel smiled and winked at me. I smiled back and blew him a kiss.

Mel finished with, "Don't worry, Gabe or Amy, I won't do anything that might be a detriment to them."

Gabe was brought up a little short, and he stammered a little when he spoke. "Mel, I wasn't worried about you; I was worried about Jeffrey. I just don't want him to be a bother."

Mel smiled. "He won't be, Gabe. I love his interest and his enthusiasm, and even though I've never had any children of my own, I have nothing but their best interests at heart. Heck, I never gave birth to any animals either, and I love all of them!"

That broke the tension, and we all laughed.

The month that summer that the kids spent with us was the best summer month I ever remember. The kids were a joy. Autumn and Hank shared them. We had kids coming and going all over the place. Christie spent more overnights with Grandma Autumn and Grandpa Hank because she loved being with the babies and helping Autumn take care of them. Jeffrey spent every night at our house and every day at the clinic with Mel. They really grew close, and within a week, Mel shared with me that Jeffrey would indeed make an amazing veterinarian. Sean was all over the place showing us a little more ADD than I had been aware of previously. Gabe had told me that Sean had attention deficit disorder, but I had laughed thinking, he's just a young boy, they all do. That was proven to be an understatement. Sean was so full of energy; he nearly wore me out. He loved spending time at the stables. It wasn't just the riding he enjoyed. He liked mucking the stalls, currying the horses, filling the water troughs, and he loved just hanging out with Old Bill who also assured me that Sean's hanging with him was just fine and dandy.

When Gabe and Gilliam returned to pick the kids up, they remarked that they seemed to have grown a foot and filled out.

The boys definitely were stronger and had added a few new muscles. It was difficult to wave good-bye as they drove down the road. Gabe and Gilliam were so excited to have their children back it was touching. They had missed their babies so much; I wasn't sure if they would let them return next summer.

Gabe kept touching Sean and saying how much bigger he'd gotten in a month. He told his Dad about working at the stables, and Gabe glanced at me for verification. I nodded. "Sean, you never cease to amaze me, son. Did you really like working with the horses?"

Sean looked at his dad and said, "Dad, I think it's totally awesome." Gabe shrugged. Mucking stables, to Gabe, was not awesome. I was pretty sure that to Sean, neither was history.

The house seemed unusually quiet, and it took weeks before I could get back to any established order in my life that felt comfortable. I was still doing my tram tours and the docent job. I had maintained that commitment even when the kids were here.

Mel was gloomy for the first time ever. He really missed Jeffrey.

The kids called us frequently, and Jeffrey called Mel at least three times a week. Each conversation was about the clinic and the animals that Jeffrey had met. I loved listening to the one sided conversation as I realized that Mel really did care deeply about Jeffrey. There was something very endearing about a man in the role of grandfather and the way he relates to a young boy, a grandson. Mel was becoming a mentor, guide, friend, and teacher to Jeffrey.

Every summer, Jeffrey, Sean, and Christie came to stay. Then when Jeffrey was fifteen, he came alone. Sean who was thirteen had decided he'd rather go to football camp that summer, and Christie who was eight was so involved in her dance classes and acrobatic competitions that it was difficult to come to the island for an entire month.

The boys Devon and Dodge were now five and would be starting into kindergarten in the fall. I was still working at the Jekyll Island Club. I wasn't doing the tram tours any longer, but I was still working as a docent four days a month in the museum. Thanks to Mr. Parker, I finished my book about Jekyll Island. It had been published and was on the shelves in both the town bookstores and the museum store as well as on Amazon.com. It hadn't flown off the shelves even though I had done several book signings at nearby bookstores, but it had sold enough to make it worthwhile for the publisher.

Hank had taken Gabe and the children's advice and had made Jim a partner. Jim had been thrilled, and the five years for achieving the full twenty-nice percent ownership were almost at their end. Jim worked even harder than he had originally now that the success of the company also meant success for him. Jim had always worked hard, but now he had climbed on our kids' bandwagon and was also encouraging Hank to spend more time with his wife and children. Hank actually was working, for the first time in his adult life, a forty-hour week like a normal business person rather than the sixty and seventy hours a week he had worked for so many years.

Hank had rewritten his will setting up the division of the Rivers Construction Company into the percentages that he had discussed with me that day at the diner. Autumn had been touched that Gabe and Gilliam and their spouses had wanted to see the division of the assets of their father's company go mainly to her and the two little ones. I was glad that Hank and I had raised our children to be charitable and loving. I was proud of them.

Mel had come to me last year and asked if he could leave the clinic to Jeffrey. He wanted to know if I would object to that. I was thrilled. So Mel has rewritten his will, leaving the house and investments to me if he should predecease me and the clinic and all the stock for the business to Jeffrey, with me as the trustee of that asset until he completes veterinary school. If he does not go to veterinary school then the clinic reverts to me, and I can do with it as I see fit.

That summer when Jeffrey came, he didn't come for one month. At age sixteen, he wanted to stay the entire three months of summer vacation. His parents agreed if we did, and it took us about five seconds to give our excited consent. Over dinner one night, the second week that Jeffrey was here, Mel told Jeffrey about leaving the clinic to him and what the conditions were. Jeffrey was so touched; he almost cried. You could see the effort he made to shove down the emotion that was showing on his face and in his eyes. Mel also told him that we'd like to help him, monetarily, with his tuition, and other expenses to get through veterinary school if that was what he wanted and decided to do.

Jeffrey, now a grown man, gave Mel a huge hug; and with tears running down his face, he said to Mel, "Thank you, Grandfather. I love you."

Jeffrey was so appreciative that it touched me deeply. The tears falling from my own eyes were tears of love for two wonderful men, my husband, and my grandson.

I hadn't realized until those three months that summer how much like Mel that Jeffrey was. They were growing to be like two peas in a pod. Both men were kind and loving, quiet and yet fun, and they enjoyed just hanging around.

One day at the clinic, something quite remarkable happened that we hadn't expected. Jeffrey had been helping Mel for about a month when Jennifer Hanley came rushing in the office one day with her little short legged Welsh Corgi, Bridgette, who had gotten out of their house by accident and run into the road. A passing motorist had tried to avoid hitting the dog but had grazed her with the front tire, which had thrown the little one into the air. The dog's fur was full of blood, and there was evidence that she was still bleeding. Although the seven-pound Bridgette was still breathing, she was not in very good condition. Neither was Jennifer who was crying hysterically.

Hearing the commotion in the reception area, Jeffrey came out through the double doors and calmly lifted the dog from Jennifer's arms into his own. He told her to follow him. He carried Bridgette to the examining table and laid her down gently. Mel was at the stables with a sick horse. Jeffrey told the nurse who had followed him into the exam room to call for Mel to come back as soon as he could.

Reaching over to the instruments that were laid out by the table, he put the stethoscope into his ears and listened for the dog's heartbeat. It was present but faint and somewhat erratic. He examined the dog's body and couldn't find any broken bones, but he was fearful of internal bleeding.

He grabbed the oxygen mask from the wall and looking at the chart for small animals, determined the level to turn the concentration gage, and then he slipped the mask over the dog's mouth to help him breath more comfortably.

That done, Jeffrey looked up at Jennifer to reassure her and was amazed at the look of admiration in her eyes. She admired him for helping her dog. What a discovery. Jeffrey didn't remember ever having anyone admire him before.

He looked at Jennifer and thought he should say something. "Bridgette seems to be comfortable at the moment. Her heartbeat is weak but regular. That's a good sign. There doesn't appear to be any broken bones. I am somewhat fearful of internal bleeding having been propelled into the air by the car tire. I'm going to call my grandfather who is on his way and see what he thinks I should do next. I am here from Atlanta for the summer assisting him."

Mel had walked in the back door in time to hear what Jeffrey has just said. "No need to call me Dr. Rivers; I came as soon as the nurse told me you needed me to return." He winked at Jeffrey and walked up beside him.

"I heard your report, doctor, and I think you have taken all the correct first steps. Now, I think we should run an x-ray to verify that there are no broken bones, and it might also give us a look inside to see if anything appears to be punctured. Do you agree with that assessment?"

"Yes. Yes, Dr. Daniels, I do agree. What is it that you would like me to do to assist you?"

Jeffrey and Mel were all business and putting on a wonderful show to boot, which should have more than impressed Jennifer who didn't look like she needed any more impressing than she already had.

"Dr. Rivers," Mel said, "If you will just bring the portable x-ray unit over here and be sure that it is plugged in, we can position Bridgette and get on with taking the required pictures."

"Yes, doctor," Jeffrey replied as he turned to bring the unit over. He also reached in and brought four blank films with him. Mel wondered how Jeffrey knew that he had planned to take four pictures. Was it a guess or was he that good already? At the time it happened, Mel made a note to himself that he would need to question Jeffrey about that when it was all over. Or, maybe, Mel thought, he'd do it now.

"How would you suggest we proceed?" Mel looked at Jeffrey, and Jeffrey looked back at him. Jeffrey seemed to exude confidence. Mel remembered thinking, as he recalled all of this to me later that he wondered if this was real or the excellent act of a teenager trying to be grown up? Mel shared with me that he thought Jeffrey knew exactly what to do, and that his feelings were soon to be found correct.

Jeffrey began, "I believe we should take one picture of Bridgette looking straight down on her while she is lying on her back. That will show us what is happening in her abdomen and also show us the spine. Then for the second picture, I think we should attempt to position her on her stomach, with her legs spread out to the sides if possible so that we can have a closer look at the organs and spine. The third and fourth pictures should be from her left and right sides respectively so that we can look at her ribs and her legs checking for fractures and anything that might be puncturing an internal organ."

If that wasn't enough information, Jeffrey continued to tell Mel about the x-ray process reinforcing to Mel that Jeffrey wasn't faking this, he really knew what he was talking about. "Since the dog is so small, each picture will also give us a good look at her neck and head since her full body, from the top of her head to the tip of her tail will fit on one piece of film. Does that sound like the appropriate way for us to continue, doctor?"

Mel responded quickly, "It's exactly what I would do, Dr. Rivers. Would you like to position the dog for the first photo?"

Jeffrey positioned the dog for the first and all the remaining x-rays, and as it turned out, there were no broken bones, no head injury, and from what the two of them could see, nothing that would foretell any internal bleeding. Mel told me later that he loved standing in front of the light box, where the x-rays were hung, while Jeffrey and he had their heads together, literally, studying the images.

Jeffrey had turned off the oxygen and hung the mask on the wall in its proper place while he and Mel were doing the x-rays. When they were through, the dog appeared to have a much stronger heart beat, and it wasn't necessary to put the oxygen back on. Mel told me that he had checked the oxygen concentration level when he had first entered the clinic and found that it was right on. You could tell when he relayed this story to me that Mel was so proud of Jeffrey that he was about to burst. Jeffrey had handled his first solo emergency perfectly. He had calmed both the animal and the owner. He had been poised, assured, and professional. He had not been rattled, and his patient came before everything else. I could not wait to tell Jeffrey's parents.

Mel was one hundred percent confident that Jeffrey was going to make a fine doctor.

This is my favorite part of everything. Mel sat there sipping on some wine that night as he told me all that had happened. He said to me, "The next part is just so much fun. I suggested to Jeffrey that perhaps he'd like to walk out with Jennifer and let her know what the next steps would be."

Hank laughed and said, "Jeffrey didn't miss a beat, Helena. That's one heck of a grandson we have. I couldn't be prouder or more amused with the boy."

As he continued relating the day's story to me, he said, "So Jeffrey looks at me and he says, 'Yes, I would be happy to walk out with Jennifer and fill her in on the next course of action to be taken with Bridgette.' With that he walks over to Jennifer who is looking at Jeffrey like her knight in shining armor, and he puts his hand on Jennifer's back and begins to gently guide her to the door. Then I hear him say to her, 'Jennifer we'll need to keep Bridgette overnight for observation just to make sure that she doesn't have anything wrong that we haven't been able to detect. I'll walk out with you and answer any questions you might have.'"

Mel stops and laughs to himself with a little twinkle in his eye as he continued the story. "Helena, I wasn't sure if I was going to be able to contain myself when I heard Jeffrey's next words to Jennifer. These were Jeffrey's, excuse me, I mean Dr. Rivers's exact words: 'Jennifer, it was very smart of you to bring Bridgette right in. I know you were very scared, but you did exactly the right thing for Bridgette.'"

Mel chuckled. "Then Grandma, Jeffrey held the door open for Jennifer, and the two of them went off leaving me to stand there and just marvel at what I had witnessed."

Mel shook my head and shared with me that at the time, he had wondered if he had that much composure at age sixteen. He said that he highly doubted it.

"Helena, I loved animals. The animals were always the biggest part of it for me. Jeffrey has been working with me for four summers now. He has apparently learned a lot more from observation and what I had been teaching than I realized. I couldn't be more proud of him if he was my own son."

I was touched. Mel had gotten his boy after all. What an amazing thing. I think of Sidney Lanier. I think of my Sidney's poem that Mel and I love so much. I think of the *Hymn of the Marshes* "Sunrise" and of the words from that poem that Mel has hung in his office and what he told me those words meant to him. "Jekyll—a Limpid Labyrinth of Dreams." So many dreams have come true for all of us on this island.

Reader's Aid and Book Club Synopsis

Helena Andrea Marchant Rivers isn't a typical Georgia peach. Each morning and night, she brushes her long blonde hair one hundred strokes until it shines but seldom does more than pull it back in a convenient ponytail. Clad in blue jeans, plaid shirt, riding boots, and a baseball cap, she sits erect in the saddle of either her Blue Blue or Grey Streak. On winter mornings Helena dons a suede jacket and chaps to ward off the cool breezes coming in from the Atlantic. She loves the sun and wind as horse and rider, joined in spirit, sprint across the fields, trot along the paths, and frolic through the surf of Jekyll Island. Helena has dedicated her last thirty years to being a loving and supportive wife and mother. Now, after a personal disaster leaves her raw, she finds herself unfocused and alone. This is the story of her struggle to find a way through the uncertainty of the future. With a warrior's rugged resolve, the probing investigative mind of a journalist and the softly beating heart of a poet, she is led to new adventures with the faint whisper in her ear: *"Fear not, for I am with you."*

Characters

Helena Andrea Marchant Rivers, the narrator, a healthy, reflective, fifty-five-year-old woman of courage and strong resolve.

Hank Rivers—Helena's ex

Gabe Rivers—Helena and Hank's son

Amy—Gabe's wife with young sons Jeffrey and Sean

Gilliam Rivers—Helena and Hank's daughter

Mike—their son-in-law and newly born granddaughter, Christie

Blue Blue and Grey Streak—Helena's horses

Victoria and Celeste—owners of Victoria's Stables

Old Bill—the stable man

Dr. Melvin Anthony Daniels—the local veterinarian

Autumn—Hank's new love

Devon and Dodge—the surprise package

Paige and Victor Durant—introduced to the reader in "The Glass Divider"

Book Club Discussion Items

1. Was Helena's reaction to Hank's announcement that he was leaving her realistic?
2. Do you think that someone can fall in love with someone else while they are in the middle of a good marriage?
3. If you were Helena, would you be as forgiving and accepting?
4. What did you think of how Helena was moved into the direction of being a docent and a tram tour guide?
5. Were you surprised by Mel's declaration to Helena? How about his timing?
6. Did you like the part where Helena decided to give the house back to Hank so that he and Autumn could raise their family where Hank and Helena had raised Gabe and Gilliam? If you were Autumn, how would you have felt about that? Did you like the trade arrangements?
7. After Mel's house burned down, were you surprised by Hank's action? How about the action of the strangers whose home building was temporarily put on hold?
8. If you read *The Glass Divider*, was it interesting to run into Paige and Victor again?
9. Did you like how Paige and Victor were introduced into the last third of the book and how they became friends with Mel, Helena, Hank, and Autumn?
10. Do you believe the instructions Gabe and Mike wrote for Hank about how to take care of a baby was meant to be funny, or was there more written between the lines?

11. What did you think about how Mel's dream was answered?
12. Did you like the title, *Transparent Web of Dreams*? Would you name it something else? What?

If you would like to visit more with these characters in future books, please let the author know. E-mail her at todalu@embarqmail.com.